Nice People
New & Selected Stories II

Also by David Jauss

Fiction
Glossolalia: New & Selected Stories
Crimes of Passion
Black Maps

Poetry
You Are Not Here
Improvising Rivers

Nonfiction
On Writing Fiction

NICE PEOPLE

New & Selected Stories II

DAVID JAUSS

Press 53

Winston-Salem

Press 53, LLC
PO Box 30314
Winston-Salem, NC 27130

First Edition

Cover design by Kevin Morgan Watson

Cover art, "The Silent Wings of Dissent," Copyright © 2013 by Jack L. Geiser,
used by permission of the artist.

Author photo by Alison Jauss

Library of Congress Control Number 2017954774

Printed on acid-free paper
ISBN 978-1-935708-59-2 (softcover)
ISBN 978-1-941209-60-8 (hardcover)

for my brother

Acknowledgments

Earlier versions of these stories, sometimes under other titles, appeared in the following magazines:

Arkansas Literary Forum: "The Bridge"
Arts & Letters: "Trespassing"
Crosscurrents: "The Jury"
Descant: "The Late Man"
Great Stream Review: "Brutality"
The Maryland Review: "Providence"
Seems: "A Brief History of My Scars"
Short Story: "Firelight"
upstreet: "Blizzards" and "Depositions"

Earlier versions of some of these stories also appeared in previous collections: "Last Rites" in *Crimes of Passion* (Chicago: Story Press, 1984) and "Brutality," "The Late Man," and "Firelight" in *Black Maps* (Amherst: University of Massachusetts Press, 1996). *Crimes of Passion* and *Black Maps* were republished in eBook format by Dzanc Books in 2013.

I am grateful to the National Endowment for the Arts, James A. Michener and the Copernicus Society of America, the Minnesota State Arts Board, and the Arkansas Arts Council for fellowships that enabled me to write several of these stories, and I am deeply indebted to the teachers and friends whose advice and support have sustained me throughout my writing life: Frederick Busch, Philip Dacey, Stephen Dunn, George P. Elliott, James Hannah, Dennis Vannatta, David Wojahn, Delbert Wylder, and Edith Wylder. I am also grateful beyond measure to my colleagues and students at Vermont College of Fine Arts, from whom I have learned much and without whom both my life and my fiction would be greatly diminished.

NICE PEOPLE
New & Selected Stories II

I

Nice People   3

Brutality   17

The Jury   27

Depositions   39

Providence   49

Trespassing   61

II
Last Rites   83

III
A Brief History of My Scars   147

The Late Man   157

Tourists   169

Blizzards   181

The Bridge   195

Firelight   201

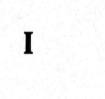

I

NICE PEOPLE

Where I'm from, stories often begin with snow and sometimes they end with snow, too. This story is no exception. It begins on a night more than a decade ago, when the snow started falling in St. Paul shortly after dusk and kept on all through the night. But Sarah and I didn't even know it was snowing. We had the curtains drawn tight and all the lights off. We had just made love for the first time, and we were lying there in her bed, silent except for our breathing in the dark. I didn't know what to say to her. We had been law partners and friends for six years, and I'd never had any trouble talking to her before. In fact, that was one reason we had finally become lovers: we could always tell each other what we were thinking and feeling. But now, lying where her husband would be if he weren't in Omaha on business, I couldn't think of a single word to say. Sarah didn't seem to be able to think of anything either. But after a while, she laughed a little, almost as if to herself, and said, "I wonder what the nice people are doing tonight?"

I didn't find out until years later that she was quoting a line from a movie. My wife and I were flipping channels one night, trying to find something worth watching, and we lit on an old film noir called *While the City Sleeps*. I don't remember much about the movie now, except that at one point Dana Andrews was in a taxi in the middle of the night with a woman who wasn't his fiancée. I mostly just remember how it felt, sitting there on the couch beside Lily, to hear him say those words. For a moment, I couldn't breathe and everything inside me seemed to turn liquid, then my cheeks began to burn as if I'd just been slapped. I was glad that the lights were off, so Lily couldn't see what those words had done to me.

By "nice people," Sarah probably meant what Dana Andrews's character meant: everybody but us. But at the time, I thought she was referring to our spouses, Lily and Jake. I thought they were as nice as people got, but now I wonder if anyone's really nice. I used to think Sarah and I were nice people too. But if we were, we would never have slept together, would we? Our affair didn't last long, but that doesn't make us any less guilty.

That first night so much snow fell that by ten, when I left Sarah to go home, the world was completely white and empty, a ghost world. I looked through a veil of falling snow at the darkened houses around me, their roofs thatched with snow, their trees and bushes flocked like Christmas trees. The only car in sight was mine. I'd parked it on the street—it had felt wrong to park in the garage, where Jake's car would normally be, or even in the driveway—and it was already covered with nearly a foot of snow. I brushed the snow off the windows and the driver's door as best I could, got in and started the engine, then got out to scrape the windows. The snow was the wet and heavy kind that freezes almost as soon as it lands, so it took me a long time to get the ice off. I must have stood there, hunched over the car, scraping as hard as I could, for at least ten minutes, all the while shivering and scrunching my shoulders up to try to keep the frigid snow from seeping down the collar of my coat. I knew Sarah was watching me from her window, but I didn't look up. Somehow, I was too embarrassed to.

By the time I'd cleared the windows, the car was so warm my glasses fogged up as soon as I sat behind the wheel. I wiped them off, then started down the hill, between the mounds of last week's snow left at the curbsides by the snowplows and beneath the archway formed by the snow-laden elms. I felt like I was driving into a dark cave, one that led deep into the earth. I had to pump the brakes constantly to keep from sliding off the slick street. It took me forty minutes to drive the twelve miles to our home in Eagan. So it was nearly eleven when I finally got home, two hours later than I'd told Lily I'd be back from the office, where I'd told her I had to work late on a brief that had to be filed the next morning.

To my shame, Lily wasn't angry, or suspicious; she was worried. She opened the door before I could even take out my key and said, "Thank God you made it, Ben. The weatherman said no one should be out on the roads right now." She was wearing a maroon terrycloth bathrobe over plaid flannel pajamas, and she had on my felt-lined hunting boots, which she always said kept her feet warmer than slippers. She looked cute and warm and I wanted to hug her. But I didn't. I just stepped in and brushed the snow off my coat sleeves and stamped it off my galoshes.

"I tried to warn you the storm was getting worse," she said, pushing her blond bangs back off her forehead. "I called your office a dozen times but you didn't answer."

I'm a good liar. Without even a pause, I said, "I thought that was you. The phone would ring and I'd pick it up, but then there was nothing. The snow must've done something to the phone lines. I kept trying to call you but I couldn't get through."

Then she gave me a quick hug, and when she let go, she kissed my cold cheek. Her lips felt soft and warm. "It's late," she said. "Let's go to bed." And once we were there, I made love to her, partly so she wouldn't suspect anything and partly because I was happy to be back home and in her arms again, safely out of the storm.

The next morning, when I woke and opened the curtains, I was blinded by the sunlight reflecting off the snow. Lily was already up; I could smell coffee brewing and I could hear her telling the twins they had to finish all their oatmeal before they could go outside and build a snowman. Because of the snow, school was cancelled for the day, and I could tell from their high-pitched voices that they felt excited and free. I'd felt the same way the night before, and I stood there at the window, thinking about Sarah, the way her moans had gradually softened until they seemed almost like a whispered prayer. Standing there, I could feel her breath on my neck, feel her fingers tangled in my hair, clutching and unclutching as she came. I felt guilty thinking about her, but it was a guilt so contorted by pleasure that it almost felt good. I stood there a long time, wondering what we would do now, all of us, the nice people and the not-nice people, before I finally went down to the kitchen and kissed Lily good morning and tousled the boys' hair.

When Jake came back from Omaha, the four of us went out for dinner at Raffi's, a new restaurant on Nicollet Mall. We always went out together once a month or so, usually to some place we'd never tried before. I'd thought about cancelling, but I didn't want Lily or Jake to think that something had changed and start to get suspicious. And I wanted to see Sarah again. We saw each other every day, of course, since we worked for the same firm, but that wasn't the real Sarah, nor was it the real me. I wasn't sure who those people were who chatted in the hallways or each other's offices and met in conference rooms with our colleagues to discuss torts and briefs and depositions, but I knew they weren't the two people who had made love in her bedroom that snowy night.

Jake is a salesman for a company that specializes in elementary school textbooks, and he was celebrating a big sale to the Omaha School District. We all had too much to drink, especially Jake. He is a big guy—big enough to play tight end at the U of M until he blew out a knee—and it takes a lot to get him drunk, but that night he was plastered. Usually the more he drank, the quieter he got, but that night, he started to tell a story. It, too, began with snow. We'd been talking about a blizzard that was headed our way, and how glad we were that we had snowblowers and didn't have to shovel like we did in the old days, and he started to tell us about something that had happened when he was a kid and had a paper route. It was the morning after a blizzard and he was trudging through the deep snow that had drifted across a customer's sidewalk when he saw something brown sticking out of a snowbank near the front steps. At first, he said, he thought it was an animal—a cat or something. And then he realized what it was: someone's hair. And then he saw a face, a shoulder, and an arm, all sticking out of the snow.

"Jake," Sarah said, as if warning him to stop. But he just took another swallow of his cognac, leaned back in his chair and looked up at the ceiling. In the candlelight, his jowly face was full of shadows, like a storyteller's around a campfire. At tables all around us, people were talking and laughing quietly, and a jazz trio was playing some slow ballad in the corner across the room. Jazz and Middle Eastern food: I could tell this place wasn't going to last.

"It was Old Lady Simonson," Jake said, then looked back down at us. "That's what all of us kids called her. She wasn't old, though. She was probably in her mid-forties. But when you're just twelve that seems old. Anyway, she was frozen to death, just a few feet from her front door."

Of course, all of us had heard similar stories. In Minnesota, people have been known to lose their sense of direction in a blizzard and die right in their own yard, never knowing how close they were to saving themselves. But what Jake told us next I had never heard before.

"Old Man Simonson killed her," he said. "They'd had a fight—all of this came out at the trial—and he hit her so hard he knocked her out. The coroner said the blow broke her cheekbone. Then he just lugged her outside and threw her off the steps into a snowbank. He said he thought the cold would wake her up so he went to bed. He claimed he had no idea she'd be out there all night, unconscious, in the snow. But she was. The snow had almost completely covered her by the time I found her. I started to shovel her out with my hands, but I could see she was already dead. Her skin—"

Sarah put her hand on Jake's and cleared her throat. "Don't tell the rest, Jake. This isn't exactly good dinner conversation."

"Hey," Lily said. "You can't stop now. You've got us all curious!"

Jake looked at Sarah, and she looked back. A moment passed. Then Jake turned to Lily and said, "Sorry. My attorney advises me to plead the fifth," and he raised his hands like someone under arrest.

Sarah told me more of the story the following week. We'd just made love, and she was lying naked on her side, her head propped up on her hand, and looking at me. The neon light of the motel sign shone through the room's thin curtains, tinting her pale skin a bruise-blue. "When Jake found her, the woman was naked," she said. "The bastard had fucked her before he beat her."

"Jesus," I said.

"She'd been screwing around, so he thought he'd teach her a lesson."

I sat up. "Does Jake—"

"No." She shook her head. "He doesn't suspect anything. You don't have to worry."

"But why'd he tell that story then?"

She shrugged. "Who knows? Maybe that's what he thinks of every time he gets horny."

I couldn't tell if she was joking.

She laid her head back on the pillow and looked up at the ceiling, her face in blue shadow. "He always ends the story by saying, 'It was the first time I ever saw a naked woman.'"

"How romantic," I said, trying for a joke.

"Yeah," she said, curling her lip. "How fucking romantic."

But then she started to cry.

I stroked the side of her face. "What is it?" I said.

She wasn't crying hard, but she still couldn't answer for a moment. Then she said, "There's something wrong with me. I hear that story and I feel sorry for the wife, of course, and I even feel sorry for the man, too, in a way. But I can't feel sorry for Jake."

I looked at her. "Why not?"

But she didn't answer. Instead, she just started crying harder.

I took a breath, as if I were going to say something. But I didn't.

Sarah and I broke it off in early April, during one of the last snowfalls of the winter. We'd driven an hour outside the Cities and had just parked in the lot of a small-town Best Western. Usually, we talked nonstop when we were alone together, but she had been quiet during the drive. I asked her a couple of times if something was wrong, and she said no, but I knew there was something she wasn't saying. By the time we reached the motel, the snow was letting up. We sat there a moment, watching the flakes fall and land on the windshield. They looked like little shards of light. I was about to turn off the car when she said, "No. Don't."

I stopped, my fingers on the key. "What do you mean?" I said, though I knew exactly what she meant.

She looked out her window. "I want to go back to the way things were before," she said. "When we were friends."

"Are you sure?" I asked, a knot in my throat.

She turned to look at me. "This isn't right. I love you but it's not right."

And that was the end of everything, basically. We'd been together little more than four months.

I said, "Okay," then turned the windshield wipers back on and put the car in reverse. I felt sad, but I also felt relieved. Now I wouldn't have to lie to Lily anymore. Now I could be one of the nice people again.

For the next three years, I imagined that Sarah and I had managed to erase all traces of our time together as lovers. We sat across from each other at legal meetings and, sometimes, lunch, and occasionally had a drink together after work with some of our colleagues, just as we always had. She laughed at my jokes and I laughed at hers. When one of us won a case, we'd hug the other and say "Good job." And when we went out for dinner, a movie, or a concert with Lily and Jake, we talked and joked the way we always had. The four of us were the best of friends, and more than once Lily told me she thought of Sarah and Jake as family. One winter when the twins played two of the three wise men in the junior high Christmas pageant, Sarah and Jake sat beside us and applauded just as hard as Lily and I did. They had no children themselves and they treated ours as if they were nephews, if not their own sons. You could have asked anybody and they would have said we were all good friends, all nice people.

I'm not sure why Sarah told Jake about our affair. Since so much time had passed, it's possible she thought she could safely tell him. Or maybe she just couldn't bear the guilt anymore. Or perhaps some detail just slipped out, something incriminating, and Jake harangued her into confessing. I don't know. I asked her once, but she wouldn't answer. All she said was, "I love Jake. Despite everything, I love him." And she must because she's still with him.

The night everything blew up, there was a freak snowstorm— one of those spring blizzards that seem to hit Minnesota every year. Lily and I were supposed to go to Jake and Sarah's house for dinner but the snow was coming down pretty hard, so I called to cancel. Jake wouldn't hear of it. "The streets are fine," he said. "And the weatherman says the snow'll stop anytime now. Besides, Sarah's been cooking and cleaning all day and she'll be heartbroken if you don't come."

The way his voice cracked when he said "heartbroken" should have tipped me off, but it didn't. At any rate, Lily and I got dressed, told the boys to microwave some frozen dinners for their supper, then headed to Jake and Sarah's house. The snow wasn't letting up at all; in fact, it was getting worse, and the wind was picking up too. The snow slashed in front of our headlights as if it were trying to blot out the light. "This is insane," I said more than once, but we kept on driving to their house. The truth of the matter is that I wanted to see Sarah. Even though we hadn't been anything more than friends to each other for three years, I still felt the excitement of doing something illicit every time we were together. It's possible I confused that feeling with love, but it's also possible I really did love her. Is there any way to tell the difference between loving someone and just thinking you love them? If there is, I don't know what it is.

When we got to their house, Jake opened the door and beamed at us. His face was red, and I immediately knew he'd had too much to drink. "Come in, come in!" he said, the most jovial of hosts. Then, as he helped us remove our coats, he said, waggling his eyebrows like Groucho Marx, "Take your clothes off and stay a while."

Lily and I laughed. Then Jake ushered us into the living room, where, he said, we'd have a couple of drinks while Sarah put the finishing touches on the dinner. Lily and I sat down on the leather couch. As always when we visited Jake and Sarah, I tried not to think about the fact that just one floor above the couch was the bed where Sarah and I had made love whenever Jake was out of town. Jake sat down in the overstuffed armchair opposite the couch, then called out, "Oh, *Sarah*. Our guests are here. Come see Benny-boy and his blushing bride."

When she didn't respond, he called out, "Sarah, don't be shy. We need you out here."

He was acting so strange, I started to wonder if there was something wrong with him besides being drunk.

"Honey!" he yelled. "Get your ass in here!"

Lily and I looked at each other. I still didn't have any idea what was going on.

Then Sarah appeared at the entrance to the living room. Lily saw her first. "Oh my God!" she said.

I followed Lily's horrified gaze. "Jesus," I said the instant I saw Sarah's face. "What happened to you?" Her cheek was red and puffy, and her lips were split and crusted with blood.

"Now, it's not nice to ask personal questions, is it?" Jake said to me. "That's not something friends do to each other, is it? But then again, maybe they do lots of things I don't know about."

And then I knew.

Lily got and up and hurried over to Sarah. "Are you all right?" she asked, then touched Sarah's arm gently, as if even the slightest touch could bruise her.

Sarah just said "No" and looked down. I noticed with a shiver that some of her hair had been ripped out: on the crown of her head, a small white circle of skin shone in the hall light.

I turned to Jake. "You son of a bitch," I said.

He leaned back in his chair. "Is that right, Benny-boy?" he said. "*I'm* the son of a bitch?"

Then Lily turned toward Jake. "How could you do this?" she said. "I thought you were a good man." She looked like she couldn't decide whether to curse him or cry.

Jake looked at Lily. "No," he said. "No, I'm not. I learned that about myself when I was twelve." Then he said, "Have I ever told you the story about the first time I ever saw a naked woman?" Lily just glared at him. "Well, sit back down and I'll tell you all about it."

Lily looked at me and said, "I want to go." Then she took Sarah's hand. "Sarah, you're coming with us."

"The hell she is," Jake said and stood up, his fists balled. "Not till I tell you my story, at least. Now you go sit down and you listen like a good, sweet little wifey."

"What is wrong with you?" she said. Then she turned to me. "*Do* something, Ben," she said. But I just shook my head. I was feeling sick to my stomach, like I was standing in a rowboat that was rocking in the wake of a passing ship.

"I mean it," Jake said. "Sit your ass down."

I hung my head. I was sure I was going to throw up.

Lily crossed the room silently and sat down beside me. I noticed her fingers were trembling, probably more from anger than fear. And I was sure she was as angry with me as she was with Jake. And in a few moments, I knew, she'd be even angrier at me.

Jake sat back down. "It was a dark and stormy night," he began, then chuckled. But he wasn't smiling; his face looked like a death mask. "The worst blizzard in a dozen years. But the next morning there I was, out trudging through the snow, delivering the paper to everybody on my route." It was the story he'd started to tell us three years before, but he didn't seem to remember telling it—and this time he finished it. But he didn't finish it the way Sarah had finished it that night we made love in the blue shadows of the motel's neon sign.

"I kept on scooping the snow away from her body with my hands," he said, "and it soon became clear she didn't have a stitch of clothes on. Not even a necklace or an earring. She was as naked as—well, as naked as Sarah or Ben."

I lifted my head. "Please don't," I said. "For God's sake, Jake, please stop."

Lily said, "What's going on?" She was talking to me, not Jake. I shook my head, like I didn't know. But I did know, of course; I knew all too well what was happening, and why.

Sarah was still standing in the entranceway. "Can you make him stop?" I asked her. She didn't answer.

"Her skin," Jake said then, "was a pale, bluish-white color, almost translucent. Like marble, in a way. She looked like a statue, only she was no Venus. She was fat, and she had these little wispy hairs around her nipples, I remember." He laughed. "Yeah, I was taking a pretty good inventory for a kid who was scared to death. I mean, how often do you get a chance to see someone naked when you're twelve? So I took a good long look."

He leaned forward in his chair and looked at me. "Maybe you think I'm a sick bastard. Maybe you'd like to call me that right now. Go ahead. The words aren't hard to say. You can say them if you really, really try."

"Finish your story," I said.

He laughed. "Okay," he said. "I will." Then he looked at Sarah. "Or maybe Sarah will finish it for me."

She said nothing.

"What's the matter, dear?" he said. "Have you forgotten how it ends?"

I stood up then. "Leave her out of this," I said.

He measured me with a look. "The big hero," he said. Then he finished the story: "I should have called the cops the minute I realized she was dead. But I didn't. Instead, I touched her tits. They were ice-cold, but I felt something warm shoot through me when I touched them. Only then did I run next door—or at least I tried to run through all that deep snow—to tell someone Old Lady Simonson was dead." He leaned back in his chair again. "For a long time afterward, I tried to tell myself that anyone else would've done the same thing in my situation—touch her, I mean. But deep down, I knew better. I knew I was a bad person." He looked at me. "What I want to know now is whether you know you're a bad person too."

My chest felt brittle, as if my ribs were made of glass and merely breathing could break them.

"All you have to do is say yes and you can go," he added. Then he nodded toward Sarah. "And you can take that slut with you."

I gritted my teeth and whispered, "Yes."

"I can't HEAR youuuuu," he said, in a drill sergeant's voice.

"Yes," I said again, louder.

"Okay," he said then. "Now get the hell out of here. It's your turn to call the cops."

But I didn't call the police. I knew I wouldn't even before Sarah urged me not to, later that night, saying through her sobs that it'd only make things worse and that she deserved what he did to her because she'd hurt him so much. I knew it the moment we stepped out of the house. The snow was still falling, and the wind was blowing so hard the snow stung my skin. Sarah started to cry. Lily wasn't crying yet, but I knew she would be, when I answered all of the questions she was going to ask.

The sidewalk was slick with ice under the deepening snow, and we walked carefully to the car. I brushed the snow off the front passenger door and opened it for Lily, but she pushed it shut. Then she opened the back door, letting the snow cascade into the car, and she and Sarah got in and closed the door. I walked around the car, brushing the snow from the windows with my gloves, watching them all the while through the icy glass. In the light from the streetlight, their skin looked pale, almost blue, as they sat there in the cold car, silently, not looking at each other, and waited for me to get in there with them. I wanted it all to be over, but I knew it was only starting. I knew that as soon as I got in the car, everything would change. I knew it wouldn't be long before Lily would file for divorce and I'd lose my wife and sons. I even knew I'd have to leave the firm, though I didn't know I'd be forced to resign after Jake complained to the partners, saying I'd made "inappropriate and unwelcome advances" toward Sarah, an accusation she didn't refute. I didn't know just how ruined my life would be, but I knew it was ruined. And I knew there was nothing I could do to salvage it.

When the windows were clear, I stood there awhile in the falling snow, took a deep breath, then I opened the door and got in.

For seven years now I've worked in a small firm in Anoka for barely half of my previous salary, and most nights I go home to my apartment and sit in front of the TV with the sound off, drinking one beer after another until I can sleep. I've had several relationships but nothing that's lasted. A couple of years ago, I had a girlfriend for a few months, a sad-eyed local schoolteacher whose divorce I had handled. One night after we made love, I told her this story, and she said I was wrong to blame myself, that I was a nice person. She said Jake, Sarah, and Lily were the bad people because they didn't forgive me the way I'd forgiven them. Sarah forgave Jake even though he beat her as cruelly as Old Man Simonson beat his wife, and Jake forgave her for her infidelity, but neither one forgave me. They didn't blame Lily at all, but Lily wouldn't have anything to do with them after that last night, depriving our boys of the family friends they'd always called Aunt Sarah and Uncle Jake, and she never forgave me either, of course, and did everything she could to ruin my life, including turning our sons against me. So Lily was the worst of all of us, my girlfriend said, and what she did proved she didn't love anyone, not really. All I'd done, she said, was love two women at the same time, so my only sin was too much love.

I knew she was wrong, that she was saying all of this just to win my affection, but I didn't contradict her. And I confess there have been times when I almost believed what she said, and times when I decided that Sarah or Lily or even Jake was the nicest of us. But all I know for certain is that that terrible night, and Jake's story, return to me in dreams, and sometimes I'm the one lying unconscious in the snowbank, the snow slowly drifting over me, but other times—I admit it—I'm the one doing the beating, my fist slamming into Jake's face, or Lily's, or Sarah's. And when I wake in the dark those nights, my heart is pounding like a fist, and even if it's the middle of summer, I shiver like it's the coldest night of the year and snow is falling all around me, all around all of us, and it'll keep falling until it covers us all.

BRUTALITY

It was late on a dark, moonless night, and they were driving home from a party at their friends' house on the other side of Little Rock. Although they had been married for almost twenty years, Elliot still loved Susan very much and found her attractive. At the party, he'd glanced at her across the room, and the way she crossed her legs when she sat down made him desire her. Now he was anxious to get home so they could make love. He thought she must be feeling the same way because her hand was resting on his thigh and she was looking at him while they talked.

They were talking about their friends' little boy Tommy, who had kept running in and out of the living room with a toy machine gun, pretending to shoot everybody. He had laughed like a crazed movie villain while he sprayed the room with bullets, the gun's plastic muzzle glowing a fiery red. At first, everyone laughed too, but after the fourth or fifth time it stopped being funny. Finally, his father lost his temper, spanked Tommy hard three times, and sent him crying to his room. Then his mother apologized to the guests. It was his grandmother's fault, she said; every time she came to visit, she brought him a gun. He had a half-dozen in his toy box, most of them broken, thank God. But the next time she visited, they were going to tell her they were opposed to children playing with guns. They would have told her earlier but they didn't want to hurt her feelings.

Elliot and Susan had married during the Vietnam War and, like many parents then, didn't buy toy guns for their son. But Elliot had played with guns when he was young, and now he was telling Susan about the rifle his father had carved for him out of an old canoe paddle. "I loved that rifle," he said, as he drove down the deserted street past the sleeping houses. It had been almost as long as a real rifle, and he had worn it slung over his shoulder wherever he went the summer he was nine. Even when his mother called him in for supper, he wouldn't put it away; he had to have it propped against the table in case the Russians suddenly attacked. As he thought about the rifle, its glossy varnish and its heft, he moved his hands on the steering wheel and could almost feel it again. A thin shiver of pleasure ran through him. "It was my favorite toy," he said wistfully. "I wonder what happened to it."

"I used to think it was so awful for kids to play war," Susan said, lifting her long dark hair off her neck and settling it over her shoulders. "But now I don't know. Look at this generation of kids that were raised without toy guns—they're all little Oliver Norths. They're playing with *real* guns now. And kids like you— you turned out all right. You wouldn't even think of going hunting, much less killing someone."

"At least not anymore," he said.

"What do you mean?" she said. "You mean you used to hunt?"

Susan was a vegan, and she did volunteer work on Saturdays for the Humane Society. Elliot had told her many stories about his childhood—he had grown up in a small town in Minnesota and didn't meet her until they were in college—but he hadn't told her he'd been a hunter. It wasn't that he considered that fact a dark secret; he just knew she'd be upset and didn't think it was worth telling her. He hadn't meant to mention it now either—it had just come out. Perhaps he'd drunk too much wine at the party. Or maybe he'd gotten so lost in his memories of the toy rifle that he spoke before he could think. Whatever, he didn't want an argument. He was in a romantic mood and he didn't want anything to destroy it.

"I was a kid," he explained. "I didn't know any better."

"How old were you?" she asked.

"What does it matter?" he said. "You know I wouldn't even kill a spider now."

"But you killed something then?"

He could lie now, he realized, and say he'd gone hunting but never shot anything. He could make up a story or two about his ineptitude as a hunter, and she would laugh and everything would be fine between them. But as he'd gotten older, lies had become harder for him. They had come easily to him in his youth, but now they tasted like rust in his mouth.

"Yes," he said.

She took her hand from his thigh and sat there silently. They passed under a streetlight, and her face flared into view. "Come on, Susan," he said. "Don't be mad."

Then she said, "How could you do it? Why would you even *want* to do it?"

It was a question he had asked himself from time to time. He had enjoyed hunting and trapping animals as a teenager, but now that he was an adult, he had no desire to do either. He thought of his brutality as a phase he had gone through, a period of hormonal confusion, perhaps, like puberty. But he still remembered the pleasure hunting and trapping gave him, and he still understood it.

"Do we have to talk about this?" he said.

"I want to know," she said.

He sighed. "Okay. If you really want to know, I did it because I wanted to see if I could hit something a long ways off." It was the simple truth. It was a thrill to shoot at the empty air half a sky in front of a pheasant or duck or goose and see that emptiness explode with the miraculous conjunction of bird and shot. It was a kind of triumph over chance, over the limitations of time and space, and each time it happened, he felt powerful and alive.

"But you could have shot at targets," she said.

"Targets don't move," he answered.

"What about clay pigeons? They move."

He wished they hadn't started this. "Can't we talk about something else?" he asked. He tried to make his voice as warm as he wished hers would be.

"First answer my question. Why not shoot at clay pigeons instead?"

He considered several lies while he turned onto the avenue that led toward the suburb where they lived. Then he sighed and said, "Because they aren't alive."

Susan looked at him. "I can't believe this," she said. "My own husband."

"Come on," Elliot said. "You're overreacting."

"Maybe I am. But I feel like I'm seeing something in you that I never saw before."

"You're making me sound like a criminal or something," he complained.

"I think killing *is* a crime," she said. "It doesn't matter if it's an animal or a person, it's still murder."

He'd heard her make this argument many times before, but this was the first time she'd directed it at him personally. He wanted to defend himself, but even more he wanted to regain the romantic mood they were in when they left the party. He drove on in silence. Then she asked, "How did you feel when you killed something?"

He was glad this question had a more humane answer. "I felt bad," he said. "I felt sorry for it."

"But you kept on hunting?"

"For a while."

"If you felt so sorry for the animals, why did you keep on killing them?"

He looked at her face then and knew he would have to tell her everything. If he didn't, she would never forgive him, and everything between them would be changed. He looked back at the road. "It may sound crazy," he said, "but the first time I shot something, I did it *because* I felt sorry for it."

"I don't understand," she said.

"Do you want to?"

"Yes."

"All right then. I'll tell you the whole story." He took a breath. "The first real gun I owned was a .22 pistol. I was thirteen. I'd had the pistol for two or three months, and I'd never shot anything with it except Coke bottles and tin cans. I'd *tried* to shoot squirrels and birds, you understand, but I'd never hit anything. Then I met this boy. He was a couple of years older than me, and I looked up to him. Frank Elkington. He taught me to shoot and trap."

"Trap?" she said. "You trapped too? Elliot, I just can't believe this is you you're talking about."

"It isn't. Not anymore."

"But it's who you were. And who you were is part of who you are, isn't it?"

He didn't like the way she was interrogating him like a police officer, and he thought about making some sarcastic joke about the statute of limitations. But he just stared straight ahead. They were driving through a business district now, and the reflections of neon lights crawled on the windshield. Finally he said, "I don't have to tell you this. I'm telling it because I love you."

"I know you do," she said. "And you know I love you."

He went on. "Frank trapped mink and muskrat and beaver along the Chippewa River and sold the pelts to a fur processing plant in town. I used to tag along with him when he did his paper route, and one day I went with him while he checked his traps. He was talking about trappers and how they lived off the land. They didn't breed animals just to slaughter them, he said, and they didn't keep them penned up either; they let the animals live free in the wild and gave them a sporting chance. He made it sound so noble that I told him I wanted to start trapping too. And he gave me my first trap."

He paused, remembering that trap. It was a rusty number eleven Victor Long-Spring, and it smelled oddly sulfurous, like the air just after a match is struck. Thinking of the trap did not give him the same pleasure that remembering the wooden rifle did, but it gave him some. He could not deny that.

"Frank showed me how to set the trap," he continued, "and the next day when we went to check it, there was a weasel in it." He paused again. "Are you sure you want to hear this?"

Susan's back was against the passenger door now and her arms were crossed over her breasts as if she were cold. She nodded.

"Okay. It was a black weasel. It wasn't worth much, but I was happy as hell. Frank was congratulating me, shaking my hand and patting me on the back, and I felt proud to have caught something on my first try, even if it was only a weasel. Then I noticed the weasel's mouth was bright red. I didn't understand at first, but then I saw its leg. It had started to chew the leg off, but we had gotten there before it could finish."

"Oh, Elliot, that's awful," Susan said, and hugged herself tighter.

"I know. I know. I felt so sorry for that weasel I took out my pistol and shot him two or three times, to put him out of his misery. Frank yelled, 'What are you doing!' and grabbed the gun from me. 'You idiot,' he said, 'you're supposed to shoot it in the *head*. Now the pelt's *worthless*.'"

Elliot could feel Susan looking at him, and he gripped the steering wheel a little harder. "That was the first animal I shot. The next one, I shot in the head, between the eyes, just to prove to Frank—and, I guess, to myself—that I could do it right."

"And you sold their fur?" she asked in a quiet voice.

"Yes. And that's how this farmer found out about me. Mr. Lyngen. He got my name from one of the men at the fur processing plant, and he hired me to trap gophers in his bean field. They were damaging his crop, and he didn't have time to trap them himself. He bought me a case of traps, and he gave me twenty cents a tail. By midsummer, I'd earned enough to buy a .22 rifle, and by pheasant season I owned a 12-gauge shotgun too."

"You cut their tails off," she said. This time it was an accusation, not a question.

Yes, he had. When he'd found a gopher trapped in the entrance to its own burrow, he'd killed it with a single shot to the head, cut off its tail, then buried it in the grave it had dug for itself. He kept the tails in a marble bag tied to his belt, and every week or so when the bag got full, he took it to Mr. Lyngen and collected his bounty.

Neither of them said anything for a moment. Then Susan said, "What made you stop?"

"Another trapper. A kid named Luke Weckworth. I'd been trapping for a couple of years when he moved to town, and he started trapping too. One morning I went to check my traps, and they were missing. I didn't know who'd taken them, but I suspected Luke. A few days later, I found the traps set along a creek that ran into the river. I'd scratched my initials into them with a nail, but Luke had filed them off and scratched his own in. I collected the traps and took them to Luke's house and showed his father what he'd done. That afternoon, Mr. Weckworth brought Luke to my house and made him apologize. Luke mumbled he was sorry, and his father gripped his arm and said, 'Say it louder.' So he said it again. I could tell Luke was mad: his jaw muscles were working, and he wouldn't look at me. But I never expected anything to come of it." He paused. "I was wrong, of course. The next morning, when I went down to the river to set my traps, he was there waiting for me."

"Did he beat you up?" Susan asked.

Elliot shook his head. "No. Not really. Mostly, he just threatened me. I was walking along the river, looking for good places to set my traps, and all of a sudden he just stepped out from behind a tree and pointed his 12-gauge at my face. I stopped dead. Then he said, 'Hello, Elliot' and smiled. For a second I thought he wasn't going to do anything. But then he stuck the muzzle of his shotgun against my throat. 'I ought to kill you,' he said, and poked me with the shotgun, hard. And he kept on poking me until I was crying and gasping for breath."

It had happened thirty years ago, but as he described it, he could feel the cold steel against the soft flesh under his Adam's apple. He touched his throat gingerly with his fingertips as he steered the car through the dark tunnel formed by the huge oaks that lined the street. In a few minutes, they'd be home. In a few minutes, he'd walk into his house, a grown man with a son who was himself almost grown. It seemed amazing that all these years had passed and, at the same time, somehow not passed too.

"That's terrible," Susan said. "What happened then?"

"Not much. He took the traps back and warned me not to tell his father or ever show my face in the woods again. If I did, he said, he'd kill me."

"He couldn't have meant it," she said. "He must have just been trying to scare you."

Elliot thought for a moment. "Probably. But I don't know. He looked like he meant it." He turned to Susan. "There was something in his eyes. It may sound strange, but it was something like fear. Not fear exactly, but close to it. I remember thinking, Here he is, the one with the gun, and he's afraid."

"Afraid of what?" she asked.

He looked away. "I'm not sure. Afraid he might actually do it, I think. Afraid he was capable of it. Maybe even afraid he'd *enjoy* it."

He didn't know whether he should say anything more. Then he did. "I wanted to kill him, Susan." And as he said those words, he remembered picturing Luke dead, his face turned to pulp by a shotgun blast, and for an instant he felt again the comfort and pleasure that thought had given him then. Leaning back in his seat, he let out a slow breath. Then he continued. "I never did it, of course, but I thought about it for weeks. And night after night, I dreamed about it. I must have killed him a hundred times in my dreams."

Susan was silent. He waited for her to say something, and when she didn't, he turned to look at her. He had thought she was punishing him with her silence, thinking thoughts she didn't dare let bleed into words, and he expected to see her glaring at him, her face a mask of anger and disgust. But even in the dark, her face looked pale, and she was wincing as if his words had wounded her. "Susan?" he said. And then she put her hands over her face and began to cry.

Elliot turned away. He had tolerated her self-righteous questions, but her tears angered him. She wasn't crying for him and what he had gone through; she was crying for herself, pitying herself for having married a man who had once killed animals and dreamed about killing a human being. She had no right to take his past so personally. It was his past, not hers. And she had no right to judge him.

"In one dream," he went on, his voice thick with a bitterness that was directed more at her now than at Luke, "I trapped him just like an animal. His foot was caught in the trap, and he couldn't get it out. He kept asking me to let him go, but I just—"

"Stop it," Susan said. "Please stop it."

And then he was ashamed of hurting her, and of wanting to hurt her. He cleared his throat. "I'm sorry," he said. "I just don't want you to—" But he couldn't explain. He sighed, then drove on without talking for a while. When he finally spoke, his voice was gentle. "I know it's awful even to think about killing someone," he said, "and I don't know why I did it. I've never felt that way about anyone else, not ever. All I know is that it wasn't real, it was just a fantasy. I never really considered doing it." He glanced at her. "You know that, don't you?"

She was drying her eyes with a Kleenex. She nodded.

"At any rate, that was the end of my hunting and trapping. I never went back to the woods, and the next time my mom had a garage sale, I sold the rest of my traps and all my guns."

He looked at her and tried a smile. "That's it," he said. "The whole story. The End. *Fini.*"

She didn't return his smile. "I've never wanted to kill anything," she said. "I can't imagine feeling that way." Then she added, almost as if she were talking to herself, "It makes me wonder. What if he hadn't threatened you? Would you have kept on hunting and trapping? Would you be the same person you are now? Would you even be married to me?"

"You're making too much of this," he said. "It happened years ago. I didn't even know you then."

"I know," she said.

"It was a big mistake to tell you this," he said. "I shouldn't have said anything."

"Don't feel bad," Susan said. "I don't mean to make you feel bad. It's just that I never thought of you like this before. I always thought you were different from the kind of people who hunt and trap."

"I *am*," he said.

"I know. I just had too much to drink tonight, and I'm taking everything too serious. I'll feel fine tomorrow."

"Good," he said. "I'm glad to hear that."

Then they were out of words. They drove the last few blocks in silence, and when he had parked the car in their garage, they got out and went quietly into the house. Stepping softly so they wouldn't wake their son, they went down the hall to their bedroom. There, they undressed slowly in the dark, then put on their pajamas, got into bed, and lay on their backs, breathing quietly. Susan's hand was lying palm down on the sheet beside him, and he traced its small bones lightly with a fingertip. After a while, she moved her hand away. "Goodnight," she said, and turned her back to him.

Elliot lay there for a long time, looking at the dark ceiling. He could tell by Susan's breathing that she was still awake, but he knew she didn't want to make love now, or even talk, so he didn't say anything. But after a few more minutes, he couldn't bear the silence anymore. Turning to her, he said, "I love you."

"I love you too," she answered.

But still she kept her back to him. He lay there on his side, facing her rigid back, awhile longer, until the distance between them was too much of an affront. Then he put his hand on her shoulder and, whispering her name, turned her beautiful body toward him.

THE JURY

I don't know why I picked Liz to tell about it. I have other and better friends. Maybe I picked her because she's divorced and has been living alone for a year now. Or maybe because she's not the kind to gossip—she's one of those "If you can't say anything nice, don't say anything at all" types. Whatever the reason, when I realized it was all over between Billy and me, I drove out to Liz's house. She lives on the east edge of town, where you can smell the paper mill in Pine Bluff when the wind's wrong. The odor almost made me say no to her offer of coffee.

Liz poured two mugs full, then sat down on the other side of her gray Formica table. Her kitchen countertops were Formica too. I'd told her about the great buy I got on new granite countertops two years ago but she still hadn't replaced her tacky old ones. And she was still in her housecoat though it was almost noon, and I doubt if she'd run a brush through her hair all weekend. I thought to myself, This is what I'll probably look like a year from now.

She was waiting for me to say something, so I started. "Something's gone wrong with Billy," I said.

Liz sipped her coffee, making a slurping noise. She always makes that noise. I hate it but I never say anything about it to her.

"Yes," she said, meaning, Go on. Her eyes were tiny behind

her thick lenses. I wondered how she saw me, whether I looked larger or smaller than I was.

"I mean, something's happened," I said. "I still love him, of course, and I think he might still love—" I stopped because I sounded so corny, like some hormonal teenager or something.

Liz took another slurp of her coffee. The steam was fogging her glasses; she took them off and wiped them with the hem of her dingy blue housecoat. I noticed her hand was trembling.

"What's the matter?" I said.

She looked at me, blind without her glasses.

I pointed. "Your hand," I said.

"Oh," she said. "It's nothing." Then she looked down. "I suppose I should tell you," she said. "Gerry's back in town."

Gerry was her ex. He was a driver for Greyhound until Liz finally talked him into going to that detox center in Gurdon, the one they advertise on TV. "Come to the beautiful woodlands of Gurdon," they say, like drying out is a nature hike or something. At any rate, when Gerry got out, he'd lost his job and Liz'd lost her husband.

"Have you seen him?" I asked.

Liz put her glasses back on and looked blankly through the yellow dotted-swiss sheers on the window at her driveway.

"If you still love each other," she said, "what's the problem?"

She hadn't seen Gerry, then, but she was still hoping. I could tell.

I shifted in my seat. "Mind if I smoke?" I asked. I hadn't had a cigarette all morning, and I was dying for one. Liz doesn't smoke—that's one reason she's so overweight—so there wasn't an ashtray set out.

"Feel free," she answered. But she didn't get up to find an ashtray.

"Don't feel bad," I said. "He might call yet. You can never tell."

Here I had come to get some comfort and I was the one doing the comforting. But I didn't complain.

Liz didn't say anything. I looked around the kitchen. Pots and pans, unwashed, piled on the counters, dishes in the sink, grease splatters all over the stovetop.

"Where do you keep your ashtrays?" I finally had to ask.

"Oh, I'm sorry," Liz said, like she was just waking up. "I'll get you one." She raised herself up from her chair by pushing against the table the way fat people do. Some of my coffee slopped over the lip of my cup onto the table, but I didn't say anything.

While she was looking in one of the cupboards for an ashtray, I lit up a Salem and took a long drag. I could tell Liz didn't want to hear my problems, but I had to talk about them. "Billy's changed," I began. "You wouldn't know him back. He's—"

Just thinking about what he was like now made my head hurt so suddenly I closed my eyes.

"Are you all right?" Liz asked.

I opened my eyes. "Yeah," I said. "I think so."

Liz set the ashtray on the table and sat down heavily. The ashtray was one of those cheap orange jobs you buy at Kmart. I tapped my ash into it.

"Tell me about it," Liz said, and took a slurp of her coffee.

I didn't know where to begin, so I started with the end. "Last night I told Billy I couldn't take it anymore, and I wanted a divorce," I said.

At the word *divorce*, Liz's face went pale, then blotchy. She took my hand. "No," she said. "Tell me you're not getting divorced too, Barb."

"I don't know if we are or aren't," I said, "because Billy won't talk to me. I told him I wanted a divorce and he just laughed and said, 'We've been divorced for years, don't you know that?' I said, 'I'm serious, Billy,' but he just laid there, staring at the ceiling like it was a television set or something. I said his name, twice, but he didn't answer. Finally, I went out of the room. He hasn't said a word to me since."

"That's awful," Liz said. "I can't believe Billy would say something like that. Maybe it's his work. Maybe he's under too much pressure. Didn't you tell me he was promoted to assembly foreman?"

"Work!" I said. "He hasn't gone to work for two weeks. After the jury broke he just never went back. He wasn't even going to call in sick or anything, so I did it for him. Mr. Parker keeps calling and I keep telling him Billy's still sick, but one of these days I'm going to tell the truth, I'm going to say he just doesn't feel like working anymore, he just wants to lay around and smoke cigarettes and stare at the ceiling."

My headache was getting worse. I opened my purse and found my Excedrin bottle. But I knew the Excedrin wouldn't help, I knew my pain was bigger than any cure, so I put the bottle back.

"I don't understand," Liz said. "What's happened?"

I shook my head. "I don't know, Liz. We just haven't been getting along the last couple of years. We've been fighting a lot, but I've read that that's good for a marriage. You're supposed to get your aggressions out. But Billy, he'd fight about anything. It didn't matter. Once, I remember, we were watching some movie on TV about a guy who thought his wife was running around with some other guy. The guy hires a detective to watch his wife, but as it turns out, the detective's the guy his wife is running around with. So the guy has to turn detective in order to catch the detective and his wife in the act. It was a pretty good movie, and I was enjoying it. But then Billy started in with the questions. 'Why did you marry me?' he said, out of nowhere. I said something like 'What?' or 'Why are you asking?' and he said, 'Just answer the question'—like he was a lawyer cross-examining a witness or something. So I said, 'Because you asked me,' but he wasn't in the mood for teasing. 'Just answer the question,' he said again. So I said something like 'You know why, now can I watch my show in peace?' About then, he got mad and jumped up and turned off the TV. 'I want to hear you say it,' he said. 'Or can't you say it, Barb?' So I gave him what I thought he wanted, I said, 'Love, of course,' and then he really got mad. '*Love!*' he said. And he paced around the room, just saying '*Love!*' over and over, like he couldn't believe I could say such a thing."

Liz was looking at me very seriously, her forehead wrinkled up like Billy's when he talked about Keathley and the trial. "Oh, Barb," she said, "I'm so sorry."

"So am I," I said, and took a long drag on my cigarette, then blew the smoke toward the window. "And that isn't the worst of it. That was just the beginning. After the trial, everything got worse. No matter what we'd start talking about, he'd end up talking about the trial. One day, out of the blue, he said, 'Keathley loved her, you know. He never stopped loving her, even after she stopped loving him. He was no monster, like the prosecutor said, he was just like anybody else, only he loved her too much. That's why he didn't shoot her boyfriend too. He said he couldn't kill someone whose only mistake was to love her the way he did.' Then I said, 'You call that love? A shotgun blast in the chest?' And then he told me I didn't know what I was talking about. 'If anybody ever loved someone, he loved her,' he said. 'You don't have any right to judge him. You don't know what it means to love somebody that much.' Then I said, 'You don't kill people you love.' And he said, 'Sometimes you do. And sometimes they kill you if they don't love you.' 'Well, I love you,' I said. 'No,' he said, 'no you don't. I thought you did once but now I know better.' So I said, 'What do you want me to do to prove I love you? Kill you? Is that it?' But he just laughed. 'You can't kill me,' he said. 'I'm already dead.'"

"I can't believe this is Billy you're talking about," Liz said. "It doesn't sound like Billy at all."

"It isn't Billy," I said. "It isn't and it is."

"Maybe a vacation would help," Liz said. "Maybe a trip. He could visit old friends. Or maybe a second honeymoon."

"He doesn't want to do anything," I said. "*Any*thing," I repeated, so Liz would get the point. But she didn't. I could tell by her blank round face, a perfect zero. "What I'm saying," I said, "is that he doesn't even want sex."

Liz looked out the window when I said that. I took a drag on my cigarette while I waited for her to say something. Then she said, "It sounds to me like Billy needs to see someone, like Gerry did. You know, a doctor, someone like that."

That was just like Liz. Here I was, pouring my heart out to her, and she was thinking about her and Gerry.

I stubbed my cigarette out in the ashtray. "No," I said. "He won't go see a doctor. He won't do anything."

"Barb," Liz said, taking my hand again, "this sounds serious. If Billy doesn't get help, maybe he might *do* something."

Liz didn't have to say that to me—I knew it already, and I'd been thinking about it day and night for weeks. Billy never talked about killing himself, not in so many words, but every now and then he'd say something like, 'When I'm gone, how long will you wait to get married again?' When he talked like that, I'd see him laying in his coffin, his head propped up on a little satin pillow, and I'd have to sit down until my heart stopped pounding.

"Oh, Jesus," I said, "I don't know what to do. I try to be strong, I make his favorite meals. But he's so *angry*. He's holding it in, but he's so angry he could do anything, maybe even kill me."

And then I started to cry like a fool.

"Oh, Barb," Liz said, "I'm so sorry for you." She was holding both of my hands now. Her fingers were cold and damp, like she'd just been rinsing dishes and hadn't had time to dry her hands all the way. I took my hands from hers and wiped my eyes with a Kleenex from my purse.

"He won't kill himself," I said almost bitterly. "He just wants to make me go crazy with worry."

After that, neither one of us said anything for a while. Then Liz said, "Do you want to move into the living room? It's more comfortable there."

I shook my head no. "This is fine," I said.

Liz took another slurp of her coffee. The noise is bad enough, but she always makes this face too—a kind of fish-face, with puckered lips. I looked away until she was done.

"Would you like some more coffee?" Liz said. "I have half a pot left."

"No thanks," I said.

Then Liz looked out the window again, and it suddenly occurred to me that she might be watching the driveway for Gerry's car.

"Maybe I should be going," I said, to see what she would say. "No," she said. "Stay."

I'm not sure she meant it, but I lit another cigarette anyway and blew the smoke toward the ceiling.

"You're an attractive woman," Liz finally said. "I'm sure Billy still finds you attractive. That can't be the problem."

To Liz, *attractive* means *slender*. I am that, and I've always had nice blond hair and a peaches-and-cream complexion, but I'm no starlet. Still, I can remember times when Billy wanted me so bad he'd practically beg for it.

I shook my head. "I don't know," I said. "One night last week I got into bed and cuddled up next to him, but he just laid there. So I started touching him. He didn't move or say anything. Nothing at all. After a minute, I just took my hand away."

"You don't have to tell me this if you don't want to," Liz said.

"I've got to talk to someone," I said. I was already beginning to feel I was talking to the wrong person, that I should leave and go see Jeanette or Bev, but I went on anyway. "If only Billy hadn't been called for jury duty," I said, "if only Mr. Parker had said they couldn't spare him from the plant, maybe things wouldn't be so bad."

Liz said, "I'm sure Billy was under a lot of pressure. All those hearings and then the jury was hung so long. Maybe in a little while, after he rests up, things will get back to normal between you two."

"There should never have been a trial," I said. "Everybody knew that Keathley killed her. Didn't his own neighbors testify they heard the shot and saw him come out of the house carrying a shotgun—the very same gun the police proved was the murder weapon? And her best friend, that McGuire woman, didn't she testify that they'd been fighting for weeks and she'd threatened to leave him? What more proof did anybody need? And Keathley, he never denied anything. He just sat there stone-faced as could be. He was as guilty as they come. Everybody could see that.

They should've sent him to the chair the day they caught him, with no trial or anything."

"That's what everybody was saying," Liz said. "The paper made it look like an open-and-shut case. I couldn't figure out why it took the jury so many days to reach a verdict."

She raised her cup to her lips. I wondered if I should say anything, then I decided to.

"Because Billy voted to acquit," I said.

Liz stopped in mid-slurp, then set her cup down on the table.

"Billy was the one who kept the jury sequestered," I went on. "He was the 'anonymous juror' the paper said wouldn't change his vote. They argued with him for one whole day, then gave up. But Judge Munden wouldn't accept a hung jury. He sent them right back to the Marriott and told them to try again. The state hates a hung jury in a trial that's gotten that much publicity. And, of course, the judge must've known Keathley was guilty as hell."

"Didn't Billy think Keathley was guilty?" Liz asked. Her voice was a little trembly, like she was excited. It almost seemed like she *hoped* he was innocent.

I'd told her so much already, I thought I might as well tell her the rest.

"Billy told the other jurors there was 'reasonable doubt,'" I said, "but he told me he voted to acquit because of Keathley's eyes."

I stubbed out my cigarette, even though it was only half-smoked.

Liz looked at me. "What do you mean, his eyes?"

"That's what I asked Billy," I said. "I said, 'You don't judge a man's guilt or innocence by his eyes, you judge it by the evidence.' He just said, 'I wasn't judging his guilt or innocence.' And I said, 'Then what the hell were you judging?' But he only shook his head."

Liz shook her head too. "I don't understand," she said. "What did Billy see in Keathley's eyes that made him vote for acquittal?"

"He said he saw how sad he was," I answered. "Can you believe that?—how *sad*? The man's killed his wife, and Billy's thinking how sad the poor guy is."

And all of a sudden I started crying again, thinking how sad *I* was. It wasn't fair. It just wasn't fair.

This time Liz didn't hold my hands or comfort me. I don't think she even noticed I was crying, she looked so caught up in what I'd told her.

I wiped my tears. I mean, I've got some pride. Even if my life is falling apart, I've got to hold my head high.

"And he held out against the other jurors for three days?" Liz said. "He kept them away from their families and jobs all that time just because of Keathley's eyes?" Liz's voice annoyed me— she sounded more impressed than puzzled.

"He said they were all yelling at him, threatening him," I told her. "Bob Jacobs, the insurance agent, even tried to hit him once. But Billy stayed calm, he was as emotionless as Keathley himself."

"It must have hurt him a lot," Liz said, looking out the window again.

"He said he tried not to listen to them after a while," I said. "He'd just watch their mouths move and their fists shake and when they were done, he'd just say, 'I still don't think we have enough evidence for conviction.'"

"No," Liz said, looking back at me. "I didn't mean the arguing."

I wasn't sure what she had meant, and I doubt she was either. "If you ask me," I said, "Billy's the one who did the hurting. He hurt all those other jurors and their families and businesses, and he hurt me. And he did it all because he thought he was smarter and better than everyone else on the jury. He told me, 'No one knows what's happened to him, no one knows what he's been through.' 'No one except you,' I said back. 'You think you know everything. What makes you such an expert on murderers?' I said. Billy didn't say anything for a minute, he just looked at me, but then he said, 'I changed my vote, didn't I?' That's the last thing he's said about the trial."

Liz sat there and didn't say anything. She just looked at her hands.

I figured it was time to leave, so I took out my compact and looked at my face in the little mirror. My eyes were puffy and red, like I had pink eye, and my mascara had streaked onto my cheeks. I clicked the compact shut.

"I can't go home like this," I said. "I don't want Billy to see me like this."

Liz looked up from her hands. "The doctors did wonders for Gerry," she said. "He hasn't had a drink in over a year—at least that's what I've heard. Maybe if you can talk Billy into seeing someone . . ."

"Billy says he won't see any doctor," I said. "What's more, he says there's nothing wrong with him, that *I'm* the one with the problem. He blames it all on me. He says I'm the monster, not Keathley."

Liz looked down at her cup, like she was searching for words in the coffee. Then she looked up. She seemed sadder than I'd seen her since Gerry left, her face suddenly pale, even her lips drained of color.

"Maybe you should see someone too," she said. "Maybe you two should go together."

"Look," I said, "are you joking? It's Billy that has the problem, not me."

"I'm serious," Liz said. "Maybe a doctor could help you understand what Billy's going through."

"But there's nothing to understand," I said. "It doesn't make any sense. You can't understand something that doesn't make any sense, can you? How can anyone feel the way he does about a murderer? He almost *admires* the guy, if you want my opinion."

Liz said, "When Gerry left me last winter, I felt like I was dead. I stared at everything, a dead stare, but I didn't see anything. I was so far inside myself I couldn't see out. I was completely gone. He'd killed me. Gerry'd killed me, and I wasn't here anymore."

She looked out the window. "Sometimes I still feel that way," she said.

I lit another cigarette. I was mad, and I admit it. Just because she'd had a bad marriage didn't make her an authority on misery.

"I don't understand what all that has to do with me and Billy," I said. "All I want to know is who you think has the problem, me or Billy."

"Barb," she said, "I have no right to judge either of you."

"Come on," I said. "Who is it, Billy or me?"

Liz just sat there and looked at me. "There were times I dreamed Gerry had drowned," she said. "Night after night I saw him lying, face down, at the bottom of a lake. Boats would pass over, people searching for him, but they never found him. In my dream, I'd try to yell out to those people, tell them where he was, but when I opened my mouth, I'd feel water come in and burn in my lungs. I'd wake up then, crying and gasping for air."

"I want an answer," I said.

She looked around her kitchen. "I have some company coming tonight," she said. "I'd better get the house cleaned and everything."

"I'm not going until I get an answer," I said.

But instead of answering, she took another drink of her coffee. Even though it must have been cold by now, she still slurped it like it was boiling hot.

I stood up, my fist clenched. "*Stop that!*" I said.

DEPOSITIONS

THE NEIGHBOR

I'm pretty sure I heard the shot that killed her. The storm woke me up—I don't know what time it was but it was the middle of the night—and I was standing at the bedroom window, watching the lightning and wondering if I should head for the basement, just to be safe. If my wife were still alive, she would have been frantic. She hated storms, and that was a terrible one. I'd never heard thunder that loud before. It'd boom, just like fireworks do right before the sky lights up, and then there'd be this long growl-like rumble. But once I heard something that sounded a little different, something like the echo of thunder. It never occurred to me that it might be a shotgun. But in the morning I saw the ambulance and police cars and I knew he'd finally killed her, or himself, or maybe the both of them, and I started to think it was a shotgun blast that I'd heard. But even if I'd dialed 911 the minute I heard it, no one could have saved her. But you already know that. Like your partner over there said, the bastard shot her from such close range there was almost nothing left of her face.

THE KILLER

I remember the noise—it was so unbelievably loud—and I remember standing there, beside her, and lowering the shotgun. So I know I did it. No one else was even there with us when it happened, so it had to be me. But I don't remember pointing the gun or pulling the trigger, or even why I would want to kill her. I should be able to remember those things, right? But I can't even imagine doing it. Is it possible you could actually do something and it would *still* be unimaginable?

THE VICTIM
Now I know why they call it phantom pain when a limb you lost still hurts: being a phantom hurts. The pain is like liquid fire, an ocean of it, lapping against where you no longer are.

THE DETECTIVE
In her dresser drawer we found all these birthday and Christmas and Mother's Day cards. All the usual sentiments. And all of them signed "Love" or "Love Forever," things like that. She kept them all. I'll bet there are millions of women all over the world with cards like that in their dressers. My own wife, too, I bet.

THE KILLER
Maybe I was asleep when I did it, maybe I was walking in my sleep and I didn't know what I was doing. Maybe it was all one of those dreams that vanish the moment you wake up and that's why I can't remember it. Or maybe I'm asleep now, maybe I've always been asleep, and I was only awake for the second it took to pull the trigger.

THE NEIGHBOR
Once he threw her out the door without a stitch of clothes on, and in the middle of the winter, too. She was out there half an hour at least, stark naked in the broad daylight, pounding on the door, begging for him to let her in. She knocked on my door, too, but there was no way I was going to get involved in their fight. An old man like me, what chance do you think I'd have if that bastard decided to give me some of the same medicine he was giving her? Some people would say that was wrong of me, not to let her in, but

anyone who knew those two would have done the same thing I did. She knocked on other neighbors' doors, too, and no one was stupid enough to let her in. She was naked, for Christ's sake, and probably high on something. And she was just as much an animal as he was. Believe me, she could give as good as she got, kicking and biting and scratching like a madwoman. For all I knew, that's why he threw her out that day. Anyway, I did call 911 but by the time you guys got here, everything was over, like it always is, and nothing happened. Same old story. A few minutes before the police cars pulled up, he finally opened the door and let her in. Her skin was blue and she was hugging her skinny ribs, she was so cold. She was a walking skeleton. I was watching through a crack in my blinds and I saw him hit her the second she was inside, a closed fist up against the side of her head, right on the temple. The *temple*: Christ, the words we use. That head of hers was anything but a temple. I don't say she deserved what she got—nobody deserves that—but she was no babe in the woods. Just look at the way she treated that little girl of hers. What is she—four or five? And already she's been exposed to all that sex and violence and drugs. With a mother like that, there's no telling who the girl's real father is. You can call that woman a victim if you want, but she was no goddamn saint, I can assure you of that. Ask anybody who lives around here.

THE VICTIM'S DAUGHTER

He isn't my daddy. My daddy is God. That's what Momma always told me. She said God gave me to her. God the Father. That's the god who's not a bird, or Jesus. He's the main god, the one who gives children to mommas.

I wonder when he'll give my momma back to me.

THE DETECTIVE

My wife. I don't know who she is. Sometimes I look at her and I think we should go our separate ways. But then I think, We already have. Still, if she left me, I'd be sad. Maybe worse than sad.

THE DETECTIVE'S WIFE

I wonder what he says when he talks about it to the other officers. Whatever it is, I'm sure it's a lie. Tough guy talk, whistling in the dark. He was so shook up when he came home that day, he couldn't keep his hands from trembling. He told me there'd been a murder, then he sat down at the kitchen table. *Her face,* he said. And then he said *Jesus.* That's all he said after that. I asked him questions, I hugged him, I rubbed his shoulders, but all he'd say was *Jesus*—nothing else, just that. Everything I know about the murder, I read in the paper. He still won't say a word about it to me. He thinks he's protecting me, but his silence scares me more than anything he could say. And he's been so distant. Last night, we made love for the first time in a month. I was on top of him, doing all the work, and he just laid there with his eyes closed. Afterward, I switched the light on so I could find my panties, and I saw tears had run down his temples. Even his ears were wet with them.

THE VICTIM

When you look at something up close, it gets larger. Go closer still and it disappears. That's what happens when you die: you're so close that everything's gone.

THE VICTIM'S DAUGHTER

They only hit each other when they got really mad. When they were mad just a little, all they did was yell. And the only time they ever hit me was when I was bad.

THE KILLER

Sure, we fought. But I was crazy about her. She had these freckles on her shoulders and back. God, how I loved those freckles. I'd kiss them, one by one by one. "Connect-the-dot kisses," she called them.

Could *you* kill someone who said something like that to you?

THE NEIGHBOR

Once I went out to mow my yard and as soon as I stepped outside I heard them screaming like banshees. Their windows were open—it was cool that day, at least for summer—and I'm sure everybody could hear them up and down the block. At first I thought they were fighting again, but then I realized it was something else. They were making love. I could tell by some of the things they were saying. Jesus, I thought, they make love the same way they fight. Like I said, they were animals. And the whole time they were making all that racket, saying words no little girl should ever hear, her daughter was sitting there on the front steps, blowing soap bubbles. She had this little pink bottle and she'd dip the wand into it, puff up her chubby little cheeks, and blow out bubble after bubble, then watch them float away. Seeing her blow those bubbles like that just broke my heart. I hope someone adopts that little girl. She should have been taken away from her mother years ago. Hell, she should have been taken away from her at birth. She deserves a mother as loving and good as my Eleanor would have been, if we'd had any kids.

THE VICTIM

What if I hadn't been her mother? What if I'd just been one of her teachers or the lady who lived next door—would my daughter still love me? Is love nothing more than an accident of birth?

THE VICTIM'S DAUGHTER

Once my momma was spanking me and she started to laugh. I don't know what was so funny, but she laughed so hard she started to choke. And then she was crying and holding me, calling me *Baby*. I'm not a baby. I'm almost five.

THE NEIGHBOR

I have to admit I didn't always hate the guy, or the woman either. When my Eleanor died, the two of them brought over a casserole. It surprised the hell out of me, since I'd hardly ever talked to them before. We were just neighbors, not friends, but they sat in the living room with me for nearly an hour, talking. They could have ignored me, the way some of the other neighbors did. I thought for a long time that they were good people, underneath. But I changed my mind.

THE DETECTIVE'S WIFE

Sometimes I wonder if he'd love me more if I were dead. That seems like such a pure kind of love. Every June I fly to Denver to spend a week with my mother. I always make sure I'm there for her wedding anniversary. She misses Dad all the time, she says, but especially then. And my husband misses me while I'm gone too. When I come home, he can't take his hands off me. And it's not just the sex he misses, I can tell that. It's me. Or whatever he thinks is me.

THE KILLER

Sure, I've always wanted to be loved more than I deserve. Doesn't everyone?

THE VICTIM'S DAUGHTER

When I grow up, I'm going to marry a girl. Girls are nicer than boys.

THE KILLER

Only God knows why I did it. But He's not talking. And does killing her make me evil? That was just one second of my life; think of all the billions and billions of other seconds, when I didn't do anything bad. And there are worse sins than murder, anyway. I remember back in high school, we had to read this book about hell. It was called a comedy, but it wasn't funny. Hell was a lot like this prison, only instead of floor after floor of cells it had circles and each one was hotter than the one before, and the hottest was for those who didn't do anything when they should have. They were worse than the murderers, the rapists, worse than everybody except maybe Satan himself. They were the ones who stayed neutral, above everything and everybody. Now, doesn't that sound a lot like God?

THE VICTIM

When he was in me, I was outside of myself. It was like heroin—all feeling, no body. Gone.

Now there's nothing to be outside of. Now I am the outside.

THE NEIGHBOR

If I hadn't started to hate that woman, I don't know what would have become of me. When my wife died, I thought I was dead, too. For months I felt like a ghost. I'd be in the kitchen one minute and it'd be morning and then I'd find myself, at night, in the bedroom, and I wouldn't remember anything in between. I felt like I was nothing but vapor, like I could walk through walls. I don't know how I came out of it, but I know that woman had something to do with it. I saw her yelling at her daughter in the yard one day and I was angry for the first time in I don't know how long. Why did God take my Eleanor and let someone like her live? I remember standing at my window, watching her ugly, contorted face and that sweet little girl crying, and hatred just came over me. It felt so good to have someone to hate. You can understand that, can't you, officer? I mean, how else could you do the job you do?

THE VICTIM'S DAUGHTER

Once we went on a roller coaster. We were way up high and screaming and he put his arms around both of us. I screamed louder and louder, so he'd hug me tighter. When the ride stopped, I almost called him Daddy.

THE DETECTIVE

It's crazy, I know, but in some ways I envy the guy. Here he is, hated by everyone and locked up in prison waiting to die, and I envy him. All he has to do is wait for the end. Everything's out of his hands now. He's free.

THE DETECTIVE'S WIFE

When I saw her picture in the paper, she looked familiar, though I couldn't say where or when I might have seen her. This is a pretty small town so I probably passed her on the street a hundred times, or sat behind her at the movie theater, or saw her playing in the park with her daughter. It's funny: all day long we pass people on the street or in the grocery store and we don't stop to think that someday those people are going to die, that we're all going to die. We see someone and we don't realize that this might be the last time we'll ever see that person alive. And all we do is say hello or nod or just walk past them as if they aren't even there. Amazing.

THE KILLER

I remember once we went to the playground and we started to swing, trying to see who could go the highest. We were laughing and acting just like kids, and that little girl of hers just sat there in the dirt watching us, a frown on her face like *she* was the adult. That just made us laugh even harder and swing even higher and higher, until we were almost completely upside down, our feet pointed up at the sky and our heads thrown back, laughing. It was a happy day. But even then I wondered, was that person who was laughing so hard me, or just someone I wanted to be?

Maybe that's why I killed her, to find out, once and for all, who I was.

THE DETECTIVE'S WIFE

Sometimes I just start crying and don't even know why.

THE VICTIM

All I remember of that last moment is the noise. All the thunder seemed to coalesce into one sound that blew through my brain like a comet trailing flames. The flames have stayed but not the sound. Now there's nothing but silence, the only language God speaks.

THE VICTIM'S DAUGHTER

Tears are so hot sometimes, they almost burn you. That doesn't make sense. Water can't be fire.

THE KILLER

When I think of all the millions of things that had to happen to make the murder possible, things I had no control over, I don't know how anyone can say it's my fault, or at least my fault alone. What if we'd never met, what if I hadn't gone to the café where she waitressed, or if I'd sat at another table, one she wasn't responsible for—would I be sitting here waiting to be murdered myself? And what if my father hadn't given me that shotgun when I turned fifteen, or my great-grandfather hadn't moved here for work when the Depression hit? If even one little thing had happened differently, I would have had an entirely different life. Maybe I chose to pull the trigger, but I didn't choose everything else that led to that choice. And they say everything happens according to God's plan, so why isn't everybody blaming *Him*?

THE VICTIM'S DAUGHTER

Why isn't everybody crying all the time?

THE DETECTIVE

Is God just the name we give to everything we don't know?

THE NEIGHBOR

According to the paper, he claims he loves her, that he always loved her. Does he actually expect us to believe that load of crap? At least I can admit the truth—I hated her. She was scum, just like him. But there's one thing I don't understand: he's the one who killed her, so why do I feel guilty?

THE VICTIM

If only you could take me into you, breathe me into your lungs and hold me there, by your heart, your hard, beating heart.

PROVIDENCE

The day the little girl drowned, Robby was sitting in the lifeguard's chair, imagining he was kissing Carrie Madigan. He'd applied for the lifeguarding job at Willow Lake Recreation World just so he could be near her. She was the boss's daughter and she worked in the snack bar, so he'd take his break there, either sipping a Coke at a table or playing on the video games that lined the wall opposite the counter, stealing a glance at her black hair and blue eyes and upturned nose as she gave someone change. Outside of ordering a Coke, he'd never spoken to her, and although they worked at the same place and they'd passed each other in the halls at school many times, he didn't think she even knew his name. She was the most popular girl in the class, and she only dated athletes. Robby was an athlete too, a swimmer, but no one cared about the swim team. At some matches, the only people in the stands were the swimmers' parents.

Robby had fallen in love with Carrie the night he saw her play Anne Frank in the junior class play. She was so beautiful and she was such a good actress that several times during the last act tears had come into his eyes. What misery Anne Frank had endured! And even though she'd suffered so much, she was able to forgive, even love, her enemies. He couldn't forget how he'd choked up at the play's last line: "In spite of everything, I still believe that people are really good at heart." When Carrie said those words, the stage was completely dark, except for the spotlight on her face. That was the moment he fell in love with her, and now whenever he imagined kissing her, the whole world around them was dark and her face was the only light. It had been three days since he last saw Carrie—she and the rest of her family were on vacation in Florida—and he missed her so much he couldn't stop thinking about her.

Because Robby was imagining kissing her in the woods behind the miniature golf course, he didn't hear the yells at first. Then he heard them. He hadn't yet understood the words, but he knew what they meant. Tearing his sunglasses off, he leapt from the chair and began running down the beach, thinking *No*.

A frail blond woman was standing knee-deep in the lake, holding her temples as if they were about to burst. "CeCe!" she yelled. "Oh my God. CeCe!"

As Robby ran up to her, he remembered seeing her earlier that afternoon and noticing some brown hairs curling out from the crotch of her yellow swimsuit. It was a terrible thought to have at a time like this, and he tried to push it out of his mind.

Before he could say anything to the woman, she grasped his arm with both hands. "You have to *save* her," she said. She squeezed his arm so hard it hurt. "She's *drowning!*"

"Where?" he asked, ashamed he did not know.

But the woman didn't seem to hear. "Oh," she said. Just "Oh," as if she'd discovered a pain so far beyond any she'd ever known that it surprised more than hurt her.

By now they were surrounded by the swimmers and their mothers. One of the mothers put her arm around the woman and said, "Don't cry, Julie," even though she was not, in fact, crying.

"Where *is* she?" Robby repeated, looking from face to face. "I need to know *where*."

"I don't know," another woman said, her hand trembling on her forehead. "When Julie and I looked up, she was gone."

Then a red-shouldered little boy with goggles around his neck said, "She was jumping off the platform." His eyes were open wide.

Almost before the boy finished talking, Robby was in the lake, swimming toward the diving platform with the big green Recreation World sign on it. But something was wrong: he was swimming like a beginner. He couldn't coordinate his strokes and kicks. And his breaths: he had to lift his face out of the water repeatedly and gulp for air, and each time he did, he broke his momentum and floundered a moment. It seemed like his arms and legs had gone numb, like they belonged to someone else. He prayed, *Dear God*, but couldn't finish the prayer.

When he reached the diving platform, he held onto the warm concrete side for a dizzy second, took a deep breath, and dove down. His eyes open, straining to see, he swam to the lake bottom. Above him, the platform loomed like an iceberg, and he suddenly remembered an old movie he and his mother had watched on TV one night. It was about a magician named Harry Houdini, and in it Houdini was trapped under the ice covering a river. All the people on the bridge above him were waiting for him to reappear, but the magic wasn't working, there wasn't any magic really, and Houdini was lost and searching frantically for a way out. But everywhere he swam he found only ice.

For a second Robby shut his eyes against the stinging dark. Why was he thinking such odd thoughts? He didn't know, but he knew he had to find the girl before it was too late. He swam around the platform's rusty girders, and everywhere he looked he expected to see the girl, her mouth and eyes open, accusatory, and her hair streaked across her face like seaweed. Every moment he was afraid he would find her, and terrified he would not. He swam until his lungs were throbbing, but he did not find her.

When he burst up into the light, Robby saw that some of the mothers and even some of the children were swimming out to help him. "Call 911!" he yelled to the women still clustered around the girl's mother. He should've told them to do that before he even began searching for the girl, but he hadn't thought of it until now. He had panicked, he hadn't done anything as he'd been taught. He could almost hear what the women would tell the policemen and newspaper reporters about him. He had never felt such shame. And he was ashamed even of being ashamed: he shouldn't be thinking about himself now, only the girl. He took a deep breath and dove down again.

This time he widened the circle of his search. It was so dark where the platform cast its shadow into the brown water that he had to search more with his hands than his eyes. He felt everywhere, but all he touched was mud and rock and weeds. For a moment he stopped his search, treading water, but then he started again, feeling his way through the dark, until his ears and throat were aching, his lungs ready to explode, and he couldn't stay under any longer. He came up gasping, a good thirty feet away from the platform. He'd had no idea he'd gone that far. Under the water, everything seemed distorted, transformed.

He treaded water for a moment, watching the other searchers dive and surface around the platform, waiting for his head to stop ringing. He didn't want to go back under. But he knew he had to find her—it wouldn't be right for anyone else to find her—so he took another deep, searing breath and dove back into the darkness.

His eyes burned from staring through the murky water. He was happy they hurt. And he was glad when his lungs began to pound. He'd been daydreaming; he hadn't seen her drown. It was only fair that he drown too. He vowed he wouldn't come up until he found her.

But he had to come up for air three more times before he finally found her. She was a few yards away from one of the girders, in the shadow of the platform. Her drowning had so roiled the lake bottom that he felt her before he saw her. He had been feeling his way along the bottom when suddenly he touched her hand. It was rigid, clawlike, and he jerked his hand away. Then he saw the dim shape of her body: she was lying on her side, her knees tucked up against her chest like a baby. He thought about swimmers who crossed the English Channel, how they wore hat pins in their swimsuits so they could stick themselves and uncramp their muscles. If she'd only had a pin, he thought. A simple pin.

Then Robby put an arm around her thin waist and, kicking off the bottom, swam one-armed to the surface. When they broke the water, he gasped for air, almost retching from holding his breath so long. He was so dizzy he could barely see.

"He's got her!" a boy swimming nearby yelled.

Mr. Murphy, the old guy who ran the kiddie carnival, was in the water now, too. He splashed toward Robby, his bald head bobbing up and down, his breath huffing. "Let me help you," he said between breaths, but as soon as he reached out for the girl, Robby pulled her away and said "No!" He was surprised at how angry he sounded.

"Okay," Mr. Murphy puffed. "Okay." And then he turned and swam back toward the shore.

When Robby carried the girl up onto the beach, her mother cried "CeCe!" as if her name were a prayer, and it suddenly struck Robby as impossible—impossible and evil—that God would let a little girl named CeCe die.

"I'm sorry," he said to the girl's mother, but she was sobbing so hard she couldn't hear. Mr. Murphy was holding her up, trying to soothe her. "The ambulance will be here any minute," he was saying. "She's still got a good chance."

Then Robby knelt down in the sand beside the girl. She was small—maybe seven years old—and she had strawberry-blond hair and freckles. The bridge of her nose was white where her mother had put sunblock to protect her from burning.

"Step back," he said to the people who had gathered around him, then he tilted the girl's head back, pinched her nose shut, and began to breathe into her, breathe for her. And suddenly he remembered, as from a time almost beyond memory, his daydream of kissing Carrie. His eyes began to sting, and his breaths came out like sobs.

Sometime later—it could have been a few minutes or an hour—Mr. Murphy came over and put his hand on Robby's shoulder. "You might as well stop, son," he said. "It's over." But Robby did not stop.

And awhile later Robby heard the siren and after that the two men from the Rescue Squad were there, talking to him as the siren wound down to a moan. But he didn't understand what they were saying, and he kept on trying to breathe his life into her.

By the time Robby finished giving his statement to the police officer and drove his moped home, his mother had already left for her weekly Parents Without Partners meeting. There was a note on the refrigerator door that told him he'd find a chicken pot pie in the freezer. Robby read the note twice before the words made sense to him. Then he crumpled the note and dropped it on the floor.

He sat down at the kitchen table and put his head in his hands. The Formica tabletop was decorated with rust-colored flecks that looked like freckles. He closed his eyes a moment, then stood up. He had to do something. Maybe he'd try to watch some television. Maybe that would help.

But when he went into the living room, he forgot what he'd gone in there for. He stood in the middle of the room and looked around, but all he saw was the little girl, her eyes closed and her hair caked with wet sand. He tried to think of something, anything, to take his mind off her, but all he could think of was Carrie, and he couldn't think of her now without thinking also of the drowned girl. For a moment he imagined Carrie drowning, saw her struggling in the dark, her eyes shut against her terror, water burning in her throat.

He forced the thought out of his head, then remembered the television and switched it on. But instead of lying down on the couch to watch, he went to his room. Just inside the door, he stopped. Somehow the room seemed strange, a friend's room maybe, but not a place where he'd done homework and slept for years. The poster of Michael Phelps over the bed; the district freestyle trophy on his desk; the yearbook beside it, open to a picture of Carrie and the rest of the Student Council—everything seemed to belong to someone else. Even the photograph on his bulletin board. Who was that boy with a crew cut holding up a small stringer of sunfish? And that man who had his big hand on the boy's shoulder, who was he?

Before he even realized he'd left his room, Robby found himself sitting on the edge of his mother's bed, holding onto her chenille bedspread. He had always loved the way her room smelled of talc and sachet. He sat there inside that smell, breathing it in and waiting for her to come home.

The next day Mr. Madigan called from Orlando. He was in a motel room and there was a sound, like someone showering, in the background. Robby wondered if it was Carrie, then felt sick, thinking of her standing there, enjoying the water pulsing against her body. "Murph called me last night," Mr. Madigan said. "He told me what happened. It's a horrible thing. I know you must feel awful about it, even though you did all you could. So I'm calling to give you a week off. With pay, of course. We'll get Dane or Joy to take your place. You just take it easy for a while and forget about all this, okay?"

Robby didn't plan to go back to Recreation World ever, but he didn't say that to Mr. Madigan. It would have taken too much of an effort. Mr. Madigan would have asked him to reconsider, and he would have had to say something. Every answer would have led to another question. No, it was better just to say "Okay." But he had no intention of returning. He didn't want to see that place ever again, or Mr. Madigan, or even Carrie.

That afternoon, his mother sat on the edge of his bed and smiled at him. "I've got an idea," she said. "What do you say we go to a movie, just the two of us? Something funny."

Robby shook his head no. His mother smoothed the lap of her plaid dress, then looked away a moment. When she looked back, her forehead was creased but she was still smiling.

"Or maybe we could drive down to Shreveport and visit your cousins," she said. "What do you think about that? I'm sure I could get Leonard to give me a couple of days off. Effie's been asking for overtime anyway; she could take over my station. What do you say?"

Robby couldn't look at her any longer. She looked like she was afraid she'd start to cry if she stopped smiling. He turned onto his side and faced the wall beside his bed.

His mother put her hand on his shoulder. "Robby, I know how you feel. Believe me, I do. But you've got to do something. You can't just lay here and think about it all the time."

Robby was silent. He wished she'd just go away and leave him alone.

"I remember how I felt when your father left," she said then. "I thought I'd never get over that. But I did, and so have you. That's something you have to remember: human beings can get over anything. We adapt. That's what makes us so great."

Robby didn't believe her. And if it was true, if people could adapt to such horrible things, that was something to be *ashamed* of, not proud. There were some things you shouldn't be able to get over, not ever.

"Do you see what I'm saying?" she asked.

Robby closed his eyes. "I'm tired, Mom. I want to go to sleep now."

"You can't sleep forever."

"I'd like to."

She took her hand away. "Robby, please don't talk like that. It hurts me to hear you talk like that."

Robby didn't say anything.

His mother stood up. "Maybe it'd help if we prayed for her. Maybe if we went down to church and lit a candle and said a few prayers."

Robby didn't answer. Nothing could make him pray again. But if he told her that, she'd only cry.

"Robby?" she said. "What do you say?"

He didn't want to answer. He just wanted to go to sleep.

"Robby?" she repeated.

"No," he finally said.

For a moment, his mother was silent, then he heard her leave his room and go into her own across the hall. Through her door he could hear the faint sound of her sobbing. He wanted to get up and go put his arm around her, tell her he was sorry he'd hurt her, but he couldn't. He didn't even have the strength to turn over. He lay there on the bed, waiting for her to stop.

A few minutes later, she came out of her room. "I'm off to get groceries," she said, her voice straining to be cheerful. "I'll see you later, honey." Robby wanted to call after her then, tell her how much he loved her. He took a deep breath and dove down for the words, his head light and woozy. But he could not find them.

For the rest of that day, Robby stayed in bed, refusing to get up, go outside, or even watch television in the living room. He just lay there, trying not to think, trying to empty his mind of everything. But the girl was always there, curled up rigid on the sand, her dead face pinched with shock.

But by the next day, Robby was no longer trapped in the moment of the girl's death. He would sit there in bed, propped up on his pillows, and his mind would swim around that moment, almost never touching it. And when he did touch it, he'd feel his heart turn over, and he'd quickly make himself think of something else. Late that morning, he found himself remembering how the girl's mother had stood in the lake, her hands gripping her head, and he called out for his own mother. But she was at Mass. She was praying that very moment, he knew, praying for the drowned girl's soul, and for his drowned soul. He looked out the window for something to fasten his thoughts onto, but all he saw was the rusty old swing set in his backyard, and he imagined the little girl swinging on it, laughing and pumping hard, her mother watching and smiling. And then, to shut that image out of his mind, he reached over to the nightstand beside his bed and took up an old *Reader's Digest* his mother had put there the day before.

He opened the magazine and began to read an article called "Vitamin C and You." He didn't care what the article said, he just wanted the words, and he let the meaningless vowels and consonants flow through his mind and carry him out of himself.

After he'd read for a while, he felt a little better. And later that day, he picked up the magazine and read some more, this time just for something to do. At first he read mostly without interest, but then he found himself smiling at one of the anecdotes in the section called "Life in These United States." He was ashamed of himself for finding anything funny after what had happened, and he put the magazine away. But a few minutes later, he picked it up again and read some more.

The next day, he read the *People* magazine his mother bought for him and the sports section of the newspaper. And that afternoon, he worked on a "TV Facts" crossword puzzle, solving all but six of the clues. Thoughts of the little girl hovered just beyond the words he read, but they did not break in as often or for as long as they had the day before.

That night, his mother came into his room with a big bowl of popcorn. "Guess what's coming on in five minutes?" she said. "One of your favorite movies."

Robby looked at her standing there, holding the bowl before her like an offering, and felt such a sudden sad love for her that he tried to smile. "What is it, Mom?" he asked.

She smiled. "*The Day the Earth Stood Still.* Remember that one? We saw it one night when you were little—too little for such a scary movie. The three of us stayed up late and ate popcorn and watched it. And that night you woke up crying and came in to sleep with us. But the next day you were telling everybody you weren't scared at all."

Robby could see that she was trying not to cry.

"I remember, Mom," he said. "Let's watch it again, okay?" And he started to get out of bed.

There were tears in her eyes now, but she was smiling. "I'll go pour us some Cokes," she said.

Robby wasn't sure when he decided to go back to Recreation World, or why. He needed the money, of course, but that wasn't the reason. Maybe he wanted to find out if he was all right, see if he could bear to watch a little girl jump off the diving platform and disappear, even for a moment. Or maybe he just wanted to show everyone he wasn't a coward. He tried to examine his conscience for his motive, but he couldn't be sure what it was. He even asked himself if he was going back so he could see Carrie. But he really didn't care if he ever saw her again. He was a different person now.

His first day back was a Saturday, so there was a good-sized crowd on the beach waiting for the signal that they could begin swimming. He didn't recognize anyone from the day the little girl drowned. Taking a deep breath, he climbed up into his chair, then blew his whistle. All of the kids ran splashing and yelling into the lake, while their mothers and a few fathers waded in behind them.

It was a hot, bright day, so Robby put sunblock on his nose and shoulders while he surveyed the stretch of lake before him, watching kids toss beach balls and Frisbees near the shore and swimmers bob out near the buoys that bordered the swimming area. He started to look out at the diving platform once, but he shifted his eyes away and watched two little boys splash water on their mothers, who were sitting on lawn chairs at the water's edge. But a few minutes later, he forced himself to look at the platform. Somehow it seemed smaller than he remembered, and the waves lapping at its sides made it seem to float, light as a dream, in the water. He stared at it for a long time. After a while, a boy and a girl climbed up the ladder on its side. Robby watched them stand there talking about something. Then the boy pointed toward the spot where Robby had found the drowned girl, and the girl held her arms like she was shivering. When they finally dove in, it was on the other side of the platform.

Robby turned away. For a second, he thought of going up to Mr. Madigan's office and quitting. But then he saw Carrie walking down the beach toward him. She was wearing a dark green Recreation World T-shirt over white denim cutoffs and she was carrying a can of Coke in each hand. As she walked up to him, she smiled and said hi. Robby said hello back, then she put her bare brown toes on the bottom rung of the ladder leading up to his chair and looked up at him. "My name's Carrie," she said.

"I know," he answered. Then, he thought to add, "Mine's Robby."

She nodded. "I thought you might be thirsty," she said, and held up one of the cans to him.

He took it, hoping she didn't notice his hand was trembling. "Thanks."

"It's so hot today," she said. She looked around the lake, then down at her toes. When she looked back up at him, her brow was furrowed, the way Anne Frank's had been in the play. And then she said, "If you ever want to talk about it—you know, what happened—I want you to know I'd be glad to listen."

Robby's heart was beating so hard his head felt light. Now he knew why all of this had happened; it wasn't for nothing; it was all to bring him and Carrie together, just as he had dreamed. "Okay," he said and smiled. And for a second—a second that could have destroyed his life had he not immediately forced it out of his mind—he was almost happy the little girl had drowned.

TRESPASSING

The first time Richard saw the boy and girl making love on his property was in late June, three months after he'd retired and started spending all of his time at home. He and Ellen had quarreled at lunch, so he'd stormed out and headed toward the southern edge of the woods that surrounded their house. There was a narrow creek that ran through a small grassy clearing in the hollow, and he planned to sit there and watch the water swirl lazily around the rocks until he calmed himself down. He'd gone to this place many times since he and Ellen bought this land in 1967. Back then, the nearest neighbor was a farmer who lived a quarter section away, but in the past few years developers had moved in and now the woods were surrounded by houses and apartment complexes. Sometimes Richard would come across kids from the new neighborhoods playing hide-and-seek or climbing trees or hunting squirrels. It infuriated him. They had no right to be on his land, and they knew it: to get there, they had to climb over a barbed wire fence posted with No Trespassing signs.

As Richard wound his way through the thicket of oaks and hickories, he tried to enjoy the breeze grazing his cheek, the songs of hidden birds, the way the sun flickered through the green leaves and mottled the ground with a strange underwater light. But somehow he couldn't. For the past few months he hadn't been able to enjoy anything. He was on edge all the time, it seemed. He knew the quarrel was his fault, but sometimes he got so bored he couldn't help but take it out on Ellen. He had thought he was bored with his medical practice—forty years of sore throats and broken bones and ulcers and pregnant women—but now he knew what boredom truly was. Ellen, though, she just went from one household task to another, humming. And she was forever suggesting they *do* something—take a trip, throw a dinner party, join their church book club. "You've got too much time to just sit and think," she said. She even suggested that he "talk to someone," as if the way he'd been feeling lately wasn't normal for a man who'd recently retired.

As he worked his way toward the clearing, clenching and unclenching his jaw, Richard suddenly glimpsed flashes of color in the cracks between some trees that flanked the clearing, and a second later he heard the murmur of voices. The two little boys he'd chased out of the woods the week before were back, he was sure of it. This time he'd teach them a lesson; this time he'd sneak up on the brats and grab them by their necks, then march them home and make them confess their crime to their parents.

Richard stepped quietly from tree to tree, keeping to the mossy patches as much as possible, until he reached a large elm at the edge of the clearing. Then he had an open view of the creek. There, just four or five yards away, a boy and a girl were lying together in the grass. They couldn't have been more than sixteen or seventeen, about the same age his son had been when he died. They had their clothes on, but the boy was lying on top of the girl and Richard could tell from the way they were kissing that it wouldn't be long before they'd be naked. The girl had red hair and thin freckled arms and she was lying so close to the creek that if she had wanted she could have reached over and trailed one hand in the slow-moving water. But both of her hands were on the boy's back. Richard couldn't see their faces, just the back of the boy's head, the black hair curling over the collar of his white T-shirt. Still, he could tell they were kissing gently, as if they felt so much passion they had to hold it back or it would overwhelm them. He stood there, listening to the breeze rustling the leaves all around him, and watched the girl's hands slide slowly down the boy's back to the top of his faded, beltless Levi's. When she hooked her thumbs through two of the belt loops, the boy moaned a little, and then she moaned too, as if in answer.

Richard wanted to shout something at them—"What do you think you're doing?" or "Get off my property!"—but he was too shocked to say or do anything. So he just stood there and watched them kiss. Even when the boy sat back and started to unbutton the girl's blouse, he didn't move. But when her blouse was open and the boy began to touch her small, pale breasts, Richard made himself lift his eyes to her face. He thought she looked familiar. She wasn't one of his patients, he didn't think. Maybe she was one of the children he'd delivered, now almost grown up? Or did she go to his church? Whatever, there was something familiar about her. And there was something about the way her eyes were closed and her lips parted that made him feel ashamed. He should not be here, watching her feel this way. Then the boy unzipped the girl's jeans and Richard saw her arch her pelvis up so that he could pull them down more easily. He felt his insides go hollow, and he turned and walked away, slowly and quietly at first, but then, when he was far enough away, as fast he could.

When he came out the other side of the woods he was winded and stood for a long time, his hands on his trembling knees, catching his breath. His heart was thudding. He should know better than to walk so fast, as old and overweight as he was. Besides, it wasn't like they were chasing him or anything. He shook his head at his folly.

After he began breathing evenly again, he stood up straight, sighed, and started through the knee-high grass of the meadow toward the house. As he walked, he tried to think of what to say to Ellen. He knew he should tell her what he'd seen but he wasn't sure how to do it. If he just came out and said, "I saw two teenagers making love down by the creek," she'd start asking questions and before long he'd feel like he was being interrogated, as if he were the one who had done something wrong, not the kids. Maybe he should just say he came across a couple of little boys and chased them off. But he didn't want to lie. The more he thought about it, the more he thought it'd be best not to say anything, at least right now.

When he got home, Ellen was in the kitchen, stirring something in a bowl. It smelled like cookie dough. From behind, she still looked like the girl he'd married all these years ago. He'd put on a lot of weight since then but she hadn't; she'd always been tall and slender. And her blond hair had only a few streaks of silver, while his was the dull gray of weathered wood.

He coughed, to let her know he was home, and she looked over her shoulder at him and smiled. The smile was a peace offering, he knew, a way of saying she was willing to pretend the quarrel hadn't happened if he was. Then she said, "Did you have a nice walk?" There was no way she could have known what he'd witnessed, but her question made his heart speed up. She had turned back to her work as soon as she asked it, but still he felt as if she were watching him, waiting for an answer.

He cleared his throat. "Yes," he said. "It was fine."

"Good," she said.

The room was suddenly too silent. Richard wasn't sure what to do or say, so he coughed again, then sat down at the kitchen table and picked up the weekly edition of their local newspaper, even though he'd read it that morning. He sat there looking at the front page while Ellen worked, but he wasn't really reading it; he was thinking about the girl's red hair spread across the green grass, the look on her face as the boy touched her breasts, the way she arched her pelvis to help him remove her jeans. He wondered if they'd heard him sneaking away through the woods. If they had, they'd probably thought he was an animal, a raccoon or possum, slinking through the underbrush. He wondered if they went to the creek often, if they'd be back.

At Mass the next morning, Richard found himself looking around the congregation, hoping to see the girl. There were two young girls with red hair, but he didn't think either one was her. One of them—Kent Riley's girl—couldn't have been more than twelve. The other was Mary Louise Arnold, whose father Hank had been a classmate of his son's. She was about the right age. He tried to imagine her hair spread out, loose, on the grass. But no: it seemed too short and not wavy enough. And she was also a little too tall; the girl he'd seen in the woods was shorter and more petite, kind of like Kristin, the girl Timmy had taken out a few times before he died. Though Richard was pretty sure she wasn't the one, he kept stealing glances at her throughout the service. Once he saw her smooth her dress down over her thighs when she stood to sing a hymn, and somehow he found that gesture both touching and erotic. He looked at Ellen then, to see if she'd seen him watching the girl, but she was singing away, her eyes on her hymnal. He noticed her knuckles, how knotted they seemed, now that she'd started to have trouble with arthritis. *Arthur*, she called it. *Arthur is visiting again.* He looked away, tried to find the black-haired boy in the congregation. There was one who was clearly too old—in his late twenties at least—and another who was too short and stocky. A third looked about the right age and height, but his hair didn't curl over his collar.

Just then Ellen nudged his arm, startling him. "Here," she said, and handed him the offering basket. Then she whispered, "What's wrong with you today? You seem so distracted."

Richard put a twenty-dollar bill in the wicker basket and passed it on, then leaned toward Ellen. "I'm just tired," he said. "Didn't sleep well." She nodded and patted his hand.

He felt ashamed then and for a long time tried to pay attention to the homily. Father Martin, their new priest, was talking about the two thieves who were crucified with Christ, how their stories still had meaning for us today. Ellen thought the world of Father Martin, saying he was a born priest, the most devout young man she'd ever met, but Richard couldn't stand him. He hated that he had to call a man thirty years younger than he was "Father"— especially one who'd vowed never to have children. And he hated the way Father Martin stood beside the pulpit instead of behind it, the way Father Schmidt, their old priest, always had. He said the same sorts of things Father Schmidt said, but the words didn't seem right coming out of his mouth. With his blond hair, blue eyes, and dark tan, he looked more like he belonged in one of those old beach party movies than in a church. Richard remembered Ellen saying once, "For a man that good-looking to take a vow of celibacy, well, that tells you something about the depth of his faith." He'd almost laughed. They might as well have taken a vow of celibacy themselves, for all the lovemaking they did. For years now, Ellen had acted as if there were a boundary line running down the middle of the bed, and he crossed it only when his need was too strong to resist.

It hadn't always been this way. He remembered back when they were first married, how she used to make a little moan each time he entered her. He couldn't remember how many years it'd been since she'd made that sound. Now she always said "I love you" when they made love. But it was that little moan he wanted to hear.

Richard tried again to concentrate on the sermon, but he couldn't bear to look at Father Martin, so his eyes wandered to the stained-glass window above the altar. It bore the image of Christ on the cross, His face turned to the side, as if to allow those He was saving to stare at His agony without embarrassment. Timmy's face had been turned like that too, when Richard went to identify him. Only later did he realize that the coroner, an old friend of his, must have turned it that way, to hide the wound made by the impact with the windshield.

Richard squeezed his eyes shut for a moment and when he opened them again, he looked over at Mary Louise. She was leaning toward her father, whispering something behind her hand. Richard watched Hank nod, then smile. The same crooked smile he'd had even as a boy. Almost a smirk.

In just a few years, Richard realized, Hank could be a grandfather. A *grandfather.* The thought stunned him. He couldn't imagine Timmy old enough to have grandchildren. Everyone else got older and older, but Timmy had remained a tall, lanky kid of seventeen with big hands and feet. He'd never gotten to be a father, much less a grandfather. And Richard would never be a grandfather either, now that he was no longer even a father.

How he wished Ellen hadn't refused to have any more children after Timmy. She had been the oldest of nine children and had already done her share of mothering, she said. But Richard had grown up an only child, lonely and often depressed, and he didn't want his son to suffer the same fate. Still, nothing he said could change Ellen's mind. After Timmy died, she told him over and over how much she wished she'd agreed to have at least one other child, but her regret didn't give him any comfort. Even now, the mere sight of a father pushing a stroller or a mother buckling her baby into a car seat would sometimes hit him so hard he'd have to hold his breath to keep from weeping.

Richard forced his eyes back toward the altar and tried again to listen to Father Martin. "Did the thief deserve forgiveness for his sins?" he was saying. "No, he did not. But the Lord granted it to him anyway, and He will grant it to us too, as long as we ask it of Him."

Lord, forgive me, Richard thought. But he wasn't sure what he was asking forgiveness for.

Over the next two weeks, Richard tried to forget about the girl, but almost every afternoon he'd find himself thinking about her, then succumbing to the temptation to hike down to the creek in hopes of seeing her and the boy again. To keep Ellen from getting suspicious, he told her he'd decided to take a long walk every day so he could lose some weight, get in shape. "Good for you," she said. "Maybe you're starting to snap out of your funk after all." Her words made him flush with shame, but still he went out the door and walked down to the creek, and he continued to go there every day after that.

One day in mid-July he found evidence that they'd been there again. It was a hot thick afternoon and by the time he reached the clearing, he had sweated through his shirt and his heart was drumming in his ears. Then he saw that the grass beside the creek was matted down in the place he'd seen them before. He must have just missed them. He was still breathing hard from the long walk, and for an instant he thought of lying down to rest in the space they had made. Then he saw something on a rock beside the creek bank. At first he thought it was the sloughed skin of a snake, but he quickly realized what it was: a used condom, dried and stuck to the rock. He stared at it a moment, then knelt down on the bank and scooped handfuls of water onto it until it came unstuck and washed off into the creek, swirling away in the slow current. And as it disappeared, he felt a strange, lightheaded sensation, as if he were swirling away too.

He put his hand to his forehead. He must have walked too far too fast again. He should know better. He closed his eyes and waited for the dizziness to pass, then stood up. He had to get away from here. He had to get home. He wanted to lie down beside Ellen and sleep dreamlessly all night, and he wanted to wake up in the morning and be happy, the way he used to be, when they were first married and he was still foolish enough to believe his life would turn out the way he wanted.

He started back into the woods and began to pick his way toward home. But soon he felt dizzy again, even a little queasy, so he sat down beneath a tall oak to rest. Leaning back against the trunk, he looked up through the gnarled branches and sun-flecked leaves at the scraps of blue sky and remembered the time Timmy climbed halfway up the cottonwood tree beside the house and then was so afraid of falling he couldn't climb down. He was just six or seven then, and he wrapped his arms and legs around the trunk as tightly as he could and cried for his mother. Richard had climbed up after him and carried him safely back down, then spanked him so he'd never do that again.

Remembering this, Richard felt the same roiling grief he'd felt the night Timmy died and he first realized he would never have a chance to make things right between them. He pressed his back against the rough bark and made himself think about the girl, the way her hands slid down the boy's back so slowly, as if her fingers were trying to memorize every sensation they felt. But it didn't work. There was Timmy's face again, turned to the side, resting open-mouthed on the steel table.

That evening, as they sat silently eating dinner, Richard decided he couldn't wait any longer, he had to tell Ellen about the young couple now. Telling her would make him feel better, relieve the burden. But why did it feel like a burden? And why hadn't he told her already?

He cleared his throat. "Ellen," he began, but as he looked at her face across the table, he thought of the woozy pleasure on the girl's face and wondered if Ellen had ever looked like that. If she had, he'd never seen it—they always made love in the dark, with their eyes closed.

"Yes?" Ellen said.

Richard cleared his throat again. Ellen's eyebrows were so blond they were almost invisible, just as Timmy's had been. Still, he could see them knit as she looked at his face.

"Richard? Is something wrong?"

He looked down at his liver-spotted hands and was surprised to see they were trembling a little. "No, nothing's wrong," he said. Then he looked up and showed her the same calm face he'd learned to wear with his patients. He raised the corners of his mouth into a small, sheepish smile. "I just forgot what I was going to say."

Ellen reached across the table and took his hand between hers. "I understand," she said. "Take your time. You'll get used to this new life of ours."

He nodded.

The next day, Richard felt even more burdened by his secret. He wanted to tell Ellen, but he just couldn't, so finally he decided he had no choice but to go to Confession. He hadn't been to

Confession since Father Schmidt retired; he hated the idea of confessing to someone young enough to be his son. So when he arrived at the church that afternoon and found it empty, he felt a spurt of relief: Father Martin was already gone, he could go home, he wouldn't have to confess today. But then he heard, behind the purple velvet curtains of the confessional, the quiet hum of someone's voice, followed by the murmur of Father Martin's response. He hesitated a minute, then made himself sit down in a nearby pew to wait his turn.

A short while later, Esther Pedersen, one of his oldest former patients, shuffled out of the confessional clutching a rosary as if looking forward to her penance. She nodded grimly at him, then, her back bent with osteoporosis, started slowly up the aisle toward the votive candles and the statue of the Virgin Mary. Again Richard wanted to leave, but he knew he couldn't. He had to do this. He entered the confessional, closed the heavy curtains behind him, blocking out all the light, then eased his stiff knees down onto the hard wooden kneeler beneath the latticed grille. When Father Martin slid back the partition, the small bulb that glowed on his side of the window allowed Richard to see the dim outline of his profile. But he knew the priest couldn't see him; he was invisible in the dark, nothing more than a voice. He took a breath and slowly let it out. "Bless me, Father, for I have sinned," he began. "It's been four months since my last confession. These are my sins." Then he stopped. All the words he'd planned to say had just vanished.

After a moment, Father Martin said, "Please go on. We are all sinners and there is nothing we can do that God will not forgive." Richard could see him nodding, as if to encourage him.

Then Richard remembered part of what he'd planned to say. "I've been having—inappropriate thoughts," he said. Then he corrected himself: "Impure thoughts."

"We all have impure thoughts," Father Martin said. "That is human nature. But we have to think about how those thoughts hurt our Lord, whose life shows us how important purity is. We do not all have the strength to be celibate, like Christ, but we should strive to confine our sexual feelings to our spouses and to avoid all occasions of sin. Is there something, or someone, in particular that has prompted your impure thoughts?"

"Yes," Richard said, and suddenly, even though the silhouette of Father Martin's profile had not moved, he felt as if he were looking directly at him, as if he could see his face. Richard hesitated, then said, "A movie. I rented an X-rated movie." For a moment, he held his breath.

"Will you promise God that you will avoid that occasion of sin from now on?"

"Yes, Father."

Father Martin nodded again. "Good. Good. Please continue."

Richard just knelt there. He couldn't believe he had lied to him. Even if he was just a boy, he was a priest. A *priest*. How could he have done such a thing? He looked down at his hands, folded as if in prayer on the ledge beneath the grille. Father Martin was waiting for him to answer. "I spoke angrily to my son," he finally said. Then he paused. He hadn't known he was going to say that. "That's all," he added.

"That's all? Are you sure?"

"Yes, Father."

"You've committed no other sins in the past four months?"

"No."

The priest was silent a moment, then he leaned his head closer to the grille, as if about to whisper a secret, but all he said was, "I will pray for you." Then he leaned back and said, "For your penance, please pray each day to the Blessed Virgin, to ask her to help you avoid your impure thoughts, and to God the Father, for help in treating your son with love and respect." When he finished saying these words, he bowed his head and began to say the prayer of absolution. Richard watched without listening until Father Martin raised his head and made the sign of the cross, then he stood to leave.

When he stepped out of the confessional, the light was so bright it seemed to echo through the church. Esther Pedersen was kneeling at the feet of the Virgin Mary, and Richard heard her rosary beads click, a sound like the ticking of a clock. He turned and fled.

A false confession was a mortal sin, and for penance Richard resolved to stay away from the creek. He decided, also, to spend more time with Ellen, to take her out to dinner and to the movies, maybe even join that book club she'd been talking about. He'd smile at her more, too, listen attentively when she talked, touch her hand across the table. And once he'd overcome his temptation, he'd go back to Confession and tell Father Martin he had lied to him. He would tell him right now if he could, but he knew he had to stop giving in to occasions of sin first, to prove that he had truly and fully repented and was worthy of being forgiven.

But after three days of pacing around the house and picking little arguments with Ellen, Richard returned to the creek, and after that he continued to go there every day. If he could see the girl just once more, then it would all be over, he was sure, and things could go back to the way they were. But as the days passed, he began to despair of seeing her, and one morning, as he approached the clearing, he found himself praying she would be there. This was one more sin he would have to confess, he knew, and he promised God that he would, just as soon as he'd seen her one last time.

Two days later, his prayer was answered. It was a bright sunny Saturday, the kind of day he'd take the girl to the clearing if he were the black-haired boy, and he spotted them as he crept toward the large elm at the edge of the clearing. They were sitting on the grass, a picnic basket beside them, and they were laughing and feeding cake to each other, as if they were at a wedding. The boy got some chocolate frosting on his chin and the girl leaned over and licked it off. Then they began to kiss. Richard knew he should look away, or leave, but he stayed there, still as a statue, watching them undress each other, then watched the boy lie down on her and the girl spread her legs for him and the boy's white buttocks clench and unclench as he made love to her. Richard felt his penis stir and he gazed, transfixed, at the girl's face, her eyes closed and lips parted in that same look of rapturous languor he'd thought about so many times since he'd first seen it. He stood there and watched her wrap her pale, scrawny legs and arms around the boy. On the boy's back was a constellation of dark moles. Somehow, Richard knew that she liked to trace those moles with a fingertip after they'd made love. He imagined him lying on her, spent, and her finger drifting from mole to mole as she lay there in that peaceful place, feeling private and safe, as if no one could ever rob her of her happiness.

A thought crept into his mind then. Had Timmy ever taken Kristin to this place? No, no. He wouldn't have. He was a good boy, an altar boy, an Eagle Scout, a volunteer at the tri-county nursing home—the place he'd been driving home from the night of his accident. Richard had always been so proud of him, but now he felt a sudden sadness: his son had never gotten to feel the way this boy and girl were feeling. Timmy had been denied that. And so, he realized, had he.

The next thing he knew he had stepped out into the clearing. He heard himself shouting "Get out of here!" as fiercely as if it were a curse. "Get off my property! Now!"

"Jesus!" the boy yelled and scrambled up, his flushed face swiveling toward Richard. He covered himself with his hands, but not before Richard saw his swollen red penis swaying upright and wet. The girl, too, was trying to cover herself, even as she crawled toward her clothes, but he caught a glimpse of the rust-red patch of hair between her legs, the surprisingly large areolas of her small breasts.

"Go!" he bellowed. "Get off my land!" But even as he said these words, he felt oddly like he was lying, as if it wasn't his property after all, it was theirs, and he had no right to be there. He felt embarrassed, and terribly sorry for them. Still, he stood there, legs apart, fists clenched, and kept on yelling at them while they grabbed up their clothes and ran through the shallow creek and into the woods on the other side of the clearing, leaving the picnic basket behind. The girl was crying now, he could hear her sobbing as she ran, and all of a sudden, to his surprise, he began to cry himself.

He sat down, trembling. What is wrong with me? he asked himself. He looked at his hands, their liver spots and gnarled knuckles. The boy and girl were far enough into the woods now that he couldn't hear them anymore. He imagined them stopping behind some trees to dress, and he wondered what they were saying to each other. He knew they hated him, and he didn't blame them. He hated himself too. If anything, he hated himself more than they did, more than the other kids he'd chased out of the woods, even more than Timmy. For a moment, he saw his son's contorted red face, heard him shout the words "Try and stop me!", saw him run out the door and get into the car—his birthday present, given to him just weeks before—and drive away, his tires spewing gravel. When he came home that night, he'd apologized—he always apologized, he was a good boy—and Richard forgave him, as he always did. But they fought again the next day, and the next, about what he couldn't even remember—probably about Kristin, the fact that she was Protestant, or maybe he'd been slacking off on his science or math homework—but whatever it was he knew it didn't matter, that none of it mattered, though it had all seemed so important at the time. At least they hadn't fought the day of the accident. At least he had that to console him.

He waited a couple of minutes, until his breathing had slowed, then he stood up on his trembling legs and started to walk back home. But he hadn't gotten very far before he found himself thinking about the girl, naked and crawling across the grass on her hands and knees, and felt his penis begin to stir again.

That night, after Ellen turned out the lights, he crossed over to her side of the bed for the first time since the night of his retirement party. He slid up against her back, then reached his hand around her in the darkness and cupped her warm breast.

"Hmm," she said over her shoulder at him. "Somebody's got something on his mind tonight. And what's that I feel behind me?" She always tried to act lighthearted and playful when he wanted to make love, but he knew she didn't really feel that way, at least not very often, so her banter usually only made him feel sad. But tonight the sadness vanished almost as soon as it came, and a strange, new happiness bubbled up in his chest and rose into his head, making him feel almost woozy. He leaned over and kissed her neck, that ticklish spot that always made her scrunch her shoulder up, then kissed her cheek and ear. A moment later they were shucking their pajamas and then he was kissing her gently while tracing slow circles around her nipples with his fingertip, and then he was kissing her breasts and she was parting her legs for his hand. And when he had made her come, he climbed on top of her, trying to suck his belly in so his weight wouldn't bear down so heavily on her, and he entered her and moved in her until they were moving together and as he came he watched her almost invisible face in the dark. But though her lips were open she made no sound.

Afterward, he lay beside her, breathing hard, and Ellen leaned over and kissed his cheek. "I love you," she said. But he was barely listening. He had just remembered where he'd seen the girl—it was at the grocery store; she was one of the new checkout girls. He tried to think if he'd ever seen a black-haired boy there too, stocking shelves or bagging groceries, but he couldn't remember one. Whoever the boy was, Richard worried he'd get the girl pregnant. He hadn't been wearing a condom today. Maybe they were so young and foolish they thought they were safe, that nothing bad could ever happen to them.

Later, as he drifted into sleep, he saw himself delivering the girl's baby, watching her son's head crown, and heard her moan with pain.

The next morning, right after breakfast, Richard drove to the grocery store. There wasn't really anything he needed, since Ellen had already done the shopping for the week, but he grabbed a loaf of bread from the first aisle anyway and headed over to the other end of the store, where the checkout lanes were. He was worried the girl wouldn't be on duty today, but then he saw her red hair behind one of the cash registers. He was so relieved he almost offered up a prayer of thanks to God, but he stopped himself just in time.

The express lane was open, but he got in her line anyway. He picked two magazines at random out of the rack, so he wouldn't look conspicuous standing in a regular lane with just one item. Cradling the bread and magazines in one arm, he watched the girl out of the corner of his eye as the line gradually shortened. He hadn't thought about what he'd say to her. He just knew that he wanted to apologize for yesterday, to ask her forgiveness. No—that wasn't true. What he wanted to do, he realized, was just talk to her, even if only for a moment, see what she was like. He stood there, shifting from one foot to the other, behind a young woman in a bright yellow T-shirt who was bouncing a baby on her hip as she watched the girl scan can after can of Similac. And all of a sudden Richard felt lightheaded. He closed his eyes until the dizziness passed, until he stopped seeing his infant son in his arms, his tiny lips pursed around the rubber nipple on the bottle he had just warmed on the stove.

Then it was his turn. He set the bread and magazines on the counter. "Paper or plastic?" the girl said. He looked at her pale blue eyes, the freckles scattered across her cheeks and nose, the red hair that reached nearly to the nametag pinned to her green shirt above her left breast. *Marisa*, it said. He looked back at her face. She didn't recognize him, he could tell. He knew he should feel relieved, but he didn't. Instead, he found himself imagining how the boy had felt, seeing that woozy rapture on her face as he moved in her.

"Paper or plastic," the girl repeated with a sigh.

Richard blinked. "Paper," he said, then took out his wallet. His fingers were shaking. If she noticed them, she'd probably think he had Parkinson's or something. But she wasn't looking at him; she was scanning his purchases. He watched her hand pick up each item and pass it over the scanner and remembered the way she slid her hands so slowly down the boy's back, then hooked her thumbs through his belt loops. He felt vaguely sick. He shouldn't be thinking about these things. What would Ellen think if she knew? Or Timmy? And what did God think?

A few moments later, she gave him his change, and the tips of her fingers touched his palm.

That night, he lay beside Ellen in bed, staring up into the darkness, his heart pounding. He could tell from her breathing that she wasn't asleep.

"Do you know that girl at the grocery store, the one named Marisa?" he asked. Just saying her name gave him a little thrill. It felt daring, almost like a confession.

"Sure," she said. "She's Evie Blackshear's daughter. You know, the new teacher at the high school. She teaches biology, I think."

Then he felt her turn on her side, as if to look at him.

"Why do you ask?"

Even though he knew it was too dark for her to see him, Richard tried to shrug casually. "She reminds me of a girl that used to go to school with Timmy," he said. It wasn't true; he said it merely because he wanted to say Timmy's name, just as he had wanted to say Marisa's name. And now that he'd said both of their names, he felt a strange, heady relief swirl through him.

Ellen was silent a moment. Then she said, "You haven't said his name in so long."

"I know," he said. "I've wanted to talk about him, but I didn't dare. I didn't want to bring back all that pain."

"You couldn't bring it back," she said. "It's never gone away."

"I know," he said again. Then: "I'm so sorry."

"It's not your fault," she said.

"It's not yours either," he said. But in a way, he knew, he believed it was. She was the one who'd encouraged Timmy to volunteer at that nursing home, and if he hadn't been working there, he wouldn't have been on that dark road when the pickup swerved into his lane. And she was the one who'd refused to have any more children, so that when they lost Timmy they lost everything.

He cleared his throat. "I should have tried harder to change your mind," he said.

Her silence told him how much his words had hurt her. He turned toward her.

"I'm sorry," she said. "If only I'd known . . ." She began to cry softly.

"He'd be forty years old now," Richard said. "Almost as old as we were then. I can't picture him that old. I can only see him the way he was."

She began to cry a little harder. "It's the same with me," she said.

Then he took a deep breath. "I saw this couple at the creek the other day," he said. "Just kids. No older than Timmy was when . . ."

She stopped crying a moment, as if waiting to see if he would finish the sentence. He didn't.

"Oh, Richard," Ellen said then, and he could tell she was wiping her tears away. "I know how you feel. I think of Timmy too, every time I see a boy his age. And when I see a young man, I think that could be Timmy. Father Martin makes me think of him the most. Not that he looks like him or anything. It's just something about the way he tilts his head when he talks, and how when you're talking to him and he thinks of something to say he never interrupts but just smiles and keeps listening. I look at Father Martin and I think, that's the kind of person Timmy would have grown up to be."

"A priest?" Richard said. "Not Timmy. He would never have been a priest." But even as he said it, he knew she was right, that he was exactly the sort of boy who might have grown up to be a priest.

"Father Martin had a girlfriend when he was young, too," Ellen said. "Several of them, in fact. He said he dated all through high school, just to make sure he was making the choice God wanted him to make."

Richard lay back and stared up into the darkness again. He noticed his heart had stopped pounding. "The couple I saw at the creek—they were making love," he said. He was surprised at how easily the words came out, how light they made him feel. Then he added: "I watched them." He paused, to let her speak, but she said nothing. "I should have told you about it earlier," he went on. "I should have told you so many things."

"You *watched* them?" she finally said.

"Yes. Twice."

Ellen was silent a long moment. Then she said, "Why are you telling me this?" Her voice was thick and it quavered. "Why are you saying these things?"

Richard turned toward her again and tried to see her face, but he could barely make out her profile. It was as if she were gradually vanishing, and so was he. Somehow, this thought made him feel calm, even happy. He knew this happiness wouldn't last, that he would soon be filled with shame and sorrow, because he was about to steal something from her that he could never give back. He accepted, in advance, this anguish, though he knew it would torture him until the day he died and, possibly, forever after.

"*Why?*" she repeated.

"I wish you could have seen them," he said, then reached out to stroke her hair. "It was beautiful. They were making love in the grass by the creek. It was broad daylight, the sun shining down on them. I could imagine how the sun felt on that boy's back, a warmth that went all the way through him, and I could almost smell the grass." And even though Ellen began to sob, he went on telling her what it felt like to be young, in love, and still alive.

II

LAST RITES

It is still night. Andrew, groggy with fever, once again thrusts his head over the wastebasket beside the bed. He gags, his throat muscles buck, and saliva runs hot and sour over his humped tongue. But nothing comes, there is no relief from his nightlong sickness. He waits until the spasms stop, then lies back and wipes the sweat from his face with a corner of the sheet.

He must get back to sleep. Even the dreams are better than lying awake in this dark. He tries to forget the dreams, forget Claudia, the baby, and concentrate on the throbbing pain in his stomach. After a while, he begins to breathe, open-mouthed, in time with the throbs.

When he wakes again, the false dawn has come. The gray light sifts through the windowpane, entering the dark as if by osmosis. Andrew blinks, focusing. His lashes are so blond they are invisible in the weak light, and his blue eyes, as a result, look almost like an infant's. His skin, too, is the salmon-pink of a baby's; it burns through his thinning blond hair like the bloom of a white-hot coal.

Across the room, first the mahogany bureau, then Claudia's self-portrait emerge out of the dark and into the new gray. Claudia's brown hair covers one ear but not the other, her eyes are open above her shut eyelids, her smile curves halfway up her left cheek.

The night is over, Andrew thinks, the dreams are over. Dreams. They made sense in the Middle Ages: messages from God, allegories even children could understand. A narrative convention? Or did they dream differently than we, who have no faith?

He isn't sure whether his illness caused the dreams or the dreams caused his illness. But it doesn't matter: now that the long night is over, his fever and nausea will leave him and he won't need any more pills. He will still feel grief, of course, but it will be a reasonable grief, not the wild anguish that began four days ago, when Sybil's telegram arrived. It won't incapacitate him; he'll be able to go about his life as he always has.

Lying there, staring at the ceiling, he can almost feel his illness leaving him cell by cell. In a few minutes, perhaps, he will be well enough to rise and shower, maybe even eat a leisurely breakfast. Then, if he still feels strong, he will call a florist and order flowers for Claudia's grave. And perhaps he'll even write to his mother. Or, better yet, call her, apologize for his long silence. Yes, that's what he'll do. And with his decision, he feels a dizzy peace swirl through him. Closing his eyes, he thinks, Soon it will all be over.

All night long Andrew had strange, feverish dreams in which he, not Claudia, had died. In one, doctors and nurses wearing sunglasses hovered over him, examining his naked corpse. In another, he was somehow present at his own funeral, though he was sitting so far back in the enormous church that he couldn't hear what the priest was saying or see the casket. He sat there patiently for a while, but then he decided to complain about his bad seat. Rising to address the usher, he saw two mourners lying naked on the pew in front of him, their arms locked around each other, and abruptly he sat back again, only his seat wasn't there anymore and he fell through darkness until he woke, sobbing, in his bed.

Then, toward morning, he dreamed he was a child again, in bed in his dark room, dying of some mysterious disease. He knew his mother was outside in the lighted hall, her ear pressed to the door, listening to his moans, and he called out for her.

But when the door finally opened, it was not his mother: instead *he* was at the door and Claudia was in his bed, moaning softly. The sheet was drawn up over her swollen belly and tucked under her arms.

He went to the bed and sat down next to her, soothed her hot forehead with a cool, damp washcloth, and then, when she seemed asleep, bent over to kiss her cheek. But she turned suddenly and met his kiss. He opened his mouth in surprise, and she breathed into him, a sour, mildewy breath, then broke the kiss and laughed. He stood up and almost fell, he was so suddenly ill. What sickness had she given him?

You're trying to kill me, he said, pointing at her. But her scarred eyelids seemed an even greater accusation, and he turned away.

When he finally looked back—was it minutes or days later?—she was holding a child in her arms. Dark curly hair and brown eyes. Staring at him.

I named him Alan, she said.

Four days earlier, Andrew was in his study preparing the final exam for his Chaucer seminar when the doorbell rang.

"Mr. Kern?" said the ear-muffed Western Union man. The words were little clouds in the chilly air.

Andrew nodded and took the telegram. He knew, because they had delivered the telegram instead of telephoning it, that someone had died. He thought of his mother in Columbus, to whom he had not written since he left Minneapolis and came to Duluth last June. But he knew it was not his mother. Turning the envelope over in his hand, he read the date—February 16, 1971—and knew that from now on he would divide his life into two parts: everything before that date, and everything after.

The man was waiting. Andrew fished in his pocket for a dollar, but all he had was a five. He gave it to the man.

"Thank *you*, sir," the man said, and left.

Andrew closed the door, went back to his study, and set the telegram beside the typewriter. His hands were trembling; to still them, he pressed them together, as if in prayer. For a moment, he considered actually praying, but he knew he couldn't. He looked at the telegram. He didn't dare open it, so he turned back to his test and forced himself to try to finish it. He reread the last question: "Discuss Pandarus' relationship to Troilus and Criseyde in terms of the Augustinian distinction between *caritas* and *cupiditas*." That was a good question. Now he should write one that would require the students to relate Book V of *The Consolation of Philosophy* to Troilus' soliloquy on free will.

But he couldn't do it. He had to read the telegram now, had to find out for sure. He ripped open the envelope: yes. He stared at Claudia's name for a moment, then felt his lungs and throat constrict as he imagined her body twisted in the wreckage of an automobile. But no: Sybil had not mentioned a car accident. Yet, for an instant, he believed there might have been a subtle suggestion of an accident in the telegram, so he reread it. But there was none.

"This does not preclude the possibility, however," he said. He immediately felt foolish for having spoken, especially in his classroom voice, and he laughed. But the laugh caught in his throat and turned into a dry sob. Claudia was *dead*. The fact was so simple it was immense. What would he do now? What *could* he do? He looked around the room for something to comfort him, but there was nothing. Books, a filing cabinet, easy chair and pole lamp, his reproduction of Blake's *Chaucer and the Pilgrims*. For a mad instant, he imagined the oak bookcase falling over and crushing him. He had never felt this much grief before, not even when his brother died. He started to weep.

A drink. That's what he needed: a drink, and the oblivion it would bring him. He turned and stumbled out of the study and half-ran, half-walked down the hall.

By the time he reached the end of the hall, he was weeping so hard he had to brace himself against the wall to keep from falling.

The day after Andrew received Sybil's telegram, he went down to the grocery store on the corner and bought a copy of *The Minneapolis Tribune*. He waited until he was back in his study, then he opened it and scanned the obituaries until he found Claudia's. It read simply:

> Claudia Marie Miller, 23, a student at the University of Minnesota, died Tuesday. She was a Roman Catholic. Survivors are her parents, Mr. and Mrs. Alfred P. Miller of Phoenix, Ariz.; a brother, Philip, of Cincinnati, Ohio; and a sister, Sybil Gardner, of Minneapolis. Funeral will be at the Wagner Funeral Chapel, 2022 Lyndale Ave., Minneapolis, at 2:30 p.m. Friday. Burial will be in Sunset Garden Cemetery.

He put down the paper and stared at it. A sob rose in his throat, but he fought it back, forced himself to breathe slowly and carefully. He didn't want to lose control again. There was no reason to lose control. There would be no funeral Mass, but that didn't prove anything. She might have lost her faith. She might have requested a simple, nonreligious service. Perhaps a priest would officiate at the funeral despite its location. There were many possible explanations—many. Even the fact that the paper didn't say how she died didn't prove anything; obituaries rarely included the cause of death.

He sat there a long time, taking deep breaths and letting them out slowly. When he thought he was calm enough to leave for school, he stood up and began to put the draft of his exam into his briefcase. But his hand was shaking so badly he dropped it, and the papers fluttered to the floor.

Despite his lecture on "The Monk's Tale," his students had failed to understand Chaucer's conception of tragedy. "Chaucer was not a *Greek*," he wrote in the margin of a particularly inane answer, then felt his comment was too harsh and blacked it out.

He took another swallow of bourbon. He had to quit thinking about Claudia. He couldn't go on like this. What would his students think of him? He looked out his study window: the sun was still an hour or more from rising and the night was so dark he couldn't see the snow falling anywhere but under the streetlight. It almost seemed as if the light had burst into a miniature blizzard.

He bent over his desk again. At the bottom of the page, he wrote: "Auden once said, 'Greek tragedy makes us feel *What a pity it had to be this way* whereas Christian tragedy makes us say *What a pity it was this way when it could have been otherwise.*' Which view of tragedy do you think Chaucer holds?'"

When he finished grading that exam, Andrew had just one more left. He took another drink of his bourbon, then started to read the first page of the test, but the words blurred. He closed his burning eyes a moment, then opened them again, and the words were clearer. He read the first paragraph without any trouble, it seemed, but halfway through the second paragraph he had forgotten what he'd read, so he went back and started over again. But it was no use, no use at all. He shook his head: he just couldn't read it, not today, not this night.

He finished his glass. The student was one of his better pupils, he'd done A- or B+ work all quarter, and Andrew was certain he'd written a good test. So he turned to the last page and wrote "A"—nothing else—and put down his pen.

He must have fallen asleep after that, for the next thing he knew, it was morning. He looked at his wristwatch: it was 7:45. He was stiff from sitting at his desk all night, and he stood up and stretched, then went into the kitchen, put two slices of onion rye in the toaster and poured a glass of orange juice. But he did not eat his breakfast, nor did he shave, shower, or even change his clothes. He was too nervous for anything routine, he had to get things settled, so instead he went back to his study, packed the exams from his three classes into his briefcase, and left for the university.

There, he posted his grades by student ID number on his office door, put the exams in a box in the hall next to his office, and turned his grade reports in to Sally, the department secretary. Then all of his professional obligations were fulfilled for the winter quarter. Even the galleys for his article on *The Cloud of Unknowing* had been proofread and returned to *Speculum*. For three weeks he had nothing to do except plan his spring courses, and there was no hurry about that.

Nevertheless, as soon as he returned home, he began planning the syllabus for his upcoming seminar on Middle English Prose. He checked the table of contents in the anthology he had ordered. *The Anglo-Saxon Chronicle* was the logical place to begin: it would provide historical context for the entire quarter. And *Hali Meidenhad, The Ancrene Riwle*. Then the mystics: Richard Rolle, *The Cloud*, Walter Hilton. Wyclyf, his defenders and attackers. Mandeville, Fortesque, Malory. So many. Should he arrange the course chronologically, to illustrate the development of Middle English prose style, or thematically, according to the principal concerns of the period? He felt he had to decide now, finish his syllabus quickly, so he chose the former.

He sat down at his desk and, consulting the university calendar, determined the seminar would meet twelve times. At least four of those sessions would have to be devoted to the students' oral reports, so that left eight for discussions and lectures. He wrote "March 14: *The Anglo-Saxon Chronicle*," then realized an introductory lecture would be necessary. An overview of medieval theories of prose style perhaps. He made a note to put the fourteenth and fifteenth books of Boccaccio's *Genealogia Deorum Gentilium* on reserve, then crossed out *The Anglo-Saxon Chronicle* and started to write in "Overview of Medieval Theories of Prose Style." Then he stood up suddenly and went to the window. His heart was pounding so hard his chest hurt. He looked outside. Last night's snow had made the landscape lunar. He put his hot cheek to the cool windowpane.

It was only a three-hour drive to Minneapolis; if he left now, he could get there by noon, in plenty of time for the funeral. Yes. That was what he would do. Finally he had decided.

Even though he had more than enough time, Andrew changed into a gray suit hurriedly, and in less than ten minutes he was on Interstate 35, heading south.

He did not turn back toward Duluth until 11:30.

When Andrew returned to his apartment, he went directly to bed. He tried to sleep but he couldn't, even though he took three sleeping pills and drank as many straight shots of bourbon. He had hoped to exorcise his guilt through the ceremony of Claudia's funeral, to bury his grief with her body, but he hadn't been able to face her corpse. He could have borne the censure of Sybil and Ray, and even of Mr. and Mrs. Miller, but he could not have borne the greater censure of Claudia's closed eyes. Still, he needed some rite, some sort of sympathetic magic, to release him from his anguish, so when 2:30 came, he decided to imagine the funeral as it took place.

He began carefully, slowly, imagining the chapel, its beige carpet and oaken pews; the mourners, Kleenexes and rosaries clutched in their hands; the organist, heavy-armed, playing Bach; the formaldehyde smell of chrysanthemums. For a second, he imagined Jack entering quietly and standing, unnoticed, in the back, but he knew that was wrong, Jack would never be there, so he started over again with the mourners, the Bach, the young priest reciting the Twenty-Third Psalm, his voice solemn, nasal. Then the organist, her white fingers lost in the snowy keys, playing Haydn as the mourners filed past the casket. Andrew was there, too, now: the last in line save for the two men in gray who would screw her casket shut and wheel it on its collapsible dolly to the waiting hearse. He stood in line, watching first Sybil, then Ray weep over Claudia.

If only he could escape, find a way to leave unnoticed . . . But everyone was watching him, waiting to see how he would react. He had to go through with it.

But he couldn't. Not now. He had to stop imagining the funeral. The line was moving too quickly, in a moment he would be at the casket, and he wasn't ready, not yet. He would be ready in a few days. He could imagine everything then. But not now.

Yet Andrew could not make the line stand still, out of time. It kept moving, and he kept moving.

And then he was at the casket, looking over its burnished bronze edge . . .

But it was not Claudia in the casket. It was his brother Alan, his face the color of dried putty.

Andrew felt his heart twist in his chest. Closing his eyes tighter, he made himself see Claudia, her head propped on a white satin pillow, her short brown hair in bangs to her eyebrows; the eyelids closed, their tiny scars imperceptible under the mortician's pale blue eye shadow; her hands crossed at her wrists, forming wings.

And then, with a sudden shock, he recognized the fact he had suppressed ever since he received Sybil's telegram: Claudia was pregnant. It struck him as an amazing fact: she had a child in her. Under her crossed arms was a child. Or was there? How does a mortician prepare a pregnant woman for viewing and burial? The fetus had died; there was no doubt about that. Did they leave it in her? Or did they remove it and bury it separately? Or destroy it? They might have cremated it. But they wouldn't. Couldn't. They must have done something else. What?

He sat up and reached for the pills on top of his nightstand, shook two into his palm, and swallowed them dry. If only he could sleep, if only he could stop thinking for a while . . . He lay back and crossed his hands over his pounding heart.

An hour later, when he finally fell asleep, his last thoughts were of Alan's lover, Ryan, who had survived the car accident. He had remained kneeling, his head bowed, throughout the wake, even when everyone else rose to view the body.

When Andrew woke, it was dark. He looked at the fluorescent dial of the alarm clock: only 10:20. There was still time to call Sybil. Perhaps he was wrong after all. Perhaps there was another explanation. He rose, put on his blue terry robe, and walked shakily down the hall to the phone. His stomach ached as if he had just run a long way. After a minute, he dialed Sybil's number.

Sybil's voice changed as soon as he answered her hello. It shook him as having the same thin, ready-to-break quality that Claudia's had when she was frightened.

"Why did you call?" she said. "You knew I wouldn't want to talk to you."

Before Andrew could say anything, Sybil's husband Ray took the phone from her.

"What do you want, Kern?"

Andrew tried to ignore his tone. "I just wanted to express my sympathy," he said.

"And?"

Andrew took a breath. "The telegram didn't say how Claudia died."

"It was suicide," Ray answered. "Barbiturates. We thought you'd be able to guess."

Andrew would not answer the accusation, at least not now. "I feel just terrible about it," he said. "You don't know how terrible." Then: "Do you know why she did it?"

Asking the question made his head feel light, almost as if it were rising toward the ceiling. He had to sit down on the hall carpet.

"I have an idea."

Andrew changed the subject. "What about Jack? How is he taking this?"

"Who knows?" Ray said. "The bastard walked out on her two days before she took the pills. Left her six months pregnant. He told us they were going to get married before the baby was born, but when Claudia called, she said she'd known all along he would leave her. The son of a bitch."

"She called?"

Ray's voice was impatient. "Yes. But it was already too late to do anything."

Andrew felt dizzy. He heard Sybil crying in the background. "What did she say?" he asked.

"Nothing that would stand up in court," Ray answered.

"What do you mean?" Andrew asked.

"You know what I mean."

Andrew was silent a moment. Then he said, "Did she say anything else?"

"Yes," Ray said bitterly. "She said she wanted you to have the rest of her paintings."

Andrew's breaths started to come hard and sharp and fast.

"Don't hyperventilate yourself," Ray said, and hung up.

Andrew felt panic spread through him then, and he knew he had to do something. But what? There was nothing to do, nowhere to go. Still, he decided to leave, go for a walk, do anything but stay home and think about Claudia. He dressed quickly, put on his coat, and went outside.

Looking up and down Woodland, he wondered where to go. Though he had lived in Duluth since June, he hadn't met anyone he could consider a close friend. He had purposely isolated himself since leaving Minneapolis, passing up faculty parties and drinking alone in his apartment. But now he felt the need to see someone, anyone, so he started up the avenue toward College Street, where he would meet students walking from the dormitories and fraternities to the bars. He could see, a few blocks ahead, the night-blackened buildings of the Duluth campus of the University of Minnesota rising above frame houses and bare trees. The night was so black as to be blue; even the gray snowbanks that flanked the streets shone blue. Passing a playground, he saw some boys throwing snowballs at cars from the top of a frozen elephant-back of a hill. He watched their breaths bloom in the blue darkness.

He did not want to think about Jack and Claudia.

Houses were on both sides of him now. Inside them, couples sat on sofas across from glowing televisions. Lights blinked on and off along the length of the street.

He would not think about Jack and Claudia. Not now.

He tried to think about the bars and the students he would meet. Perhaps he would see some students from his seminar, or from one of his introductory literature courses. He could show them another, less formal side to his personality. He imagined buying them drinks, telling them jokes.

He had not thought of Jack for weeks; he'd been too busy worrying about Claudia. He would not start thinking about Jack now.

He would meet his students at Walton's, a bar he'd heard about. He would be friendly. They would laugh and toast each other. The students at the bar. Jack. Claudia. The students at the. Jack.

Andrew closed his eyes tightly and listened to the winter night for sounds his mind could hold. All he heard was the packed snow cracking under his soles. The sound frightened him strangely: it seemed to be coming from behind him, as if he were being followed. He opened his eyes and turned around. No one was there. Whom had he expected? Of course no one was there. Nor would anyone be at the bars: the quarter had ended that afternoon, and everyone would have left by now. He was a fool, an enormous fool. His abdomen tightened, and he felt a spasm rise roiling into his throat. Turning toward his apartment, he began to run, slow and stiff-legged, clutching his stomach.

When he got home, he took Claudia's self-portrait out of the hall closet and hung it over his bureau like a sign of quarantine.

A Photograph: Andrew and Alan, July 4, 1944

The Kern boys, six years old last week, stand on the beach while their mother steps forward, then back, looking into the viewfinder. Andrew wears a white T-shirt to keep his fair skin from burning. His nose and cheeks are white with suntan lotion. (Take his hand, Alan, will you? That's a good boy.) Alan is taller and acts older, though he was born three minutes after Andrew. Everyone says he looks like Daddy, so Daddy must have dark curly hair, brown eyes, and tan skin. In the picture of him they have hanging over the sofa, he's wearing a sailor hat, so Andrew can't tell what his hair looks like. And since the picture is black and white, he can't tell what color his eyes are either. Andrew looks like Mama, and that's why strangers never know he and Alan are twins. It's a secret they share whenever they go someplace where no one knows them. (This one's for Daddy. Smile for Daddy.) Andrew tries to smile, but the sun is so bright he sneezes just as the shutter snaps. (Oh hell, Daddy'll never see it anyway.) Then her chin starts to quiver, and she begins to cry. I'm sorry, Mama, I'm sorry, Andrew says, and moves toward her. But Alan reaches her first, so Andrew stops and stands there, watching him comfort her.

❧

The bedroom wall is yellow with midmorning, but Andrew has not yet risen. He lies still, breathing shallowly, and listens to the blood thudding in his temples. It sounds like words in some primitive, forgotten language, words garbled by distance and time. He thinks he can almost understand them. Then nausea spirals through him again, and he decides, for perhaps the tenth time, to get up and take some Pepto-Bismol. But he lies there awhile longer, and when he finally does get up, he doesn't go into the bathroom, where he keeps the Pepto-Bismol, but into the study. There, he takes a letter out of the bottom drawer of his desk, then feels so faint he hurries back to bed. When his head stops swimming, he sits up carefully and reads the letter.

> *Dear Andrew,*
> *An emergency. C. missed her last period and a doctor confirmed it. Due the first week in May. Send more money.*

It is typed on a piece of scratch paper and not even signed, so it could never be used as evidence. So uncharacteristically careful of Jack, who'd always been so reckless. "C." instead of "Claudia," no signature, no return address—only the information and the request, the proofs of Andrew's fatherhood and guilt by proxy.

Andrew lets the letter drop to the floor. He is so suddenly tired he can't keep his eyes open. Perhaps he'll feel better after he sleeps some more. Perhaps then he will see things more clearly. Everything is too confused now. He needs to sleep, so his mind will be clear enough to comprehend it all.

Before he falls asleep, he imagines his apartment in Minneapolis, his bedroom, the dark, and, in the dark, Jack and Claudia conceiving the child, his child. But the dark fools him, Jack is not there, and instead he is on top of Claudia, working hard, hating her, knowing she will become pregnant and die. She is not dead yet, but she is wearing the sunglasses to cover her scars. He tells her angrily to take them off but she says no, and all the while he makes love to her he watches her mouth open and close, her thin nostrils dilate, and the tiny muscles of her cheekbones twitch under the dark rims of the glasses.

A few months after Andrew moved to Minneapolis, he found in his English Department mailbox a dittoed invitation to a party. It read:

BEWARE THE IDES OF JANUARY!

Sybil and Ray Gardner invite you to join them in celebrating the much-awaited 2014th anniversary of Julius Caesar's last gasp. Party games, mingling, seduction, all in order. A new Caesar crowned and killed every hour. For faculty and friends alike (and some not alike). Saturday the 15th, beginning at 8:00.

RSVP, BYOB, SOS, RIP

When Andrew met Claudia at Sybil and Ray's party, she said she was thinking about changing her major from history to art. "I like to paint," she said. "And besides, then I could take more courses from Uncle Ray." Her head was tilted as if she were trying to hear something in the distance. Andrew had seen other blind people tilt their heads in the same way, and he wondered why they did it. Even more, he wondered why he was so attracted to her. She was certainly not beautiful. Perhaps she had been pretty once, but her face was marred now by a crooked line of tiny scars running from her left temple to her right cheek. Still, he hadn't been this attracted to a woman in years. And maybe the scars attracted him as much as they repulsed him, for the more he tried not to look at them, the more his eyes kept returning to them.

"You don't *really* paint, do you?" he asked, and was immediately conscious of sounding rude. He tried to correct his mistake: "I mean, I've never heard of a blind artist before."

Claudia smiled. "Beethoven was deaf, you know."

"Okay," Andrew said. "But that's different, isn't it?"

"Do you want to see one of my paintings?" she answered. "Maybe that'll convince you."

"Sure," he agreed.

She put out her arm for him to take. "It's in the master bedroom," she said. "Down the hall and the third door on the right."

Andrew led her out of Sybil's study, past the people standing by the fireplace in the living room, drinks and cigarettes in their hands, and turned into the dark hall. And then he thought he understood: she was trying to seduce him with her blindness the way some women tempted men with a pretended modesty. The painting was a ruse: no doubt she would laugh at him for even half-believing her.

But when he opened the door to Sybil and Ray's bedroom and saw, hanging over the bed, the painting he had not believed in, Andrew felt a confusing loss of self-assurance. The painting was as simple and innocent as Claudia appeared to be: an idyllic summer farm scene. And it was clearly her painting and not someone else's, for her blindness was everywhere evident. The red of the barn extended onto the meadow; a window was half on the farmhouse and half on the roof; the sun was hopelessly tangled in the branches of a tree; none of the colors had quite the right tint. The painting— and Claudia's trust that it had turned out perfectly—made him think he'd been wrong about her: perhaps she was the Sweet

Innocent Blind Girl she seemed to be. He thought of closing the bedroom door and putting his hand on her breast to test her, and imagined her smiling slyly at him and pressing his hand with hers. But he looked at her and knew he was wrong. He felt a desire to laugh, but the laughter was trapped inside him.

"That's really something. How did you do it?" he asked, trying to sound both incredulous and casual.

Claudia leaned against the doorjamb and smiled.

"Most people think blind people can't paint just because they can't see. That's what I thought too at first, but Ray talked me into taking a course two years ago, Art for the Handicapped it was called. I was the only blind person in it, and I learned how to do it. What I do is remember some nice place I was at before I went blind, then hold the canvas before me and try to make the picture in my mind shrink to the exact size of the canvas. Then I memorize it, sort of, and start painting." She smiled again. "I guess my first paintings were *awful*, but that didn't stop me—I couldn't see them anyway!"

"It's amazing," Andrew said, "it really is." Then he added: "How were you blinded?" He knew the question was intrusive, but he had to ask it in order to gain control of his nervousness.

The question didn't seem to surprise her. "It was a long time ago," she said. "I was still in grade school then, and I kept getting these headaches. Then one day I went blind—just like that. Something pressing on the optic nerves. I had to go to a special school for a while or I wouldn't still be just a sophomore here." She laughed a small laugh. "I'm quite used to it now," she added.

Andrew stared at her scars. He did not know what to say.

"Andrew?" she said, after a moment.

"I was just looking at your painting," he finally answered. "I really can't get over how good it is."

Later that night, Andrew sat down next to Sybil on the sofa and told her what Claudia had said about her blindness.

Sybil was drunk, and she kept opening and closing her eyes, as if she were having a hard time focusing. "Optic nerves?" she said. Then she said, "Oh yes, she heard that somewhere, so she tells it to everyone."

"She doesn't really think people believe her, does she?"

"You mean the scars?" Sybil said, wrinkling her nose. "Yes, they give her away, don't they? But she's forgotten them. She believes what she says."

"But how did her blindness really come about?"

"My, my," she laughed, "aren't we curious tonight." Then she took a drink from her glass.

Andrew didn't know what to say, so he shrugged and took another sip of bourbon.

Sybil leaned toward him then. "If you really want to know," she said, "she was blinded when she accidentally ran into a barbed wire fence. She was twelve at the time. We were at a family reunion on an uncle's farm—the same farm as in her painting, by the way. The men had gone out pheasant hunting and Father tripped and shot himself. He was wounded in the foot—he lost a couple of toes, as it turned out—and he was unconscious and losing blood, so two of our uncles picked him up and carried him back to the house. When Claudia saw him, she thought he was dead and ran off toward the woods behind the house. She was crying so hard she didn't see the fence." Sybil paused a moment, then continued, "The barbs didn't actually cause her blindness, though. Every specialist we took her to said the cuts were superficial, scratches really, and that her blindness was the result of the shock she'd had. They predicted her sight would return within weeks."

She took a long drink from her glass.

"That's fascinating," Andrew said.

Sybil looked over the glass at him, then lowered it slowly.

"It's something we don't talk to her about," she said.

In bed that evening, Andrew thought, through a blur of bourbon, about his mother. It had been two months since he'd flown to

Columbus for Alan's funeral, and he had not called or written since then, even on Christmas Day. He felt a guilty grief every time he thought of her, but still he could not bring himself to call her, to ask for forgiveness. But no: that was not it. She would not demand an apology; she would apologize to *him*. (*I don't know what I've done, Andy, but I'm sorry. Please don't be angry with me anymore. You're all I have now that Alan's gone.*) But her apology would only make him feel guiltier, for he wouldn't deserve it. And if he went to Columbus again and saw her dusting and redusting Alan's room, looking at his pictures in the photo album, or playing the old record of lullabies he loved as a child, he would feel the same oppressive love he felt in November and would have to hurt her in order to protect himself. And then he'd hate himself even more.

Just imagining his hypothetical guilt made him feel guiltier. The guilt warmed in him now, mingling with the liquor.

At the party, he had come close to being cruel to Claudia. After he talked with Sybil, he had an almost overwhelming desire to ask Claudia about her scars and her romanticized painting of the farm where her father had been shot. But why had he wanted to ask such things when he knew it would hurt her so? She was just a sweet, innocent girl who had loved her father so much that the thought of his death had blinded her. He felt ashamed for having considered hurting her.

It was funny he hadn't thought of it at Sybil's: Claudia affected him the way his mother did. She made him feel so uneasy, so strangely guilty, even when he hadn't done anything wrong. In the bedroom, talking about her painting, she had suddenly said, "I like to play a little game with people when I meet them. I try to guess whether they're smiling or not. You know, you're not easy." He hadn't known what to say after that, but he had to say something, so he said, "Well, I'm smiling." But then she shook her head. "No," she said. "You're not. Maybe you were, but you're not smiling now."

Andrew thought about Claudia often during the days that followed, and when Sybil mentioned at a curriculum committee meeting that

Claudia had asked about him, he decided to call her. In his office that afternoon, he thumbed through the student-faculty directory until he found her name, dormitory, and phone number. He wrote the information on an index card and put it in his shirt pocket.

That evening, he called her from his apartment. While the phone rang, he imagined her trying to find her way to it. He saw her short steps, her hands extended before her, feeling the wall, the furniture . . .

After the sixth ring, she answered.

"Claudia?" he asked, though he knew it was her.

"Yes?"

"This is Andrew Kern. We met the other night at—"

"Yes, I remember you."

Was she glad he'd called? Or was she already framing some excuse for not going out with him?

"I was wondering if you were free this Friday," he continued, slightly out of breath. "I have tickets to the concert at Northrup—it's Zubin Mehta and the L.A. Philharmonic. They're doing Schumann's First and Shostakovich's Fifth. And perhaps, if you like, we could have a late dinner afterwards."

He expected a pause, a hesitance, either pretended or real, about dating a man ten years her elder, but there was none.

"Why, that would be *wonderful*," she said. And she meant it. He knew it and felt a thrill of pleasure. But almost simultaneously he felt something else, something he didn't understand: disappointment. After he hung up, he wondered if he'd wanted her to be a bit more coy, elusive. Or maybe he had wished she would be less excited so he wouldn't have so much to prove to her. He didn't know. All he was sure of was that part of him wished he hadn't called.

But the next day he felt no disappointment, only anticipation. That morning, he purchased the concert tickets at the box office in Northrup Auditorium and called in reservations at Evelyn's, a new restaurant on Wayzata Boulevard, and after classes that afternoon, he drove downtown and got a haircut at The Head

Quarters, one of the most expensive barber shops in Minneapolis. The following day, he bought a new gray pinstripe suit and vest at Dayton's, even though he already owned an extensive wardrobe, then took his LeSabre to a detail shop to be washed and waxed, and when he returned home, he polished and repolished his black wingtips. And on Friday, when it was almost time to drive to Comstock Hall to pick up Claudia, he examined himself in the full-length mirror on his bedroom closet door. He liked the way the suit looked on him. He had always kept in shape—he did a hundred sit-ups and fifty push-ups every morning—and the suit was well-cut and fashionable. But the suit did not matter, just as the haircut, the polished shoes, the sparkling car, and the elegant restaurant did not matter, because Claudia was blind. None of it mattered, but he was doing it anyway and it made him feel good.

All evening long, Andrew was a gentleman. He helped Claudia into his car, took her arm in his when they walked, opened doors and ushered her through with his hand on the small of her back, and helped her into her seat at the concert. All of his courtesies were necessary because she could not see, but he tried to make her feel they were not done out of necessity or even mere manners. During the concert, he touched her hand with his while he whispered a description of Mehta's passionate conducting style. A little later, she touched his arm. He leaned toward her, expecting a whisper, but she said nothing. A few moments later, after she had moved her hand away, he took it in his and held it for the rest of the symphony.

Afterward, at Evelyn's, they talked about the concert while they waited for their dinners. They agreed that it had been extraordinary, though Claudia preferred the Schumann and Andrew preferred the Shostakovich.

"It was very kind of you to take me," Claudia said.

Andrew sensed a new tone in her voice. It was more than gratitude: she was charmed by him. He was surprised, though he had known she was not experienced with men, at how sincerely she had been affected by his simple courtesies.

"I was delighted to take you," he said.

There was a silence. Claudia looked up and sipped her strawberry daiquiri. In her purple velvet dress, she looked more attractive than he had thought possible. Almost beautiful, in fact.

"Sybil tells me you have quite a reputation in your field already," she said. "She read me the *Modern Philology* review of your book."

"Oh? And what else did Sybil tell you about me?"

Even in the dim candlelight, he could see her cheeks darken.

"That you're brilliant, but a wolf."

"She said that?" he asked.

Claudia nodded.

Andrew recalled his drunken attempts to kiss Sybil at Dean Maxwell's party. A wolf, he thought. Then he remembered his schoolmates teasing him, when he was young, during recess. He was a rabbit then. "There's Bunny Kern," they would say, then circle around him. One of them grabbed him once by the neck and gripped him hard. "Why don't we take the bunny's pants off and see if he's got a tail?" the boy had said to his fellows, but Sister Mary Margaret, the fifth-grade teacher, came walking around the corner and they left him with his pants only partially unzipped. But Sybil had said a wolf.

"I'll admit to being brilliant," he said, "but I'm more a lamb than a wolf."

Claudia laughed, her head tossed back lightly.

"You have to admit that men your age aren't generally considered safe dates for us younger women," she said.

There was another tone he had not heard her use before: she was risking something now.

"Then why did you accept my invitation—not just for the music, I hope?"

"No. It was wonderful, though. But tell me, is it true that you're not yet divorced?"

Andrew was taken aback. He had nearly forgotten that he'd told Sybil, shortly after he arrived at the university, that he'd recently separated from his wife. It was a lie—he had never been married or even engaged—but his bachelorhood had occasionally been the subject of jokes among the faculty at Syracuse, where he had last taught. Too many people got the wrong impression if you were thirty-two and single and not dating anyone. So he'd lied to Sybil. He hadn't thought his lie would return to him and demand further lies, but now Claudia had mentioned it. But what did she mean? Was she simply concerned about a legal formality, not wanting to date a married man, or was it more than that? He remembered the blush and the tone he had noticed in her voice.

"I assume Sybil mentioned that when she told you what a wolf I was," he said, brightly. Then his voice became businesslike. "No, the divorce hasn't come through yet. I stopped in to see Sandy when I flew to Ohio a couple of months ago for my brother's funeral, and she said the papers would be sent out for my signature in a few weeks. But they haven't come yet. Some delay or something, I suppose."

He wondered why he hadn't avoided complications and simply said the divorce had just been finalized.

"I'm sorry about your brother," Claudia said.

Andrew leaned toward her.

"Are you sorry about the divorce?" he said, winking. For an instant, he felt foolish for winking at a blind woman, but Claudia's light laugh showed that she recognized in his tone the quality of a wink. Leaning back, he sipped his Manhattan. He wondered if she had also recognized that he, too, was risking something.

When Andrew awoke the next morning, the lightheaded feeling of the evening was gone. He had been a fool, he was sure. The thought of the intimate, teasing risks he had taken numbed him now. The drive to Comstock Hall with his arm around her shoulders, the giddy feeling as he tilted her head back for a kiss in the parking lot, the second kiss at the elevator in her dormitory lounge: he had acted like a schoolboy. Last night he had been at ease, nearly candid, but now he was suspicious of himself. He thought of the money spent on the new suit, the dinner, the concert. Why had he spent so much, why had he even called her in the first place? Though he had always prided himself on his ability to understand himself, he was now as confused as a teenager. And Claudia, a simple girl like Claudia, was beyond his understanding. He had been so sure, when he first met her, that her innocence was feigned, and then, last night, he was certain it was not. And yet she had acted very much the same both times. She *had* been the same, but *he* had been different. Last night, he had forgotten, in the darkened auditorium and restaurant, her scars. He had forgotten them just as she had and, as a result, he had accepted her on her terms, accepted her innocence. Maybe he was attracted to her, in part at least, because of her innocence, but the fact that it was based on an illusion, a willful rejection of the truth, repelled him. He hated self-deception. Had it been willful self-deception last night when he remembered her blindness but not her scars? It didn't matter: he knew now that he'd been no better than she: last night if she'd told him that story about her optic nerves he would have believed her.

As he got out of bed and began his day, Andrew told himself he would never again forget that, despite her apparent innocence, there was deep within Claudia's brain the image of two men carrying her dead father.

⁂

A Photograph: Andrew and Alan, August 7, 1950

Andrew looks through the photo album with his mother the day after Alan's funeral. (Remember this one, Andy? The day Aunt Martha and I drove you up to summer camp?) In the photograph, Andrew and Alan are standing beside a green tent with the number six stenciled on in black, wearing matching khaki outfits bought especially for their first summer camp. Andrew is staring directly at the camera, and his smile seems stiff, as if it has been held too long. Alan's eyes are closed above his more natural smile. (You see his eyes? I must've snapped the picture just as he was blinking.) Andrew remembers how he closed his eyes as he stood beside his brother's casket during the wake. He could not bear to think of his face bloody and broken, his body crushed in the demolished car, nor could he think of the reconstruction the mortician had been compelled to do to his features. They were twins, after all, they had shared their mother's womb, they had been locked in an embrace from the moment of conception. Alan's death only made their oneness more real. He was gone, yes, but he was not gone, too. Andrew still feels his presence the way an amputee feels pain in his missing arm or leg.

(I remember your letter still. "The counselor says there are no bears in these woods but I am not convinced." You wrote that, remember?) Andrew remembers only how some of the boys stripped and tied a fat boy named Timothy to a tree and urinated on him because of what he'd been doing with himself in his sleeping bag. And he remembers the look, beyond anger and shame, on the boy's face when Alan untied him after the others had gone away. (Oh, he was such a handsome boy.)

Andrew can't look at the photograph anymore. Even the tent makes him think of the canopy over Alan's grave yesterday. He tries to think instead about his flight back to Minneapolis the next morning and the lecture he will have to prepare on *The Manciple's Tale*, but he can't. His brother is dead. A part of him is dead.

His mother reaches for another album. (I want to show you these pictures, they're from way back when. Taken with a box camera, a Kodak Brownie, all of them.) Andrew notices tears in her eyes again. The old woman tries to control her wavering voice. (Look at this one. I just said his name, and when he turned around, I snapped the picture.) Andrew knocks the photo album from her hands and strides out of the room, cursing with grief. His mother, weeping, follows him to the door. (I can't help it, Andy, I can't help it, he meant so much to me.)

In late February, Andrew took Claudia to Evelyn's again. After dinner, as they sipped their coffee, he considered asking her to spend the night with him. He knew she had never been asked before. A week ago, at his apartment, she'd told him what he had guessed earlier: he was the first man she had ever dated. "The boys never paid any attention to me in high school—because of my blindness, I think. But you don't seem to mind," she had said. He decided to ask her, to see how she would react. He took her hand in his as he spoke.

She did not seem surprised or offended, nor did she appear frightened. She only asked, "Do you want me to?"

"It has to be a mutual decision," he said.

"The other night you said that sometimes you still think of Sandy, that even though you're getting divorced you're still fond of her in a way."

"I only wanted to see if you'd get jealous," he answered. "How else am I to find out if you love me?"

"Do *you* love me?" Claudia asked.

"Yes," he said, then coughed unnecessarily. "Yes, I do."

There was nothing else he could say, but he could hardly believe he was saying it. He'd been seeing her almost nightly for the past three weeks, but still he hardly knew her. And now he was telling her he loved her and asking her to sleep with him. Why?

"You mean a lot to me, too," Claudia said. "More than anybody ever."

Andrew thought of the little girl hysterical at the thought that her father was dead. And still hysterical: hadn't the doctors said her blindness was psychosomatic, that she would be able to see again as soon as she overcame the shock?

"I hope that's true," he said.

"It is, Andrew." She finished her coffee. "I'm ready to go now, if you are, but could we stop by the dorm on the way? I have some things I want to get."

She smiled, and he realized, with a queasy fear, that she considered this the most important night of her life.

While waiting in the dormitory lounge, Andrew felt a sudden desire to leave, an imprecise longing to be home, relaxed and drowsy in a hot bath. He had made a mistake: he could not be romantic tonight. Perhaps he could never be romantic with Claudia: he didn't know. Everything seemed a series of mistakes, of misunderstood emotions, but he knew he couldn't leave.

After a few minutes, he heard a strange tapping sound and looked up to see Claudia walking into the lounge, flicking a long white cane from side to side. The cane was a surprise: he had never seen her use it before and somehow had never thought of her needing one. Whenever he had been with her, he had either taken her arm in his or held her hand.

Claudia stopped after a few steps. Andrew saw that she had changed into slacks and held a paper bag and a painting in one hand. Instantly he knew that the painting was for him and that the bag contained her nightgown and, perhaps, toothbrush, makeup, lotions, creams, perfumes, even hygiene spray: an overnight case that would raise no suspicions from the housemother. The idea of a woman spending the night at his apartment and bringing all of her trifling toiletries irritated him. He felt a sick cramp move in his chest.

"Andrew?" she said to the room.

"Here."

She folded the cane at each of its joints, then put it into the purse hanging from her shoulder and walked toward the sofa where he sat.

"Andrew?" she repeated.

"Yes."

She stopped again, beside him now, set down the paper bag, and held up the painting.

"I did this one especially for you," she said, and smiled. "I wanted it to be a surprise. I've worked on it every day now for a month, and

I just finished it this morning." Andrew took the painting from her, and she felt the sofa, then sat down. "I hope you like it."

It was another landscape. Like the one over Sybil and Ray's bed, it was unfocused, out of plumb—it seemed, however unconsciously, to combine some aspects of impressionism and cubism—but he could tell it was supposed to be a grove of apple trees beside a brook. And there was something else too. He looked closely at the upper left, beyond the grove, and saw—was it the farmhouse he had seen in her other painting?

And then he knew: this grove was the place she had been running toward the day she went blind. He felt a sudden elation at his discovery, then, just as suddenly, he felt depressed, threatened, as if she had tried to smother something in him. Once more he wanted to be gone, to leave without any excuse and never be troubled with her again.

"Why aren't you saying anything, Andrew? Don't you like it?"

"Yes, it's a nice painting, it . . ." He knew he could not say what she wanted to hear; he did not dare now, for his own sake. "It's nice," he went on, "but, I don't know, maybe it's a little *too* nice. You have a tendency, at least in the two paintings you've shown me, to prettify things, to make them seem overly romantic."

For the first time in his presence, her face showed the pain her scars suggested.

"Don't get me wrong," he said, putting his arm around her. "I'm really amazed at your talent. But do you ever try other types of paintings?"

Her mouth quivered, but she did not answer. He looked at her eyes to see if they could cry. They were not wet, and they chilled him.

"You don't understand," he said. "I didn't mean it as a criticism—just an observation. I didn't mean it the way it sounded."

"You don't like it," she said.

"Yes, I do," he said. "That's why I'm mentioning my reservations. If I didn't admire what you'd done, I wouldn't be trying to help you do even better." Then he pulled her close and kissed her on the forehead. "Don't feel bad. I didn't mean to hurt you."

But she only said, "I don't feel so well, Andrew. Maybe . . ."

She didn't finish, but Andrew knew what she meant. "Yes," he said. "Maybe tonight's not such a good idea after all. Maybe we should wait awhile. We'll talk about this some other time."

And he knew, then, that the next time he saw her, she would be a different person. He had ruined her complacence and that was a start. It was only a matter of time now.

"Okay," she said softly.

Then he kissed her. And when he was finished, she said, "Do you keep your eyes open or closed when you kiss me?"

The question surprised him. "Closed," he answered. "Why?"

"I keep mine closed too," she said.

His fever has been with him so long he's begun to imagine it as something alive, something parasitic that has been inside him all these years, waiting for this day. A devil, growing like a tapeworm.

Father Gruber. Round wire-rimmed glasses and frayed cassock sleeves. Once he told the fifth-grade acolytes about a boy who had been possessed. The boy growled like a dog and showed his teeth every time anyone came near; once he even bit his mother's shoulder so hard she bled. His parents tried doctors and psychiatrists, but they all threw up their hands. Finally, the parents called in a priest, and all he had to do was speak the ritual words of exorcism and the devil flew out of the boy's mouth with a shriek. After that, the boy slept a long time, and when he woke, he hugged his mother and cried.

He has not believed in God for years. Why, then, is he so certain the devil exists?

If only he could believe in God, if only there were some ritual that could save him.

He notices, with some surprise, that his legs have begun twitching again. His calves are chafed and sore from rubbing between the sheets, but he can't keep them still. They jerk as if they have a life of their own. And his stomach muscles are out of control, too: he watches, fascinated, as they twitch under the sheet. It almost looks as if there's a child inside him, stirring.

And then he remembers the dream. She said she'd named him Alan. His stomach cramps, and he gasps. He needs more pills. That's all. If he takes a couple more pills, he'll be fine.

But when he tries to reach for the bottle on the nightstand, his arm doesn't move. He thinks it must be asleep. Then suddenly it lurches awake and knocks the bottle onto the floor, spilling the last three tablets out. He tries to pick them up, but his fingers will not close on them.

Andrew lay in his bed for hours after he left Claudia at her dormitory. He was too excited to sleep; he felt like dancing, like staying up all night, even like calling Claudia and inviting her over again. He was amazed at how affected she had been by a few ungenerous words—her whole manner had been altered. The tip of Freud's iceberg, he thought. The tip of the iceberg was getting bigger; maybe, in time, he could turn it over. He was anxious to begin but didn't know how. If he called her, she would suspect a reconciliation—or would feel that nothing had really changed after all. But it would bother her if he called, it would confuse her, and that would be valuable, at least for now. But it would be more valuable to make her feel she had somehow jeopardized their relationship, so he decided to let her worry for a week or so before he called her again. This decision gave him a fresh excitement and, with it, a sense that the days, even that night, would never pass, that time was moving as slowly as a cat stalking its prey. He waited anxiously for sleep and its ability to carry him through time to morning in an instant.

When sleep finally came, Andrew's body jerked, as if to check a fall.

He let six days pass before he called Claudia again. Drumming his fingers on the kitchen table, he waited for her to answer. After ten rings, she had not answered, so he started to hang up.

But then he heard a voice.

"Yes?" the voice said, as if irritated at being interrupted.

Claudia had always answered the phone with a bright "Hello," so Andrew wondered for a second if he had the wrong number.

"Claudia?" he asked.

"Yes," she repeated. Her voice was even, restrained.

"This is Andrew," he began.

"I know," she said. "What do you want?"

The tone of her voice chilled him, but it also intrigued him. She was daring him to try to make her love him again. She had been hurt, was still hurt, but she was a stronger person because of it. He was certain she had learned the folly of painting idyllic scenes and inventing perfect romances. She knew now that love and pain were inextricable, twins.

"Please don't be angry," he said.

"I'm not."

"Yes, you are."

"Okay, I am. I'm angry and I'm upset. Andrew, I just don't understand you sometimes. You seemed such a loving—" She stopped herself. "What is it you want? My reader is here and we have work to do."

"I want to apologize," he said. "And make it up to you. I want you to have dinner with me tonight. Here. Beef Stroganoff, asparagus, some cabernet. How does that sound?"

There was a long pause. Finally, Claudia said, "I have three chapters of American history to read by tomorrow afternoon, and Ann can't read in the mornings. So I'd better not."

"I'll read the chapters to you."

"No. Ann's here already."

"You can tell her to go back home. I'll pay her whatever she would've earned, and I'll read the chapters to you tonight after dinner."

"I can't do that, Andrew," she said.

"*Claudia.*" He said her name as if it were a threat never to see her again.

For a moment, Claudia said nothing. Then: "All right, Andrew. All right."

Why hadn't she brought her history book? He had meant it when he said he would read to her. Didn't she believe him?

Claudia sat on the sofa, sipping her third glass of wine. Andrew put *Prélude à L'Après-Midi d'un Faune* on the stereo.

"Because I lied," she said. "I don't have any chapters to read for tomorrow."

Andrew smiled. "And Ann: was she there?"

Claudia shook her head no, and they both burst out laughing.

"You little tease," Andrew said, then sat down beside her and gave her a long kiss.

When he finished, Claudia said, "My drink. You'll make me spill it."

He took the glass from her hand and put it on the end table beside the sofa.

"Is everything all right now?" he said.

"Yes," she answered, and he kissed her again. And as he kissed her, he slipped his hand into her open cardigan and began to rub softly in slow circles one of her breasts. Claudia quickly brought her hand up to his wrist, as if to stop him, but then let it drop to her side. He felt her nipple harden under her blouse.

When he ended the kiss, she said, "Oh." It was almost a moan, almost a statement. Andrew smiled and kissed her again, more passionately this time, and all the while he massaged her breast. After a few minutes, he asked her in a whisper if she wanted to go into the bedroom, and she nodded yes.

There, she let him undress her. Slowly, gently, he removed her sweater, her blouse, her skirt, her bra, and panties, and when she was naked, his suspicions were confirmed. Scattered across her chest, abdomen, and thighs where the barbs had bitten into her were tiny, indistinct, star-shaped scars. It gave Andrew a strange sensation to think that the scars on her chest were there before her breasts developed.

In bed, he felt at first an overpowering certainty that he would fail, but after Claudia tightened, afraid, against his body, he had no trouble. When he entered her, she made a little cry, a noise more of pain or surprise than pleasure, and her eyelids fluttered. She moved under him with a jerky, taut energy, and her thighs shuddered with each thrust of his penis.

When the rush came, he became aware that he was kissing her deeply and felt suddenly empty, hollow. He broke the kiss and lay there on top of her, listening to her moan. He heard pleasure in her moans, but he also heard pain. She was a virgin, and his rough lovemaking had hurt her. But he had hurt her in another way, too: he had destroyed her romantic illusions about love, her innocent confidence that love was something simple and happy. Now he felt weak and lightheaded.

He wanted to sleep, so he came out of her and rolled over onto his back. Claudia turned toward him then and put her head on his shoulder and her hand on his chest. As he fell asleep, he thought he heard her crying softly. But perhaps he was already dreaming, for next he saw her standing beside a white picket fence drying her tears with a handkerchief, only it wasn't tears she was crying, it was blood, and her handkerchief was red and dripping.

Later, awakening, Andrew looked at the clock, released himself from Claudia's embrace, then shook her shoulder. "It's 1:30," he murmured. "I'd better get you back to your dorm." He wasn't thinking clearly yet. He had forgotten that he'd asked her to spend the night; indeed, he'd almost forgotten that they had made love. All he seemed aware of was that someone was in his bed who should be somewhere else.

Claudia sat up and dressed herself drowsily, without talking, and all the way back to Comstock, she slept with her head on his shoulder. And on his way home, Andrew imagined how she'd feel in the morning, when she woke in her room and remembered what they had done. He was certain she would be a different person then—someone wiser, more mature. Someone able, finally, to be a lover instead of a daughter.

But the next morning a friend of Claudia's delivered an envelope to Andrew at his office. Inside was a Hallmark card. On its cover, two lovers walked hand-in-hand on a beach while an orange sun dissolved into the ocean. Andrew did not even bother to read the verse inside, but he did read the note that fell out of the card. It was written in a childlike hand, its words running above and below the lines of the stationery.

> Dear Andrew,
> Thank you for being so wonderful to me. I love you.
> Claudia
> March 5, 1970

Andrew crumpled the note into a ball and threw it into the wastebasket. He couldn't believe it. Who did she think he was—her high school valentine? And she had dated the note, as if that day were so important: the beginning of an epoch. Had she forgotten the things he'd said about her painting? Had she thought sex was something *sweet?* He shook his head and swore under his breath. She'd never had her mind on what they were doing for one minute; the whole time she had been imagining orange sunsets and lovers walking barefoot in the sand.

At first he was only annoyed by her card and note, but the more he thought about them, the angrier he became. Later that morning, in the middle of his lecture on *The Harley Lyrics*, he felt a desperate need to leave, to find Claudia and tell her how she had been blinded; to make her feel her scars and understand the terrible meaning behind her seemingly innocent paintings. But as the day passed, he began to realize that he was more angry at himself than at her. He was disgusted by his self-delusion. He had expected her to understand the dark side of love right away. He knew that deep within her, deeper perhaps even than the image of her wounded father, she did understand the degradation and annihilation implicit in love. But she could not learn to face it immediately. He thought of the girl he had believed he was in love with when he was an undergraduate: the first time, he failed, and frantic evenings followed until they parted that spring, evenings when he would not leave her alone and she moaned, saying he was hurting her, she was sore and tired, would he mind not doing it tonight. It had taken Colleen time; it would take Claudia time. Andrew knew now that he would have to begin over again. This time he'd make sure she struck the bottom of sex and discovered there the love for her father that had blinded her.

⬥

A Photomontage

Pat-a-cake, pat-a-cake, baker's man, bake me a cake as fast as you can: excited, his tongue sticking out between bulging cheeks, he slaps her hands as the blue bulb on the camera flashes. There is no one as fun as her. She almost always lets him sit in the special seat on the shopping cart and makes Alan sit underneath where the potatoes go. She pushes him down the aisles and drops colorful packages in behind him until the cart is full. He pokes her in the stomach with a finger whenever she is not looking.

There are five of them, although eight were invited. All wear shiny caps fastened under their chins with rubber bands and watch as he and Alan count to three, then blow the candles out. Across the table is Wendy Jensen, who lives next door and has a mole on her cheek. She wants to be a nun like Sister Marcia when she grows up, but her mother wants her to be a concert pianist. She makes Wendy practice at the big piano in their living room every day, and sometimes Andrew sits on the floor beside her, listening to the quiet plinking and, outside, the pop of cap-pistols.

Andrew and Alan run through the lawn sprinkler in their maroon swimsuits, smiling and yelling at their mother. She sits on the back steps, waiting for the right moment, and presses the button on the new camera that takes color pictures just as they leap into the spray. Later, when Andrew sees the photograph, he cries at his salmon-pink skin and white-blond hair. (What is it, Andy, what's wrong?) He tells her what the kids at school call him, and tears come to her eyes. They sit at the kitchen table, all alone, and she tells him about genes, but he doesn't believe it can be her fault.

"Do Gentlemen Prefer Platinum Blondes?" the caption reads. Her silver gown is strapless and off the shoulders. Her lips are full, parted, and shining, and her eyes are half-closed, as if she's about to swoon with desire. If Mom ever looked like that at somebody, I would smack her one, Andrew thinks. Damn DiMaggio, he says with the other boys.

Page seventeen, second row, third from the left: Lynette Bowman, her hair teased, glasses slightly crooked. Orchestra 10, 11, 12; Concert Band 10, 11, 12; Senior Band 10, 11, 12; FHA 10, 11, 12; Candystriper 10, 11; AFS Club 11, 12; Pep Club 11, 12; Library Club 11, 12; Girl Stater 11; Yearbook Staff Co-Editor 12. She is a thin, bird-boned girl, but on the night Andrew escorts her to the senior prom her breasts are so suddenly large and pointed beneath her pink dotted-swiss formal that Kirk Aamot and his friends tease her until she runs into the bathroom crying. Andrew doesn't know what to do, so he goes out to the parking lot and sits in his mother's car. The band inside the gymnasium plays a full set before Lynette finally comes out. She is no longer crying, but she is flat-chested again. He thinks he should kiss her, to make her feel better, but instead he starts the car and asks if she wants him to take her home.

Colleen sits on the hood of his blue Chevy. Legs crossed, leaning back on her hands, her head turned provocatively to the right. As lonely as Andrew—or lonelier, because she does not have the friends among the faculty he does—she teases him continually. (Are you taking a picture or is this just an excuse to look at my legs all day?) She is good to him, and he knows it. That night, they park deep in a grove near an abandoned farmhouse and kiss for a long time. But when they take their clothes off, he goes limp and cannot enter her. She touches him but it makes no difference, and finally she gives up and puts her arms around him. (It's all right, Andy. Don't worry about it. It doesn't matter.) She is trying to comfort him, and he despises her for it.

Tucked away in his monograph on the *Confessio Amantis*, a photograph from *The Minneapolis Tribune*: the National Guard is removing the barricade of chairs, boxes and boards students laid across Washington Avenue, near Coffman Memorial Union, as part of their protest against the U.S. invasion of Cambodia. To the left of the barricade, a Guardsman stands motionless, his tightly gripped rifle separating him from a shouting student who wears a black armband. The student's neck is corded with anger. In the background, sitting on the grass, as serene as a Buddha, is Jack.

❦

That Friday, Andrew did not call Claudia. He knew she would be expecting him to call, to begin seeing her every weekend again, but he was still too upset to see her. If he called her, if they were together again so soon, she would want him to be "romantic" with her, and he could not, at least not yet. He remembered the scars on her breasts, her moans, the way she put her head on his shoulder after they made love: no, he could not see her tonight. He had to forget about her for a while, do something else, keep his mind occupied.

Thank you for being

A stack of term papers stood on his desk. He had promised his students he'd have them graded by Monday, so he could return them when they wrote their final exams. He looked at his watch. It was 7:30: if he began now, and worked steadily all evening, he could finish by midnight.

for being so wonderful

He sat down at his desk and took a paper off the top of the pile. It was titled "The Wife of Bath: Feminist Prophet." He set the paper aside and picked up the next one. Its title was "The Pardoner's Yellow Hair: Chaucer's *General Prologue* and Medieval Theories of Physiognomy."

so wonderful to me

Andrew stood up and walked to the window. Perhaps he should call Claudia after all. He had to do something. He couldn't stay here tonight. He was too restless for that. Why was he so restless? He didn't know, and he didn't care; he just knew he had to go out. But not with Claudia. He felt the need to go someplace where he wouldn't be known, where he could start everything over, fresh, undetermined by the past, and be someone else, if only for a night. He wanted to talk intimately with strangers, to drink and dance until he was so exhausted he could sleep, for once, without being awakened by bad dreams.

He didn't want to think about the dreams, but before he could stop himself he saw Alan in the casket, his eyes open, alive, looking at him out of his ghost-gray face.

Andrew shut his eyes a moment, to push the dream image back into the darkness.

Then he couldn't wait any longer; he had to go now, before he changed his mind and called Claudia. He slipped on his jacket and hurried out the door.

He was already in the car and driving before he decided where he would go. There was a new place he'd heard some students talking about, a place called The Golden Fleece, on the West Bank. That's where he would go. Perhaps he'd meet a woman there, someone who would be more his type than Claudia. A divorcée perhaps. Or maybe a young girl, an early developer, precociously pessimistic about love and marriage. Whoever she turned out to be, he couldn't tell her his real name; he had to make one up. What could his name be? He thought of several—Robert, Edward, Bruce—but none of them sounded right. Alan was the only name that would fit him, and he couldn't use it, he could never use it.

Although Andrew hadn't expected to know anyone at The Golden Fleece, when he got there he recognized Perry Waltham, an associate professor of art he had met briefly at Dean Maxwell's party. At first, Andrew thought of leaving and finding another bar, but he didn't know where else to go. And besides, Perry was virtually a stranger to him. Andrew hadn't seen him at any of the faculty parties since Maxwell's, and though he'd heard bits of gossip concerning him, he didn't know if any of it was true. Perry was sitting alone at a table in the corner where the wall-length mural depicting the trials of Jason began, so Andrew walked over from the bar and asked if he could join him.

"Why not?" Perry answered, shrugging. "It's a free country, isn't it?"

Andrew hesitated a moment, unsure of Perry's tone.

"Go ahead, sit down." Perry waved his hand.

Andrew took a seat. The room was dark enough to allow him to excuse himself before someone he knew could come in the door, adjust to the dim light, and see him with Perry.

"I understand this is your first year here too," he began, and cleared his throat nervously. "How do you like it so far?"

"I love it, of course. I meet the nicest fellows. Very bright, stimulating youngsters—and handsome as hell too, I might add. Keeps you young just to look at them."

Then there is no pretense, Andrew thought. He was embarrassed, but he had to say something.

"You're not old. What are you? Thirty-four? Thirty-five?"

Andrew knew Perry was older, but he did look young. He was one of those men whose faces remain boyish well into middle age and beyond. Or had he had plastic surgery?

"Ha ha. Funny boy. You're a funny boy. Now how old do you really think I am? I'm sure none of my students know. Go on. Guess."

"I can't really say. Thirty-seven?"

"No. *Forty*-seven."

The door opened and closed; Andrew's eyes strained at the two men who came in and took seats at the mahogany bar: no one he knew. He turned back to Perry.

"That's hard to believe. You look much younger."

"I try to keep in shape." He hooked his thumbs under his belt, then sucked his flat belly in until it caved below his rib cage. He spoke, holding the air in his lungs: "Can't hard ly fitin to mypants any more." Then he let the air out and laughed.

Andrew laughed with him, then sipped his bourbon self-consciously. Perry's answer had a recklessness in it, a certain denial of the need to avoid making mistakes, that was attractive to him, yet made him uneasy.

"Oh, here's Jack," Perry said.

At that moment, a tall, slender young man with dark wavy hair approached from the restroom nearby.

"This is Jack Bostrom, one of my prize pupils," Perry said. "I was sitting with him."

"I'm sorry. I thought you were alone," Andrew said, then stood to shake hands with Jack. "Bostrom, is it?" he said. Jack nodded. Andrew wasn't sure if Bostrom was the name he'd heard at the parties.

"Don't worry about that," Perry said. "Stay on and chat awhile. Right, Jack?"

"Right."

"Oh, excuse me," Perry said. "Your name is Kern, isn't it?"

"Yes. Andrew."

Perry stood and, flourishing his arm toward Andrew, said, "Jack Bostrom, I am pleased to introduce Professor Andrew Kern."

Jack laughed. "You've perfect manners, Perry, you really should applaud yourself."

"You're quite right." Perry clapped his palms together and laughed.

They all sat down then, and Andrew glanced around the room to see if anyone had been watching them. Four young men and two women were sitting at the round table closest to theirs, drinking beer and talking about somebody named Dennis. In the corner, a fat man in a light blue suit was sitting with a woman who looked half his age—his secretary, perhaps? He kept straightening his tie, as if he hoped it would hide his huge belly. And across the room, two college-age men were leaning over a table and talking intensely about something. The candle in the center of the table made their faces look sinister.

Andrew took another swallow of his drink and looked back at Perry.

"Mr. Kern's a medievalist," Perry was saying. "He knows all the fine points of courtly love, and he's been practicing them on this blind girl, Sybil Gardner's daughter, I believe."

There was something new in Perry's tone. Was it mockery? Or was it just a friendly facetiousness?

"Sybil's sister," Andrew corrected.

"Of course," Perry said. "I did have the sex right though, didn't I?"

It *was* mockery, he realized, and it was for Jack's sake. Perry was trying to humiliate him in front of Jack.

"Perhaps I should go," he said, and started to get up.

"No, stay," Jack said, taking Andrew's wrist lightly. Then he turned to Perry. "There's no need to be impolite, Perry. I hardly think Dr. Kern—"

"Andrew," he requested.

"Andrew. I hardly think Andrew is here to mock your sexual preference."

"Don't you think Sex With The Blind is an interesting topic?" Perry retorted. "We could have an open forum on it right here." He seemed to be trying to keep the lightness in his voice, but failing.

"You mean Sex With The Female, don't you?" Jack said. He turned to Andrew. "Never mind him, all he thinks about is sex— or something he likes to call sex."

Perry giggled.

"Tut, tut, Jackie, you'd better watch out. Andrew here might be with the Vice Squad."

It was out in the open; they spoke of it as if they didn't care what anyone thought.

"I was merely apologizing for you because somebody has to," Jack said. "Andrew, I take back what I said about Perry having good manners."

Andrew was worried the conversation would end in an embarrassing silence. "It's not necessary to apologize," he said, his voice wavering slightly. "I don't pretend to care anything for the girl anyway."

Then he took a long drink from his glass, and hoped the darkness hid the blush he felt suffusing his cheeks and forehead.

As the evening passed, and he began drinking doubles, Andrew lost his self-consciousness. What did he care what Perry thought of him? Jack seemed to like and accept him, and he liked Jack. So even if Perry told him to leave, he wouldn't go. But Perry wouldn't tell him to go: he wasn't even talking to him. He was talking only to Jack, as if Andrew were not even there. Andrew wasn't going to sit there and be insulted like that, so he kept interrupting Perry and starting conversations with Jack. That made Perry angry, but Jack only smiled, so Andrew kept it up. "Don't humor him," Perry warned. Jack laughed. "Would you rather I humored you?" he asked, and continued talking with Andrew. But it wasn't until eleven o'clock, when Perry was summoned to the telephone, that they were able to talk freely.

"Perry doesn't like me, does he?" Andrew began, with a laugh.

"He's too afraid of people to like them," Jack answered.

"He likes you."

Jack smiled. "No, he's afraid of me, too. He knows I like to have women now and then, and he's worried I'll go straight on him. But mostly he's afraid I don't love him. I don't, and he knows it, but he won't accept it."

Andrew was confused. "If you don't . . . like him, why . . ." He waved his hand in the air instead of finishing the sentence.

"Because the pay is good," Jack answered.

Andrew looked at him. He didn't understand.

Jack smiled. Then, as if explaining something that would be obvious to anyone but a child, he said, "I live with him because he pays me to."

Andrew was stunned. Perhaps he hadn't heard right. Perhaps he was drunker than he thought.

"But . . ."

"Oh, don't be shocked. It's nothing to be shocked about. Some men keep mistresses and some keep misters. That's all."

Andrew shook his head. "But to do it only for money, Jack . . ."

Jack leaned over the table. "Everybody's got to fuck," he said, "so if you're going to do it anyway, why not get paid for it? And what does it matter who you do it with? In the dark, everybody's the same, man or woman; it's all just a matter of cocks and holes." He sat back. "I'll do anything with anybody, and I think everybody would say the same if they were honest."

Andrew was feeling a little dizzy. "What?"

But Jack didn't want to talk about it anymore. "I've told you enough about myself," he said. "Let's talk about you for a while."

"What do you want to know?"

"Well, for starters," Jack said with a smile, "how long have you been such an innocent?"

Andrew stared at Jack.

Just then, Perry returned.

"Jack," he said, "it's old Winston, we've forgotten his ugly party. He says he's been calling all over after us."

Andrew began to rise from his chair, but before he could excuse himself, Jack said, "Why don't you join us, Andrew?"

Perry glared at Jack, but Jack ignored him.

Andrew paused. No one who knew him would be at the party. Even Claudia was not a reason to say no. And he wanted to talk some more with Jack. Jack intrigued him: he seemed the most complete and adventurous nihilist he had ever met.

"I don't have anything else to do, I guess," he said.

Perry shrugged. "It's your funeral," he said. "Let's go."

Andrew had been sitting on Winston's davenport talking with Jack for almost an hour. He was so drunk now he couldn't even taste the cabernet he was drinking.

"Sometimes," he was saying, "I think I love her and other times, I don't know, other times I don't even like her. It doesn't make any sense." He shook his head. "She's a sweet girl, Jack. A sweet, sweet girl. I wish I were more like her. I wish I were a better person."

Jack had quit drinking some time before. "Why are you telling me this?" he asked quietly.

"Thank God I told her I was still legally married!" Andrew continued. "I've told everybody I was married; did I tell you that, too? It's a lie. I've never been married. I've never even been in love. I don't even love my mother. I'm a horrible person."

"You're drunk, Andrew. You don't know what you're saying."

"I'm telling the truth," he insisted. "Do you realize that I haven't even sent my mother a postcard in over four months? Four months!" He lowered his head and tried not to cry.

"Come on, Andrew. I think you'd better lie down and get some rest. You'll feel better after a little sleep."

Andrew lifted his head. "What's wrong with me, Jack?"

Jack looked at him. "I don't know," he said.

"Yes, you do," Andrew said. "I can tell you do. You have to tell me."

"All I know is that you're going to be sick. You've got to stop drinking."

"What if I *want* to be sick? What if I don't care how sick I get?"

Just then, Andrew heard some people behind him laugh, and as he turned to see if they were laughing at him, he spilled his glass on Jack's lap.

"Oh shit," Jack said, and stood up quickly.

"What's wrong?" Andrew said, turning back.

Then Perry came over from across the room, where he'd been talking with Winston and a slim Asian man they called VC for a joke. "Here's a hanky," he said, and dangled his handkerchief in front of Jack's face the way a matador teases a bull with his cape.

Jack took the handkerchief and started to wipe the wine off his jeans.

"That's an interesting location for a stain," Perry laughed.

"Fuck off," Jack said.

Andrew finally understood what had happened. He stood up unsteadily. "I'm so sorry," he apologized. "I didn't mean to spill it. It was an accident."

Perry looked at him. "You're making an ass of yourself, Kern," he said. "Why don't you just run on home?"

"Leave him alone," Jack said.

"All right, Jackie," Perry said, putting his hands up and backing away. "But I'll remember this the next time you come asking for some extra spending money . . ."

Jack watched him go back to Winston and VC.

"He's mad at you," Andrew said.

"Yeah. Maybe I should go talk to him."

"Don't go," Andrew said.

"I'd better. I think I've hurt him too much this time."

Andrew caught his arm as he started to go.

"What do you want from me?" Jack said, impatiently.

What *did* he want? Andrew looked dumbly around the room for a minute, his head reeling. Then he thought of something. He held up his glass. "I need some more wine. My glass is empty."

Jack took the glass and set it on the coffee table. "You're going to be sick enough as it is," he said. "You'd better do what Perry said and get yourself home. If you like, I'll call you a cab."

"Wait a minute," Andrew said. "Just wait a minute. I'm not so drunk that I can't tell when I'm being insulted."

"What are you talking about?"

Earlier, when he was telling Jack about Claudia and his mother, he'd felt relieved, even absolved, the way he did when he was a child and confessed his sins to Father Gruber in the dark confessional. But now he began to feel a woozy horror at what he'd revealed. What was to keep Jack from telling Perry—and anyone else—what he had told him? And he was sure Jack had understood things he hadn't even said. He felt a surge of nausea and his head went light.

He pointed at Jack. "You tricked me," he accused.

He knew everybody was watching him, but he didn't care.

"A lovers' spat," someone said, then giggled. Andrew turned in the direction of the giggle, said "I swear he tricked me," and then his mind spun, the room rolled away, and he fell to the floor.

When he woke, hours later, he was lying on the davenport, covered by a yellow and white patchwork quilt. Looking around, he saw there was no one in the room, and he felt a sudden anxiety mingle with his nausea. For a reason he had not yet remembered, he was anxious to find Jack. Slowly and carefully, he sat up, shucked the quilt, and put his feet on the floor. His head seemed to sway, as if his confused thoughts were winds that blew it back and forth.

He stood up and stumbled toward the door. To steady himself, he stopped at the stairway and leaned against the banister for a second. He tried to breathe slowly, evenly, so he wouldn't throw up.

Then he heard the voices: they were coming from upstairs. He heard Perry's voice first, just a murmur, low and peaceful, and then he heard Jack's.

He barely made it out the door before he began to vomit.

The following morning, he called Claudia. He'd had two Bloody Marys already, but his head was still throbbing. His skull seemed to have tightened, like a vise, around his brain.

"Oh Andrew," Claudia said, "I've been so worried you wouldn't call."

"My work's been piling up," he said. "The usual end-of-the-quarter business: exams, term papers, grades. I'm still not done with it all, but I want to take the day off and spend it with you. The whole day, all twenty-four hours. And I won't take no for an answer."

"No," she said, then laughed. "Just teasing!"

"Good. Can you be ready in ten minutes?"

"Ten minutes!"

"Twenty minutes, then. I won't wait any longer."

"Okay. I'll start getting ready right now. Goodbye."

"Just a minute," he said. "I have something to tell you."

"Yes?"

A vein was pulsing in his forehead. He traced it with a fingertip.

"I love you," he said.

There was a pause.

"Thank you, Andrew," she finally answered. "You don't know how happy you've made me."

After Andrew hung up, he sat at his kitchen table a moment, thinking about what he'd said. He knew he didn't love Claudia, but he wanted to, and he was determined that he would. There was no reason for him not to love her. She was a wonderful woman: loving, selfless, good. He had been foolish to let her blindness bother him so much. What did it matter if she believed she were truly blind? And what harm was there in her innocent dreams? From now on, he'd let her believe whatever she wanted, and it wouldn't matter to him. Even if she started painting her kitsch again, he wouldn't care; he'd praise everything she did. He was going to make himself as deserving of her love as she was of his.

Just before he left to pick up Claudia, Andrew took down the Cézanne still-life over the living room couch and hung her landscape in its place. Then he stepped back and looked at the grove of apple trees, the quiet brook, the farmhouse in the distance. Now he was ready for her.

·❀·

A Photograph: Ryan Enevoldsen, December 22, 1967

Andrew, in Columbus for the Christmas holidays, has stopped by Alan's studio on Westcott. They sit under the skylight in old overstuffed armchairs and drink coffee. Last night, Andrew ran into Becky and Frances, two girls they knew in high school, and he thinks they should all go out together again, double-date like they used to, just for old time's sake. But Alan doesn't want to go. (Come on, you'd have a great time. You always liked Becky, didn't you? And she said she hasn't seen you for years.) Alan shakes his head. (I have a lot of portraits to finish. A lot of retouching. The Wallace wedding pictures. I'll be too busy.) Andrew puts his cup down on the coffee table. (On Saturday night? Are you kidding?) Then Alan gets up with a sigh and motions for Andrew to follow him. They walk around the flood and spot lamps, the camera on its tripod, and go behind the blue backdrop into the darkness. (What's on your mind?) Alan says nothing, just switches on the safelight, mixes D76 solution with tap water and acid fixing salt, and pours it into the developing tray. Then he takes an 8x10 sheet negative and submerges it in the fluid. Andrew looks at his brother, but Alan still says nothing, only begins preparing the stop bath and fixing solution. (I don't understand, Alan. What are you trying to prove?)

But in a few minutes, Andrew begins to understand. The photograph starts to develop, a figure seems to rise out of some unseen depths of the film. Andrew strains to see the figure. In another moment, it is clear. It is a man, a young man, about their age. Tall, blond, Scandinavian-looking. And he is naked. He is half-sitting, half-lying on an unmade bed, smiling at the camera and raising a wine goblet as if for a toast. Alan takes the photograph out of the developing tray and immerses it in the stop bath, then turns to his brother. (His name is Ryan.)

⬧

Andrew rolls his head from side to side, but he cannot escape the fever pulsing in his temples. He opens and closes his mouth as if there's not enough air, or as if he's trying to talk to someone who is too far away for words. His eyes open and close, too. For a long time he has tried to sleep. But he is still awake, though he doesn't know it because he's dreaming.

In his fever dream, the blindfold is tied so tightly that his brain throbs behind his eyeballs. The game is blind man's buff, only they call it blind man's bluff, not knowing any better. There are children all around him, calling his name, poking him, giggling. He turns each time he is prodded and reaches out: nothing. Always nothing. The laughter reverberates, and he turns in circles until he is dizzy and stops. Then he hears Alan's high-pitched laugh and moves toward it, his arms extended like a monster's or a lover's. But his hands touch only air.

The Minnesota Daily, Tuesday, May 17, 1970, page 3A:

UM STUDENT AWARD WINNER

UM junior John Bostrom was recently awarded Third Prize in the Tenth Annual Upper Midwest College Student Photography Competition, sponsored by the American Federation of Photographers. First Prize went to Kenneth R. Schall, a senior at the University of Wisconsin-Milwaukee. Second Prize was awarded to Gwendolyn Burton, a junior at Gustavus Adolphus in St. Peter.

Bostrom's prize-winning photo is "an excellent example of the surrealistic effects which can be achieved by superimposition," according to Dr. Perry Waltham, UM associate professor of art. To make his photo, Bostrom superimposed film of the Mojave Desert onto film of the headless upper torso of a man. "The effect," Professor Waltham said, "is eerie, almost as if a desert is becoming a man or a man becoming a desert."

The photograph will be displayed, along with other works by Bostrom and his fellow students, in the main gallery at Coffman Memorial Union from 9:30 a.m. to 3:30 p.m., May 18 through 24. The exhibit is free and open to the public.

At first, Andrew was going to call Jack and congratulate him, but then he thought better of it. He hadn't talked to Jack since that night at The Golden Fleece in March—and he hadn't even answered the note Jack sent the following week, asking if he was still angry at him. So he didn't call. But the next day, after his 8:30 class, he decided to walk over to Coffman and see Jack's photograph. As he walked across Northrup Mall, he wondered if Jack would be there for the opening of the exhibit.

Jack wasn't there that morning. But that afternoon, when Andrew went back to the gallery after lunch, he was. Andrew saw him as soon as he entered. He was standing by a photograph reminiscent of a Wyeth painting—waist-high weeds, a dilapidated barn—talking with a tall anemic-looking girl with stringy yellow hair.

Andrew pretended not to see Jack and casually began examining the photographs he'd already looked at that morning. He stopped in front of each one, as if scrutinizing it, and tried to decide what to say when Jack finally noticed him.

He was staring blankly at a photograph of a sailboat race on Lake Calhoun when Jack put his hand on his shoulder. Andrew turned.

"Oh, it's you," he said, and put out his hand. "Congratulations on your award. I read about it in the *Daily* yesterday."

Jack shook his hand and smiled.

"Thanks. Thanks a lot."

There was a short silence.

"How's Perry?" Andrew began, awkwardly.

"I don't know," Jack answered, and when Andrew looked at him, he explained, "I only see him in class now. We've had what he calls a 'tiff.' He drew up 'divorce papers' and everything. He still loves me, he says, so he's giving me a hundred dollars a month for the rest of the year. Then I'm 'on my own.'"

Andrew wished he wouldn't talk so loudly. He wanted to look around, to see if anyone had heard, but he was too embarrassed.

"I'm sorry," he said, almost in a whisper.

"So am I," answered Jack. "But only because I have to find a job now—or should I say, *another* job: living with Perry was hard work. If I don't make more money, I can't stay in school, and if I can't stay in school, I lose my student deferment, and if I lose my student deferment . . . But what the hell—have you seen my picture yet?"

Andrew shook his head, so Jack led him toward the center of the far wall. When they were about ten feet from the photograph, Jack said, "Stop here." Andrew stopped. "Now what do you see?"

Andrew had already seen and studied the effect of looking at the picture from a distance and then up close that morning, but he pretended to be seeing it for the first time.

"It looks like a man. A man's chest and arms."

"Okay. Now come closer."

He walked forward a few steps, then stopped.

"Ah," he said. "Now I see the dunes. It's amazing how you were able to superimpose something so rounded onto something as relatively flat as a man's chest."

He went even closer, put his face up near it.

"It's remarkable work. Absolutely first-rate." He meant it: his brother, for all his skill, had never done anything nearly as good.

"Thank you," Jack said, with a mock bow.

"Really," Andrew said. "I'm surprised it didn't win first prize."

"One of the judges said he thought it would've won if I hadn't 'beheaded' the man. He told me the picture needed a grimacing face, or a weeping face, or something like that. That's rubbish, of course."

"Did you tell the judge that?"

"No. I told him this man didn't have a face."

Andrew laughed.

"No, I meant it," Jack said.

Andrew smiled uncomfortably. He wasn't sure what Jack meant.

"The judge laughed, too," Jack continued. "I wanted him to laugh. You, too. But I'm serious. This man doesn't have a face."

Andrew wasn't smiling now. He stared at the photograph. "I don't understand," he said. "Who is it supposed to be?"

Now Jack laughed. "It's a self-portrait," he said. "It's me. Who did you think it was?"

When Andrew left the gallery, he felt a strange, jittery panic he didn't understand. He was relieved to get away from Jack—it had been a mistake to see him again—but he was trembling, and his breaths were so rapid they almost hurt. He sat down on the steps outside Coffman to get control of himself. He'd felt like this once before, years ago, when he was at camp with his brother. The counselors had taken all the boys hiking along a mountain trail, and when they weren't looking, Andrew had crawled out onto a rock and hung his head over the edge of the precipice. He felt a swooning vertigo then and, closing his eyes, saw his body falling endlessly through the empty air. But he wasn't afraid, not then. It was only later, when Alan pulled him back from the edge and he should have felt nothing but relief, that the panic started.

Later that day, Andrew met Claudia outside her biology classroom, as he had for several weeks, to take her to his apartment for dinner. She kissed him on the cheek, and he took her arm, then they started toward the parking lot. She was telling him about something funny a student had said in class when she suddenly stopped and said, "Did you have a hard day?"

"Nothing out of the ordinary," he answered.

"You seem tense," she said, and squeezed his arm.

"I'm fine."

"Are you sure?"

"I said I'm fine."

A few moments passed. Then she said, "How far is it to the car?"

"You're full of questions today," he said.

"I'm sorry," she said. "I'll shut up." And they walked the last blocks to the parking lot in silence.

But as they walked up the stairs to his apartment a few minutes later, she stopped and said, "Andrew, won't you tell me what's wrong? I know something's bothering you."

His arm began to tremble.

"Is it something I did? Please tell me, Andrew."

He did not say anything. He just continued up the steps, then opened the door and let her in. Then he turned to her worried face and said, "Remember the other night at Sybil and Ray's? Remember Sybil's little comment about 'wedding bells'?"

"She didn't mean anything by that. She was just—"

"I know what she was doing. Well, I want you to listen carefully to what I'm going to say—you *can* hear, can't you? I'm not going to marry you. Not now, not ever."

"But Andrew, you said before, you said that this summer—"

And then she started to cry.

"I know I suggested we live together this summer," Andrew said. "But living together and marriage aren't the same thing. And besides, it was only an idea." He took hold of her wrist and noted that she was trembling now and his grip was firm and steady. "Come on," he said, and started to pull her across the room.

"What are you doing?" she asked.

"I'm taking you to the bedroom."

"Andrew, don't," she said. "Let's talk. I want to understand."

He didn't say anything.

"You're hurting my wrist, Andrew. Please don't."

Then they were in the bedroom. He stopped inside the door and closed it behind them. The only light in the room was the sunlight that slanted through the blinds and barred the unmade bed.

"Oh, Andrew. Please tell me what I've done."

Then he started to undress her. She stood still, her arms at her sides, while he unbuttoned her blouse and unzipped her skirt. Tears were running down her cheeks, but she made no effort to wipe them away.

When he finished and began to undress himself, she whispered, "Why do you want to make love to me if you don't love me?"

"Do you think sex is love?" he said. "Are you that goddamned innocent?"

Then he got into bed, leaving her standing beside the door.

"Andrew," she said.

He did not answer.

"Andrew, you're frightening me."

Again he did not answer, and Claudia began walking, her arms stretching out in front of her, toward the bed. When she reached it, she got in cautiously.

"Why are you treating me like this?" she asked.

"I'm giving you something to think about the next time you paint some rosy scene."

He had wanted his words to come out sharply, but his voice was shaking. It angered him.

"I wish I could hate you sometimes," she said, in a thin voice. "But I can only be afraid of you. You've been so kind to me that I thought you loved me. You've never been really cruel to me before, but sometimes I've been afraid of you, Andrew, I have." She paused. "Sometimes you scare me."

"It's just that I'm your first lover," he said, "and you're learning what love really is."

"I just need someone to take care of me," she said, crying harder now. "You've taken care of me. We don't even have to call it love anymore. I promise I won't ever say anything about getting married. You can just take care of me, can't you?"

He did not answer.

"Sometimes I think you hate me, Andrew. I can feel it sometimes." Her voice became nearly a whisper. "I felt it when I gave you my painting, and I felt it now and then during the last couple of months. You'd get irritated and you'd try not to show it, but I could feel it anyway. I wish I could see you. Sometimes I think you're doing all you can just to keep from hitting me."

He raised a fist and held it over her face.

"Andrew?" she said.

He lowered his fist slowly and watched her face work.

When she let out a little scream and covered her face with her small hands, he came on top of her. She began to cry fiercely then, and he thought of how she would cry afterward when he told her about the scars. He forced her legs apart.

She did not stop crying.

A Negative: Andrew and His Mother, December 24, 1966

Wearing his navy blue blazer, Andrew stands next to his mother and smiles at his uncle. (If you're so smart, why don't you put your arm around that good-looking woman beside you?) His hand touches, lightly, the back of her midnight green dress, and his fingertips feel the hooks and laces of her corset. His uncle comes forward two steps, then goes back one. (Okay, I have you. Smile big now, Sis. Andy, you just think about your favorite girl. There you go.) Then the camera flashes, recording what only it can see: the whiteness within black, the blackness within white. It is not a photograph of mother and son, but of two souls, dark angels, just risen from their bodies. They are clothed in white but they are black, so black they are almost not there. Their hair, their faces, even their hands are black. But their eyes and their mouths are white, as if burning from what they see, from what they cannot say.

Sybil was standing outside Andrew's office when he arrived the next morning. "I've been waiting for you," she said. He opened the door and let her in.

"Have a seat," he said.

But she would not sit.

"I can't forgive you for what you've done," she began. "Claudia's forgiven you, but she doesn't know any better, she's so—"

"Now, wait a minute. What's this all about?" Andrew hadn't been able to sleep all night and he had a terrible headache. He didn't need Sybil to make him feel worse than he already did.

"You know what it's about."

"She knew the scars were there. She's got fingers. She's felt them."

"You bastard, you know what I mean."

He did not say anything. He started to straighten some memos and papers stacked on his desk.

"Damn it, Andrew, when I saw her last night she was wearing *sunglasses!*"

Andrew looked out the window. He tried to imagine Claudia wearing sunglasses, but he couldn't. He turned back to Sybil. "She's not blind," he said. "Not really. You told me that yourself."

But she ignored him. She put her trembling hand to her forehead as if feeling for a fever. "I don't know why you made her remember all that, and whatever your reasons were I can never forgive you for it," she said. She was trying to control her voice. Andrew was so tired of listening to women who couldn't control their voices. His mother, Claudia, and now Sybil. Why wouldn't they just leave him alone? "But Claudia's got it in her head somehow that you love her," Sybil went on, "and she thinks you two will get along better now that she knows what it is you don't like about her. So I'm supposed to invite you to a party Ray and I are giving Saturday. She told me not to tell you she'd be there, but I'm telling you anyway. If you have any feelings for her at all, you'll be there. Or better yet, you'll go and see her right now."

She paused, looking at him.

"Well, what do you say?" she asked. "Don't you have anything to say?"

"I'm afraid I can't accept your gracious invitation," he answered.

Sybil looked at him a moment. "You bastard," she said. Then she turned and strode out of the office.

Andrew was shaken, but at the same time he was relieved. He felt a sort of satisfaction in knowing that he no longer had to deal with Sybil. Their account was closed; it would never be reopened. He wished he could end his relationship with Claudia as easily, but Claudia's weakness was harder to deal with than Sybil's strength. Claudia would forgive his cruelest words; Sybil would forgive nothing. He wished he could hurt Claudia into breaking up with him, but he knew now that he couldn't. He had always preferred making his lovers hate him, so they wouldn't be hurt when he left them. It was odd: he was cruel to them because he didn't want to hurt them. And because he wanted to love them: for some reason, he could never love them unless he could feel sorry for them. If only he could explain all this to Claudia, make her understand. But he wasn't sure he understood it himself. Sometimes he thought he did, but he wasn't sure.

He tried to forget about Claudia, to read his mail, but his headache wouldn't let him. He had to do something about her; he couldn't go on like this. He thought about going over to her dorm and telling her as gently as he could that he no longer wanted to see her. But he knew he couldn't look at her and say those words. But he had to say them nonetheless, so he decided to call her. That was the only solution—a quick phone call, a simple message, then silence. He looked at his watch: she would be getting ready for her first class now. If he waited any longer, she'd be gone, and he wouldn't be able to call her until after lunch.

He took a deep breath and inhaled slowly. He had to do it now. His finger shook a little as he dialed her number. He took another deep breath and waited for her to answer.

But before the phone rang three times, he remembered, with a sudden thrill, Jack's businesslike separation from Perry, and tried to hang up before Claudia could answer. He heard her hello just as he set the phone back on its cradle.

That evening, when Andrew returned to his apartment, his headache was so severe he didn't turn on the hall light for fear it would be too painfully bright. Feeling his way down the hall in the dark, he went into the kitchen, sat down at the table, and put his throbbing head in his hands. The things he'd done that day seemed beyond anything he had ever imagined himself capable of doing, and yet, in a way, they were trifling. He'd cancelled his classes; called Jack and met him for lunch at The Paddock, a coffeehouse in Dinkytown; and he'd opened a checking account in Jack's name at the Midwest Federal on University. And then, back at the office, he'd read the classifieds in the latest issue of *The Chronicle of Higher Education* and, though most of the positions in his field had been filled months before, found two jobs for medievalists advertised, both assistant professorships, one at the Duluth campus of the university and the other at Miami University of Ohio. And even though it would mean a drop in rank and pay, he'd written a letter of application to Miami University and, because he already knew Merrell Kincaid, the chairman of Duluth's English department, called him and told him he was interested in the position. The events of the day had been nothing more strenuous than paperwork and phone calls: business. But he couldn't shake the feeling that he had done something too enormous to name.

After a while, he stood and switched on the light on top of the stove and in its weak glow made a grilled cheese sandwich and a salad. But he couldn't eat more than a few bites of either. Even water made him nauseous, and he felt so sick that he went to bed, even though it was only seven o'clock. He was too exhausted to keep his eyes open, but he couldn't sleep, so he lay there blindly, barely able to move or even think. He didn't know how long he lay there half awake; it might have been minutes, or hours.

Just before he fell asleep, he whispered, "I will make it up to you. I promise I will." But he could not have said whether his words were addressed to Claudia, his mother, Alan, or God.

When Sybil met Andrew and Jack at the door, Andrew observed that the Ides of May had passed without any official acknowledgment from her, but she ignored him and did not even ask the name of his companion. She took their coats perfunctorily, and they went on into the crowded living room. They had arrived at the party late, and everybody had been drinking for a couple of hours. Already, people were standing and walking unsteadily, as if the floor were in motion; some were even leaning against walls or the piano or another person. And all but a few who sat staring dumbly at the drinks in their hands were talking and laughing so loudly that Andrew could barely hear John Lennon, in the background, singing "Lucy in the Sky with Diamonds." But Elizabeth Gilliam, the young sociologist, seemed to hear only the song: she danced slowly, all by herself, spilling from her wineglass as she swayed, barefooted, through the crowd. Then one of the history professors—Andrew thought his name was Charley Canton—stepped up to Elizabeth, tapped her invisible partner on the shoulder, and said, "May I cut in?" Elizabeth laughed dreamily and put her arms, wineglass and all, around his neck, and they half danced, half held each other up, around the room. Somebody started to applaud, and soon everybody was clapping, though only a few knew why.

"Where is she?" Jack finally asked.

"I don't see her anywhere," Andrew answered. He was almost hoping she wouldn't be there, so he wouldn't have to go through with this. "Let's go get a drink and look around."

They worked their way through the living room to the bar, got bourbon on the rocks from the graduate student Ray had hired to serve drinks, and found a place to stand near the fireplace. Then Andrew saw her. She was sitting across the room, on a long white sofa, and she was wearing dark glasses. Andrew felt his heart constrict. For a moment, he thought he would pretend he hadn't seen her, tell Jack she wasn't there, and then they could leave. But he touched Jack's arm and said, "There she is."

"Where?"

Andrew nodded toward the sofa. But there were more people dancing now, and they blocked Jack's view for a moment.

Then he said, "I see her." The way he said it made Andrew wonder if he were nervous, too.

Just then, Sybil crossed over to Claudia and whispered something in her ear. Claudia nodded.

"She knows I'm here," Andrew said, "and she's wondering who you are."

"Let's go talk to her," Jack said. "I'm ready if you are."

Andrew was not ready yet, but he wasn't sure he'd ever be. He was thinking that everything was wrong, that he and Jack should talk about it some more. But he only said, "No. Let's wait another minute or two."

Jack nodded, and they stood quietly, sipping their drinks and watching the dancers. After a minute, Sybil and Ray danced by them.

"Come on, Andrew, join the fun," Ray said, as they passed. Andrew knew that he wanted him to dance with Claudia, and he felt so suddenly sorry for him, for Sybil, for Claudia, for everybody, that he almost started to weep.

If only I were drunk, he thought. It would be so much easier. He took a long drink of his bourbon and felt its pleasant burn in his throat and stomach.

But he knew he couldn't wait until he was drunk. If he didn't do it now, he never would.

"Let's go," he said to Jack.

"You sure?" Jack asked.

Andrew didn't answer. He just led the way through the shifting labyrinth of dancers toward the sofa. No one was sitting with Claudia then, so they sat down on opposite sides of her.

"Claudia," Andrew began, and felt his stomach lurch.

"Andrew?"

"Yes. Were you expecting someone else?" He was trying to sound harsh, but his voice trembled.

Claudia's face was tense, and she didn't turn toward him when she spoke.

"I haven't heard from you in a while," she said.

"I've been doing a lot of thinking," he answered. He'd imagined that sentence many times that day, but now that he said it, it sounded so foolish, so trite. He edited himself: "I've had to make some difficult decisions."

Then she turned to him.

"Are you still angry with me?" she asked. "I'm not the same. I won't offend you anymore, I really won't. Don't be angry, Andrew. I *need* you."

Andrew was silent. He wanted to be far away, asleep.

Claudia reached out and touched his arm.

"Say something, Andrew!"

Andrew looked at her hand.

"Yes, I know you need someone to take care of you," he said, as coolly as he could manage. "But we shouldn't talk like this when other people are around. You know someone's sitting beside you, don't you?"

Claudia nodded.

"I'd like to you to meet him. His name is Jack Bostrom. Jack: Claudia Miller."

Jack said hello, but Claudia did not respond or even turn toward him.

"What are you trying to do to me, Andrew?" she asked.

He could see his face in the dark lenses of her glasses and, underneath, the scarred eyelids, closed as with pain.

"I have to be going," he said, and stood up. He was not drunk, he had not even finished his first drink, but still he felt something like the vertigo liquor brings.

"Andrew!"

"I'll be back in a few minutes," he said. "Jack can take care of you for a little while, can't he?"

Claudia started to open her mouth, but Andrew turned and walked quickly away. He stopped at the outer edge of the dancers, near the hallway. His legs were trembling, so he leaned against the wall. On the other side of the room, Sybil stood watching him. He averted his eyes and watched the dancers drift and sway to "A Whiter Shade of Pale." When the song ended, they stopped, standing drunkenly, their arms around each other's waists, waiting for Ray to change the album. Someone called out a request for "Melancholy Baby" and someone else hooted and others laughed. Ray put on Buffalo Springfield.

Andrew finished his drink, then walked back toward the white sofa and sat in a chair near it. Jack looked at him and smiled.

"Andrew tells me you paint," he said. "That's quite an accomplishment for a blind person—or for anyone, for that matter."

"I've quit painting," Claudia said.

Andrew noticed that Jack's hand was on Claudia's, but she was ignoring it.

"Why did you quit?"

She turned her face toward Jack's.

"Because I'm *blind*."

Andrew stood up and started toward the bar—he suddenly needed another drink very badly—but before he had taken two steps, he heard Claudia's voice: "Andrew was listening, wasn't he? He was watching us, wasn't he?" She didn't wait for Jack's answer. Standing up, she said, in a wavering voice, "Would you like to see a painting I made? It's in Sybil and Ray's room; come on, I'll show you."

Andrew watched her face. Her jaw muscles were rigid, but her lips were quivering. She and Jack walked past him, around the dancers, and disappeared into the hallway.

Andrew went to the bar, got another bourbon, and drank it quickly. The student behind the bar looked at him and poured him another drink before he could even ask for it.

Fifteen minutes later, Claudia and Jack had still not returned from the bedroom, so Andrew got his coat and left without saying goodnight to Sybil and Ray, who stood watching him from the middle of the slowly rotating circle of dancers.

For a dazed hour, Andrew has felt only the slightest pain, and finally, as darkness comes, his pain lapses into numbness. His body is impossibly light now, and it drifts, as if held up by a dream. His mouth gapes; he does not hear the gurgling in his throat; he stares vaguely at the snow falling outside the darkened window. His eyes are as unfocused as an infant's, yet what he sees is clear: he sees himself, lying in his bed, his mouth gaping. But the face he sees is not his: it is a tender face, the face Claudia must have seen, in her dreams. He lies there, staring at his face, his eyes open wide in the dark.

❦

A Painting: Andrew, February 20, 1971

He is what is left before the dark window becomes an eyeless socket. What is left diminishes: the snow, brushed in by her unconscious hand, fills the hollows of his body and gathers in mounds over him. He begins to disappear. He is disappearing. The steady hand of the painter does not stop until nothing of him stands out against the snow that cannot be scraped from the landscape by a fingernail.

III

A BRIEF HISTORY
OF MY SCARS

1962

I was seven. What did I know about the law of gravity, or any other law for that matter? What did I know about matter either, a word derived from the Latin *mater*, which means *mother*? I crawled up the tree, I flew down. I went up it like a child and plummeted down it like an angel banished from heaven, wings folded like hands in the posture of prayer. On my way back towards the earth we call our mother, a branch must have reached out and cut me, a quick switchblade slice just below my left eye. The harder I cried, the more my blood seeped out of the wound, a new kind of tears.

It should not surprise you that the tree was an apple tree.

Whenever I tell this story, I'm tempted to put a snake in it. It's what the audience expects, even demands. But the truth is, there was no snake. There was only me.

1963

One summer morning I fell off my bike and when I stood up I was bleeding from my chin. I ran in the house crying. My mother washed the dirt out of the wound and put a Band-Aid on it. She smiled at me. "Now you'll have a dimple just like Kirk Douglas," she said. Kirk Douglas was her favorite actor. I'd heard her say he just about made her "swoon." I had to look that word up.

Later I went into the bathroom and lifted one edge of the Band-Aid to look at my chin. There was no dimple, just a cut, crusted with blood that had turned a rusty brown.

1963

This time, it was my mother who was crying. "I can't believe he's dead," she kept saying. She was talking to my father, who was stroking her back as it rose and fell with sobs. It was dinnertime but they were sitting on the edge of their bed. My father's workpants were covered with dirt but my mother didn't say anything about him ruining her white chenille bedspread. I just stood there, watching them from the doorway. Somehow I'd become invisible. Neither one of them saw me. My stomach hurt in a strange new way. I had heard about internal bleeding and wondered if that was what was happening to me.

Later I found out it was the president who had died. The president was like God. How could he possibly die? I thought about this for a long time and my stomach hurt even more. I was afraid the bleeding would never stop.

1965

Daniel Boone's Indian sidekick Mingo really knew how to throw his tomahawk. He could pin the sleeve of an enemy's buckskin shirt to a tree from a hundred feet away. I liked the way he never wounded anybody, just embarrassed them so much they wished he had, so I went out into the garage and sawed the handle off my father's ax, to make it look like Mingo's tomahawk. It was heavy and I could throw it only ten or twelve feet. Every time I threw it at the tree in our backyard it bounced off. Finally I stood right next to the tree and tried to sink the blade into it. All I could do was chip the bark, so I chopped at it harder. The ax blade glanced off the bark then and hit my thigh just below the hem of my shorts. It didn't stick into my skin either. In fact, at first I didn't think it had even cut me. I didn't feel any pain and there wasn't a mark on me. But then the blood began to bloom.

I thought I was going to die. I may have lain down on the grass, to calm myself, but it's possible I fainted. I don't know how much time passed but when I looked at the cut again, the bleeding had stopped.

My mother taped a gauze bandage over the cut and said it was just a scratch, really. "Your father's going to be very upset with you," she scolded.

I nodded. My throat was hurting from holding back tears.

"Axes aren't cheap, you know," she added.

I nodded again.

Later, after my father spanked me, I couldn't decide if I was angrier at him for punishing me or at her for telling him what I'd done.

Maybe you'd like this story more if I told you the tree I'd been trying to wound was the apple tree. But it was just an ordinary oak.

1968

My mother cried even harder when the president's brother died. My best friend was named Bobby and I imagined him lying on the floor with blood all around his head. Still, I wasn't able to make myself cry. Maybe I was a bad person, like the man who shot the president's brother, I thought. But that thought didn't make me cry either.

1970

I kissed her, but she didn't kiss me back. She just looked at me. Even her freckles looked angry. "What's wrong with you?" Kathleen said. "I don't like you like *that*."

1971

A few weeks after I got my driver's license, my father let me take the car to the library to study. Kathleen was there, sitting at one of the tables and looking at a world atlas. She was taller than I was now, and skinnier, but her freckles and red hair still made me tremble. One of her friends had told me she liked me "that way" now, so I worked up the nerve to go over and say hi. She said hi back, then showed me the map she was looking at. It was Vietnam. I asked if she had a test in Current Events or something but she said no. She was just feeling sad about her brother and that's why she was looking at it. She said she had an older brother there who was missing in action. She looked like she was about to cry. I felt so bad for her that I told her I was going to enlist as soon as I was eighteen and that I'd start looking for him the minute I got over there. Whenever she'd smiled at me before, her smiles were crimped, as if she were afraid to encourage my feelings for her. But this time she grinned at me. It may be hard to believe, but that was the happiest moment of my life. Nothing before or since comes close. When I drove home that night, the sky seemed full of stars.

But the next day at school, she and her friends passed me in the hall and started to giggle. "Hello, Sarge," she said, and saluted, then burst into laughter.

Later I found out her older brother was in college, not Vietnam.

1972

When my father left my mother and me, he took almost everything he considered his. But he left the ruined ax.

1973

When your mother dies, something happens to your mouth. Your lips don't work right. You can still say all the words you used to say but your lips don't feel the same saying them. It's like your mouth isn't yours anymore. And the words are someone else's, too.

A few weeks after her heart attack, I learned in English class that *matter* and *mother* are related words. Even now, almost forty years later, whenever I hear someone say "What's the matter?" I think of my mother.

And what do people say when you lose a job? They say, "He got the ax."

1974

In the newspaper one morning, an article about a boy, now six, who was born without a face. Where his eyes, nose and mouth should have been, there was only a hole opening onto soft mucous membrane. A *hole*. And he had eyelids on one side of his head. The article quoted a surgeon, who called his condition "bilateral cleft face." We actually have terms for such things. Language can handle anything, except the truth, which is that we are all born without a face. Some of us stay faceless; I'm one. You'll get no description of me.

1976

On the fourth of July, I proposed. It seemed the patriotic thing to do. Marie didn't seem to know what to do with her mouth. Her lips moved around a moment, then she said, "You know we're too young, right?" I said, "Of course." We kissed, then went back to eating our picnic lunch. I think I was relieved, at the time.

The next week, Marie started dating her previous boyfriend again. They got married six months later.

1978

Sharon was the next one. She wanted to marry me but I didn't want to marry her. Day after day scarred with words. One morning, driving to work down streets glittering like mica in the sunlight, I felt, for a moment, that she was the one. But it wasn't love: it was the morning, the sunlight glinting on the streets, nothing more. By dinnertime the sky was the color of dishwater and then the rains came, distorting everything through our apartment window, bloating the trees, the whole world a watercolor. And all that night, words and tears.

And after she left, more tears, these ones mine.

1979, 1981, 1985

Alicia. Caroline. Jenny.

The appendectomy scar on my abdomen. The crescent moon on my knee after arthroscopic surgery. The matching scars I imagined over and over on my wrists.

1985

When I came home from work, I found the note Jenny had stuck to the refrigerator. I already knew what it said but I read it anyway. I didn't cry and I wasn't angry either. I just read it and set it on the counter, then started to make my dinner. While the pasta roiled in the boiling water, I hummed the song my mother always used to sing when she was happy: *Oh, don't sit under the apple tree with anyone else but me.*

I never read that note again but I still have it. It's in a file with my copy of the divorce papers and the photos we took on our honeymoon the year before. In one of the pictures, she's sitting Indian-style on the hotel bed in the early morning sunlight, her blond hair all mussed up, and there's a pillow print running down her cheek like a scar. I remember kissing it.

1985

I thought I could win her back. I called her, wrote her letters, sent her flowers and other gifts. I followed her car home from work, honked as she pulled into her driveway. She threatened to file a restraining order but I said none was needed. I continued to follow her but kept out of sight. I didn't stop until she started wearing maternity dresses.

1985

When I lost my job, I told everyone I got the ax. It was my own private joke but even I didn't laugh.

I cannot tell a lie: when I got the ax, I chopped down that apple tree.

1987

Her little boy clung to her leg when I met them in the park. Jenny told me his name but my ears were ringing and I couldn't hear. The boy's father was carrying a cooler from his car to one of the picnic tables. I left before she could introduce me.

1988, 1990, 1993

Angie. Coreen. Suzanne. They kept leaving me, one after another. Or I kept making them leave. After a while, it doesn't seem to matter much who's at fault. The result's the same either way.

1995

On my fortieth birthday, I threw myself a party. I invited my mother, Jack Kennedy, Bobby Kennedy, and God. No one came.

1999

I rented the movie *Diamonds*, which starred Kirk Douglas. He'd had a stroke a few years before so his mouth didn't move right and his words were a little slurred. For the first time, I could see a resemblance.

2000

At midnight the world's odometer clicked over but my car's didn't move. For the past three hours I had been parked across the street from Jenny's house, something I hadn't done for at least a decade. After the light finally turned off in her and her husband's room, I stayed there for another hour. All over the world, survivalists were hoarding bottled water, canned food, and gasoline. I sat there, hoarding only the dark.

2001

At first I thought it was an accident—a pilot horribly off course. But as we all know, it wasn't an accident. Nothing is.

One after another they fell, arms out like wings.

2002

They say if you dream you're falling and hit the ground, you die. Some nights, just as I drifted off to sleep, I'd feel my body start to fall and I'd jerk awake, all my muscles tensed, my jaw clenched tight. Then I'd lie there for hours, listening to the liquid darkness around me, my heart jackhammering, my breath feathering, and think about everything I call my life.

Night terrors, we call them. And what makes them so terrifying is that we're our own terrorist.

2004

A friend was pulling nails out of old railroad ties he wanted to use to make a flowerbed and one flew up and pierced his eye. The odds of that happening.

He has a glass eye now. When he catches me looking at it, my own eyes feel like nails.

2005

I chopped the snake in half. It wasn't intentional; I was just hoeing up the soil, getting the garden ready. It was a harmless garter snake. I wondered about the word *garter* and thought of the blue garter Jenny had probably worn under her wedding dress. There was a boy I knew when I was in first grade who called it a *garden* snake. That made more sense to me than *garter*.

I watched both halves of the snake wiggle for a long time.

I decided not to look up the word *garter*.

2006

I thought it would be funny to bury my father's hatchet. So I did. But when I told my shrink what I'd done, he didn't laugh. He just said, "Burying the hatchet is one thing, but forgetting where you buried it is another."

2007

Some memories never scab over. I looked her up on the Internet. There was Kathleen's name, sixty-seven times, and one link led to a photo. Her hair a darker red now, the freckles hidden with makeup.

I moved the cursor down her face like a razor blade.

2009

I saw a woman with a tracheotomy scar smoking a cigarette. When she blew plumes of smoke out through her nostrils, I imagined the smoke swirling out of her throat instead, like words that can't be spoken.

2010

People talk about how long time is. But not how deep. When I was one, every second was only one year deep. Now, every second is fifty-five years deep. No wonder time seems to take forever, even though it's moving faster and faster toward the end.

2011

When we're wounded, our body overcompensates, creating more new tissue than we need. A razor-thin cut can heal thick and raised as a worm. *Proud flesh*, the doctors call that kind of scar.

The words we use. We should be ashamed.

2012

In my dream I'm a child again, climbing the apple tree, and when I reach the top I keep going, keep rising, but I'm not flying, I'm climbing the sky like it's a tree too, gripping invisible limbs and pulling myself up, inch by inch, my hands scraped and bleeding from the rough bark. I'm surprised; I never knew the air was as solid as the world below. Then I look down and there is no world below. Somehow I know, young as I am, that if I let go of the sky I will fall forever and never land, and therefore never die. I let go.

That's when I woke up. For a moment I didn't know who or where I was. And for that moment I was happy.

THE LATE MAN

It had been a bad day. Dana and I had a terrible fight that afternoon, our worst one ever, and I got so angry that I raised my fist as if to hit her. I didn't, but to her it was the same as if I had. She called me a wifebeater and told me to get out. I'd had more than enough by then, so I turned and stormed out of the house, slamming the door behind me. Then I saw Katie sitting on her Big Wheels in the carport, crying, and I realized she'd heard us fighting. "Don't cry, sweetheart," I said. "There's nothing to cry about." But she kept on, her little chin quivering, so I told her I was going to the store and would bring her back some cherry Popsicles, her favorite treat. Normally she would have smiled, maybe even clapped her hands, but that day she just kept on crying. "I'll be right back," I said then, and left.

But I didn't come back right away. I drove around for a while, not going anywhere particular, just driving and thinking things out. When I'd finally cooled off, I picked up a box of Popsicles and some other groceries at Safeway and started back home. But when I turned onto our block, I don't know, suddenly I felt as if I couldn't even look at our house. I just wanted to drive on by, as if I'd never lived there and didn't know anybody who did. I wanted to drive and drive until I was in another life. I saw myself somewhere far away, in Canada maybe, pulling into a motel late at night, the groceries still on the seat beside me. And

I *did* drive by. I passed Katie on her Big Wheels and didn't even wave, and I felt then the sudden pleasure of conclusion, of closing accounts, the clean pure thrill of zero. By the time that feeling faded and I turned back toward home again, the Popsicles were a red puddle on the car seat.

When I got home, Dana and I fought again, and by that night, when I had to go to work, my mind was a whirl of anger and confusion. As the *Courier*'s late man, I was responsible for proofing each page before sending it on to camera, but I was too upset to concentrate and I held up the production schedule so much that it was an hour after deadline before we turned the state edition. Even if a big story hadn't come in over the wire just before deadline—a plane had crashed in Detroit, killing everyone on board except a four-year-old girl—we would have turned late. Still, I hoped I could use that story to convince the managing editor to give me another chance. I knew he'd call me in his office the next day, and when he asked me what my excuse was this time, I'd tell him we'd had to redo page one to get the story on, and how that meant we had to move our lead story down below the fold, move another story inside, and revise the jump pages. I hoped that would convince him not to fire me, but I doubted it would.

We'd turned the state edition so late I had to run three red lights to get to the Burger Palace before they closed at ten. The Burger Palace was the only restaurant downtown that stayed open Sunday nights, mostly for those of us at the *Courier* and the *Herald*, the rival paper, and by the time I pulled into its lot, the sign had already been turned off. But two employees were still behind the counter and there was a customer sitting in one of the booths, so I knew I'd made it in time. I sat there in the car for a second, my heart still speeding, then got out and started toward the door.

I was in a bad enough mood, but as soon as I stepped into the restaurant and heard steel guitars and a cowboy's nasal twang, I felt worse. The waitresses had the radio turned to KABX, the country station. I'd lost a dozen accounts to that station when I worked for KEZN, and I still couldn't listen to it without anger. The way I saw it, KEZN was responsible for the problems Dana and I were having. After they fired me, she had to go on overtime at the beauty shop, and we didn't see much of each other anymore. And when we did, we were in such miserable moods— me, because I wasn't working; her, because she was working so much—that we fought more than usual. And now things had gotten so bad that I'd almost left her and Katie.

I stepped up to the cash register, trying to ignore the music, and one of the waitresses came over to help me. She was around my age, but she looked younger, partly because she was tiny and partly because she wore her blond hair pulled back into a ponytail. The nametag pinned to her red, white, and blue striped shirt said *Monica*. She smiled when she said hello, and I decided she was pretty.

"You just made it," she said. "Carol Sue's locking up now."

I glanced over my shoulder and saw that the other waitress, a sullen-looking teenager with greasy brown hair and acne, had come around the counter and was turning the key in the lock.

"Guess this is my lucky night," I said. Then I ordered King Burgers with fries for myself and the copy editors. They were back in the newsroom, scrolling the wire and subbing out state stories for the city edition, and when I brought them their food, they'd have to keep working at the terminals while they ate. I knew they blamed me for making them work through their dinner break, and I was sure they were complaining about me that very minute.

As Monica rang up the order, I heard a curse from behind me and turned to look. The customer I'd seen earlier had spilled some French fries on her lap. She slid out of her booth, mumbling, a cigarette in one hand, and brushed the fries and salt from her loose Hawaiian print dress with her free hand. She was a short, heavy-breasted black woman, maybe thirty-five or forty years old, and she was so drunk she could hardly stand. Her eyes were half-closed, and she tilted her head back as if to help her see through the slits. She looked toward me. "What you looking at?" she said. I'd heard drunks say that before, but she said it differently, as if she wasn't so much angry as curious.

Before I could say anything, she waved her hand, as if to erase her question, and said, "Just a minute." Then she leaned over her table, bracing herself with one hand so she wouldn't fall, and picked up a large green vinyl purse. Turning, she staggered toward the counter. I smelled the liquor on her breath before she reached me.

"Hi," she slurred, almost giving the word a second syllable. Then she stumbled and fell against me, her shoulder against my arm, her hip against my thigh. "Esscuse me," she said, but she didn't move away. She just closed her eyes and rested her head on my shoulder. For a moment I wondered whether she was a prostitute. But she was so ugly she would have had a hard time making a living on her back. Her leathery skin, broad, flat nose, and large mouth all made me think of some kind of lizard or salamander. I cleared my throat. It was a kind of speech, and evidently she understood because she shifted away from me and leaned against the counter for balance. I glanced at Monica. She rolled her eyes, then gave me my change and went back into the kitchen. The black woman took a drag on her cigarette and blew tusks of smoke out her nostrils. Then she closed her eyes for a long moment. When she finally opened them, she handed the cigarette to me.

"Here," she said woozily. "Hold this for me."

I didn't want to be bothered with her, but I didn't know what to do, so I took it.

She started to fumble with the worn gilt clasp on her purse. "Come on, purse," she mumbled. "Open up."

I was feeling foolish holding the cigarette, so I set it on the counter, letting the long ash hang over the edge. It wouldn't have taken much to hold her cigarette for a moment or two, but I didn't.

Then she got her purse open and stood there swaying and looking into it as if it were so deep she couldn't see to the bottom. "There it be," she finally said, and pulled out an almost empty pint of George Dickel. She held the bottle out toward me, closed her eyes, and said, "Want a drink?"

"No thank you," I said. Then I cleared my throat again and said I had to go. I wanted to sit down at one of the booths and relax, smoke a cigarette or two. But as soon as I started toward the booths, she took hold of my arm and said, slowly, as if each word were a heavy weight, "Ain't you my friend?"

I didn't know what to say, so I just stood there. She let go of my arm and put the bottle to her lips. When she finished, there was only a swallow left. "What's your name?" she said.

"Paul," I said. I don't know why I didn't tell her my real name. It wouldn't have cost me anything.

She moved her face toward me then, as if to see me better, and I saw her red, swollen eyes. That's when it struck me that maybe she wasn't just a drunk. Her eyes looked like Dana's had that afternoon, when I came home after our argument. "My name's Lucy," she said, her eyes closing. She seemed to have to force them open again. Then she said, "My boy is dead."

I wasn't sure I'd heard her right. "Pardon me?"

"My boy . . ." Then she saw the cigarette on the counter and carefully, as if her fingers were somehow separate from her, picked it up and put it in her mouth, though she didn't take a puff. "He died today. My boy. My Freddie."

I heard a voice from the kitchen then. "Here she goes again," it said.

I looked toward the booths. "I'm sorry," I said. But I'm not sure it was true. Mostly, I felt uncomfortable. I wanted to get my burgers and go.

"That's nice," she said, and leaned against me again. "You're nice." Then she straightened up and smiled at me. When she did, her cigarette dropped to the floor. She stared at it a moment, then looked back at me. "What did you say?" she asked.

"Nothing," I said.

"I thought you said something," she said. Then she tilted her head back and swallowed the last of her bourbon. She held the bottle to her thick lips for a long time, tapping the bottom with her finger. When she finally set the bottle on the counter, she looked at me and said, "Empty."

I nodded and glanced over at the booths. Then she grabbed my arm again. "Please," she said urgently. "Don't leave me alone. I been alone all day and I can't take it no more."

Her fingers were pressing into my skin, but I didn't pull my arm away.

"I'm sorry," I said again.

She shook her head slowly. "He was only thirteen. His voice was still changing." Her lips started to tremble. "One minute it was high, then the next . . ." She stopped and tears began running out of the slits of her eyes.

I looked around for the waitresses, but they were still in the kitchen. I heard the sizzle of the grill through the nasal whine of a country singer complaining about his woman running around. I wished they would hurry up.

"Have you talked to someone?" I asked. I meant a minister or a doctor, but I don't think she understood.

"He won't talk to me," she said. "He blame me for it all. He say I the one made Freddie do it, I the one after him all the time to do his schoolwork, clean his room." She squeezed her eyes shut.

I could have asked "Do what?" but I already knew. Now I wanted more than ever to get away from her and her grief.

"Excuse me," I said, and pulled my arm out of her grip. "I need to go sit down."

She followed me toward the booth, talking to my back. "I beg him not to do it," she said. "I beg him and beg him, but he say 'Go away and leave me be or I do it now.' And when I reach out for him, he do it. My boy, he *do* it." Then a sob shuddered through her.

It may sound strange, but I was embarrassed by her grief. I felt sorry for her, I truly did, but I was embarrassed too. Maybe it was because she was a stranger and I couldn't possibly share her grief. Or maybe it was because her grief had taken her so far beyond embarrassment that I felt some odd obligation to be embarrassed for her. I don't know. All I know for sure is that I wanted to get away from her more than I wanted to comfort her.

I started toward the men's room. "Where you going?" she asked.

"I can't help you," I answered, more bluntly than I intended, then went in the men's room and locked the door behind me.

"What's wrong?" she said. She knocked on the door. "What'd I do?"

"Nothing," I said. But the way I said it I might as well have said, "Go away." Then, her voice wavering, she started talking about her son again.

I looked around the room and tried not to listen. The walls were covered with graffiti—phone numbers, drawings of naked women and penises, a dirty limerick or two—and on the gray metal toilet stall someone had scratched the words WHITE POWER and LYNCH NIGGERS. I thought about all the blacks who came into that room and read those words, and I looked back at the door. The woman was saying something about a bridge then, and that's when I remembered the story. A teenaged boy, a student at Emerson Junior High, had climbed out onto the ledge of an old railway bridge and dove to the rocks below. But it hadn't happened that day, as she'd said; it had happened at least two weeks ago. I remembered proofing the story. It'd been too long to fit the hole in our Police Beat section, so I had to cut the last paragraph, which mentioned that the boy's parents witnessed the suicide.

"Cars be going by," she was half-saying, half-sobbing, "but nobody is stopping, everybody is just looking out at us. One of them even points at us like we are something *interesting*. And I say, I say, 'Freddie, come back, everything be all right,' and he say, 'No, Mama,' and I reach out for him but he just lean forward. He just lean forward and I feel him going like it is me going and oh, his sweet head, his sweet, sweet head!"

I opened the door. She was standing there, swaying back and forth and holding her head as if it were about to shatter.

"I'm sorry," I said. But she didn't seem to hear me.

"Ohhh," she moaned, then slumped into one of the booths. She put her face down on the tabletop and covered her head with her hands, like a soldier under fire.

The younger waitress—Carol Sue—appeared at the counter
then with a white paper bag. "Sir, your order's ready," she said.

As sorry as I felt for the woman, I was glad to have an excuse
to leave. I stepped up to the counter and took the bag. Looking
over my shoulder, Carol Sue said, "Excuse me, ma'am, but we
have to close up now." Then she came out from behind the
counter with a ring full of keys in her hand.

The woman gradually stood up. She wasn't crying anymore.
"I ain't got nowhere to go," she said.

"You can go home, can't you?" Carol Sue said. "You do have
a home, don't you?"

The woman shook her head. "No. Not no more."

Monica came out of the kitchen then, wiping her hands on a
towel. She smiled in a stiff, controlled way that didn't reach her
eyes. "Is there someone we can call for you?" she asked the
woman. "Or a taxi?"

"Ain't no one," the woman said.

By this time I was at the door, waiting for Carol Sue to unlock
it. I turned my back to Monica and the woman and tried to listen
to the radio. But still I heard Monica say *I'm sorry but* and *police*.
Then Carol Sue turned the key in the lock, and I hurried out to
my car, opened the door, and jumped in. As I put the key in the
ignition, the woman stumbled out of the Burger Palace and ran
toward me. "Wait," she said. "Stop."

But I didn't wait. I started the car and began to back up. She
ran up alongside the car and knocked on the passenger window.
"Help me," she said. As I stopped to shift into drive, she put her
face up to the window, her wet cheeks glistening in the light cast
by the streetlight. "*Please*," she said. And she leaned against the
car as if it were all that was holding her up.

I could have shifted into park. I could have rolled down the
window and asked what she wanted. I could have talked with
her for a few minutes or even offered to give her a ride. I could
have put my arms around her and consoled her the best I was
able. But what I did was reach over and lock the door.

She stood up then and watched me as I turned around and headed out of the lot. I looked in the rearview mirror and saw her standing there in the middle of the black asphalt. Then I turned onto Scott and pressed on the accelerator.

As I drove down the street, I once again imagined driving away from everything. I saw myself on the freeway, driving in my dark car through the anonymous night, on my way to a new life, a new self. But this time that thought didn't give me any pleasure. This time it scared me.

When I turned down Buchanan and saw the *Courier* building looming in the dark, I accelerated and sped past the turnoff to the parking lot. I wasn't sure where I was going. For a moment, I thought about going back to the Burger Palace and comforting the woman—*Lucy*, I told myself, *her name is Lucy*—but I didn't. Why didn't I go back? Part of it, I'm ashamed to say, was that she was black. I asked myself, would I have comforted her if she were someone else? What if she were white, and pretty? What if she were Monica? Or what if she were *Dana*? And then I saw Dana in the Burger Palace, drunk and staggering up to a stranger to tell him her life was ruined, and I felt something narrow inside me open wide, like a wound.

But still I did not go back to the restaurant that night. I went there the next three nights and then occasionally after that, but I never saw Lucy again. I asked Monica and Carol Sue about her, but they didn't know any more than I did. I thought of checking the police report for her address, but I didn't. I still think about doing it, sometimes, though I know I never will. It wouldn't make much difference now. Whatever I said or did would be too late to help.

I didn't go back to the *Courier* that night either. Instead, I went home. At first I didn't realize that was what I was doing, and when I found myself turning onto our street, I thought I must have done it through force of habit. But it wasn't habit. It was something like habit, only deeper and more powerful. Whatever it was, it's what I most miss, now that Dana and I are divorced.

When I went inside, Dana was in the kitchen, washing dishes. She turned when she heard me, and I saw that she'd been crying again. Her eyes were red, and there were some Kleenexes crumpled on the counter beside her.

I stopped next to the refrigerator. On it, held up by magnets, was a picture Katie had drawn of a purple flower with a smiling face.

Dana pushed a strand of her black hair behind her ear with the back of a wet hand. "You're awfully early," she said.

"I'm not fired, if that's what you're thinking. I just came home for a minute. I'm going right back." I still didn't know why I'd come home; I only knew that I'd had to.

"Good," she said, wiping a plate with the washcloth.

"Let's not fight," I said.

"Who's fighting? If I state a simple fact, does it mean I'm fighting?"

"No."

"Okay. Then leave me alone."

She kept on washing dishes and stacking them in the rack. I watched for a moment, then cleared my throat. "You've been crying," I said.

"Very observant of you."

"Please," I said. "Don't."

She whirled toward me then, her face red and pinched and her lips quivering. "Don't what?" she said, her voice rising. "Don't hit you? Don't yell at you? Don't make our daughter cry?"

I didn't say anything. She turned back to the sink and began violently scrubbing a pot. "Just leave me alone, will you," she said. "Just go away and leave me in peace. Leave us both in peace."

"Is that what you want?" I said.

"That's what I want."

I felt groggy, as if I were just waking up. "You mean, you want a divorce?"

"Yes," she said. "I do."

I didn't know what to say. I just stood there, watching her back. Then I heard Katie's footsteps in the hall.

"Mama," she called.

I looked at the doorway and there she was, standing in her pink pajamas, rubbing her eyes.

"Hello, honey," I said, and went over and squatted down beside her. I kissed her cheek and, as I did, I heard Lucy saying "his sweet, sweet head."

I made myself smile. "What are you doing up so late, little lady?"

"A dog was chasing me," she said. She spread her arms wide. "A *big* dog. And he was *barking* at me."

"It's just a dream," Dana said, wiping her hands on a dishtowel. "I'll take you back to bed, sweetheart."

"That's okay," I said. "I'll do it." And I hoisted her up and carried her back into her dark bedroom and tucked her in. Then I brushed her hair away from her eyes and kissed her forehead. Fear was feathering in my chest, making it hard for me to breathe. I knew this might be the last time I'd tuck my daughter into bed in this house. "Good night, honeybunch," I said.

"What if he comes back?" Katie said then.

"If he comes back," I said, "I'll chase him away."

"Don't hit him, though," she said. "I don't think he means to be mean."

"Okay," I said, and kissed her on the nose. Then I went back into the kitchen.

"Don't you think you'd better get back to work?" Dana said. She was still doing dishes, her arms sunk almost to her elbows in the sudsy water.

I thought about the bag of food in the car and imagined the copy editors checking their watches and cursing me for taking so long. "Yes," I said. But I didn't move.

Dana kept on doing the dishes as if I weren't there. I watched her for a long moment, and I thought about Lucy and wondered where she was. Then I said, "I'm sorry."

She didn't say anything; she just shook her head. I wanted to walk up behind her then and take her into my arms. I wanted to tell her I loved her. I wasn't sure it was true, at least not anymore, but it had been once and maybe it would be again. There were so many things I wanted to say, but my thoughts withered to one word. "Dana," I said.

"I don't want to talk about it now," she said. "Just go, and we'll talk about it later."

Something funny happened then. I don't know why—maybe it was because I was thinking about going back to the *Courier*— but I suddenly saw that plane going down in Detroit—not just the words of the story, the black ink, the typos and style errors, but the plane itself. I saw it rock back and forth, then begin to plunge, saw the left wing strike the Avis building, shearing stone into sparks, and the plane skid, streaming fire, beneath the railroad trestle and the interstate overpass. And through it all I saw the terrified faces in the fiery windows.

I felt lightheaded, dizzy, as if I'd drunk the bourbon Lucy had offered me. I had to do something or I'd start to shake, so I stepped up to the sink and took Dana's arm. She turned and looked at me, her lips set in a hard thin line. I knew then that it was too late to change her mind, but there was something I had to say, something I had to make her understand, though I didn't know what it was myself until I'd already said it.

"There's been a terrible accident," I said. And my voice shook as if I were breaking the news about a death in the family.

TOURISTS

LAS VEGAS

Five months after our baby died, our grief counselor suggested we go on a vacation. A change of scenery would do us good, she said. Take our minds off things a little.

"Where should we go?" Amy asked her. She was still finding it impossible to make decisions, even simple ones. Sometimes she would sit in front of the TV for half an hour, the remote in her hand, before finally clicking it on. I still felt awful too, though I have to admit that I wasn't as sad as she was anymore. A couple of weeks before, I'd caught myself whistling while I changed the oil in my pickup. I stopped immediately and hoped Amy hadn't heard me. If she had, I doubt she'd have ever forgiven me. That's how unhappy she was. It was like postpartum depression, the counselor told me, but ten times worse because the baby didn't live. "Your son may have been stillborn," she said, "but he was still born." And then she gave me a look and said, "Everybody heals at different paces, Dan. Try not to forget that."

The counselor suggested we go to Las Vegas. Why, I'm not sure. Probably because it's where adults go without their kids, so we wouldn't run into too many children to remind us of our loss. Or maybe she just figured our lives were so dark that we needed some glitter to balance things out, make the world seem almost normal again. I don't know. At any rate, she told us there were lots of group tours available, so we wouldn't have to worry about selecting a hotel, planning an itinerary, etc. We wouldn't have to worry about a thing. It'd all be taken care of for us.

That sounded good to Amy. So we said yes.

PROLAPSED

I'd never heard the word before Cynthia called to tell me what happened, so I wasn't sure what it meant. I'm a salesman for Big South Carpets and twice a month I hump carpet samples to stores in Texas, Louisiana, and Arkansas. I was in a motel outside San Antonio, fast asleep, when she called me.

Cynthia is Amy's best friend and the wife of my best friend Ken. Ken and I are more like brothers than friends; we grew up on the same street and went to the same schools from first grade on. I knew Cynthia long before I knew Amy, who didn't move to Little Rock until the ninth grade. But Cynthia had never called me before, much less at 2:30 in the morning, so I knew right away something bad had happened.

"What's wrong?" I asked.

"Oh, Dan," she said, then began to cry.

"Tell me," I said.

"The umbilical cord," she said, then her words turned to sobs.

I think I knew then but still I asked, "What do you mean?"

While she struggled to answer, I looked out the window at the parking lot, the cracks in the asphalt wild with weeds under the security lights. Some of them were as tall as a toddler.

"It was prolapsed," Cynthia finally managed to say. "They started to prep her for a C-section but it was too late. He'd gone too long without blood and oxygen. Even if they'd been able to bring him back, he would have had—would have been—" Then she was sobbing again.

"I'll be home as fast as I can," I said, then hung up. I stood there a minute, my mind blank, then started to repack my suitcase. I felt like I was doing everything in slow motion, and I didn't recognize my clothes. They seemed to belong to someone else. Or I seemed to be someone else.

I don't remember checking out of the motel. I don't remember if I texted my customers to tell them I'd have to reschedule my visits. I don't even remember the ten-hour drive back to Little Rock. All I remember is wondering, over and over, what *prolapsed* meant. I could have Googled it on my cell phone, but for some reason I didn't dare. Still, I hoped everything would be all right once I understood that word. But it wasn't, of course.

Even today, more than a year after it happened, I find myself thinking that word over and over. I'll be giving some sales pitch about our latest line of Berber carpet, but what I'm thinking is *prolapsed, prolapsed, prolapsed*, the word that changed everything.

CHECKING IN

After we landed in Las Vegas, the tour bus took us to the pyramid-shaped Luxor Hotel along with the rest of the tour group, which was made up mostly of retirees, people old enough to be our parents or grandparents. Our tour guide was a matronly former realtor with silver hair the wind couldn't budge. She never walked anywhere; she bustled. She led us into the hotel lobby, then repeated the night's itinerary for us: we had exactly two hours to get settled in our rooms and gamble a bit, if we wanted, then we were to meet downstairs at the Luxor's buffet. After dinner, we'd take in the Fremont Street Experience and the spectacular outdoor shows at the Bellagio and Treasure Island before returning to the hotel for more gambling and a complimentary nightcap in Aurora, one of the Luxor bars. On the agenda for tomorrow, she added, was a day trip to Hoover Dam, Lake Mead, and the Lost City, the remains of an ancient Anasazi village. I only half-listened to her say all this; I was focusing on the sounds coming from the casino, the bells and buzzers and coins clanging into metal trays. There was something comforting about those sounds, something consoling about being in a place where loss is certain and expected, even embraced. There's really no gambling in Vegas: everybody knows what's going to happen to their money. As the joke goes, that's why they call the place *Loss* Vegas. And that's why tourists go there, I think: to take a safe stroll through loss before returning home, where a single word can ruin their lives forever.

But I knew Amy wouldn't gamble. She'd only watch.

THE BED

Once we were in our hotel room, Amy and I unpacked without a word. We both tried not to look at the bed. We hadn't made love since our son died, or for the last three weeks of her pregnancy before that. She'd had two first-trimester miscarriages in the past three years, and both times we made love a few weeks later, anxious to try again for the child we both wanted. But after we lost our son, she stiffened every time I tried to touch her, so I'd stopped trying. I hoped she'd be willing to make love again now that we were away from home and everything that reminded us of our unhappiness. In the past, whenever we went on a vacation, we'd have sex every night and sometimes in the mornings, too. There was something about being in a strange city and a strange room that made us feel strange, too, like we were different people than we'd always thought. And the fact that we knew we'd be leaving that place soon made our lovemaking so intense that each time felt like it was somehow both the first and last time. I hoped that this vacation would turn out like those others, that we could become those people again and, this time, keep on being them when we went home. But even as I hoped this, I knew it wasn't going to happen.

I put the last of my shirts in the drawer. "I love you," I said to Amy. "I love you, too," she said back.

That's what we always said when the silence got too large. But those words couldn't shrink it anymore, and we knew it.

KEN

Two nights before our son was stillborn, Amy and I were having dinner with Ken and Cynthia at their home. We always had a great time together, laughing and telling tales on each other, and that night was no different—until all of a sudden Amy said she thought she was having a contraction. "Are you sure?" I asked. She wasn't due for another two and a half weeks, so it didn't seem possible she'd be having contractions already. She shook her head. "I don't know," she said, and we went back to eating and talking. And then a few minutes later, Amy had another contraction, and this time she was sure that's what it was. The first thing we all thought was that it was false labor. Cynthia had false labor herself with her first pregnancy, she said, and it was perfectly normal. But we weren't going to risk anything, so we said our goodbyes and hurried to the hospital. Amy had another contraction on the way there, and another one soon after we arrived at the ER. She had a couple more while we waited in one of the rooms for a doctor, but then they stopped. When the doctor examined her, he said it was a false alarm and it'd be another two or three weeks before the real contractions would begin. In any case, he said, there was nothing to worry about; both baby and mama were doing just fine. She didn't have any bleeding or anything, like she did before the miscarriages, and the baby's heartbeat was strong.

If I had known Amy would go into labor two days later, I would have stayed home. I'm usually on the road just four or five days at a time, so I thought I'd be back long before the baby came. But I wasn't, and I think there was a part of Amy that blamed me for his death, just because I wasn't there. That's not rational, of course, but grief isn't rational. Sometimes I felt like she was exaggerating her sadness in order to punish me. And she wasn't punishing just me; she was punishing Ken and Cynthia too. After the baby died, she refused to spend time with them anymore. Her excuse was that it hurt too much to see them because they reminded her of what our life used to be like and how different it was now. But I think she blamed them for the false labor and everything that went wrong after that, and for having three kids when we had none.

I used to play golf with Ken every weekend and we were on our church softball team too. But after we lost our son, Amy couldn't even bear to hear Ken's name. So I had to see him on the sly. But it felt like I was cheating on her, so I started making up excuses for not being with him. By the time we went to Vegas, I hadn't seen him for a month.

I won't lie. I missed him. It was like I'd lost both my son and my best friend. And my wife. And I wasn't just sad, I was angry.

PINEAPPLE

After her first miscarriage, Amy religiously avoided eating or drinking anything that could cause another. She had another one anyway but that didn't stop her from being hyper-careful about her diet. She had a long list of things to avoid posted on our refrigerator door. It included the things you'd expect—coffee, tea, alcohol—and a lot of things you wouldn't expect, like tomatoes, broccoli, squash, kale, Swiss chard, ginger, and sesame seeds. At the top of the list were what she called "The Five P's": pineapple, papaya, peaches, peppers, and parsley. Pineapple was the worst of them all, she said; it could actually cause contractions. She made copies of the list and gave them to all of our friends and relatives so they wouldn't accidentally serve her something she shouldn't eat. That list was on our refrigerator for three years. Then one day, about two months after we lost our son, I noticed it was gone. And later that day Amy came home from the grocery store with a fresh pineapple. She set it on a cutting board, but then her lips started to tremble and tears came into her eyes and she left the room. So I peeled and cut it into cubes for her, then put them in a bowl, covered it with Saran Wrap, and put it in the fridge. We had some that night after dinner. She took one bite and then left the room. I could hear her crying quietly in the nursery. But I didn't go to her right away. I kept eating. It had been so long since I'd tasted pineapple that I'd forgotten how sweet it was.

CONCRETE

At the buffet dinner Amy and I sat next to a retired farm couple from Kansas. They had six boys, all grown now, and they showed us pictures. One of them had taken over the farm. He was a fine boy. They were very proud of him. They were proud of all their boys.

Amy was all right during the dinner, but afterward, she went into the women's room for a long time. The tour group was lined up in the lobby, ready to leave. I knocked on the restroom door and called her name, but she didn't answer. Whenever a woman came out, I could hear Amy inside crying. Finally, the tour guide came over and wanted to know what was holding us up. I told her Amy had eaten something that disagreed with her and that we'd skip the night's events. "She'll be fine in the morning," I said.

The tour group had been gone for ten minutes before Amy finally came out of the restroom, her eyes red and swollen. "I'm sorry," she said, and I wanted to say "There's nothing to be sorry for," but instead I just nodded.

Back in the hotel room, we watched CNN for a couple of hours. ISIS had attacked another Iraqi town, the Russians invaded the Ukraine, the Ebola death count in Africa topped fifteen hundred, and a nine-year-old girl accidentally killed her instructor at a shooting range with an Uzi. Amy watched it all blankly and said nothing. Finally, I said, "Other people have a lot worse to deal with than us."

"I can't help how I feel," she said. Then her chin started quivering.

I gritted my teeth. "You can at least try," I said.

"Don't you think I am?" she answered. "And don't you even care that we lost our son?"

"You know I care," I said. "Don't give me that shit."

Then she started to cry. I thought about hugging her and kissing her forehead, like I'd done hundreds of times in the past five months, but I didn't. I just watched her cry until she finally wiped her eyes with the heels of her palms. Then I said, "We'd better get some sleep. The bus leaves early."

She nodded. Then we undressed, put on our pajamas, and got into bed. We lay there in silence for a long time, and eventually she began to breathe with the rhythm of sleep. I lay there a long while after that, looking up into the darkness. I was wishing we were home and Amy was all right again and Ken and I could head out to the golf course in the morning. But in the morning, Amy and I would be on our way to Hoover Dam. From the photographs I'd seen, it looked like the world's biggest tombstone. Some people claimed that several of the hundred men who died building the dam were buried in the concrete, but the tour company's brochure said that wasn't true. What was true, it said, was that there was enough concrete in the dam to build a highway all the way from San Francisco to New York.

When I finally fell asleep, I dreamed Amy and I were on that highway, driving fast, behind us a sky-high wall of water.

THE LOST CITY

After we toured Hoover Dam and took an hour-long cruise on Lake Mead, the bus took us to Overton, the home of the Lost City Museum. There we saw the reconstructed ruins of an ancient Anasazi village. The museum guide, a perky teenage blonde who managed to smile even while talking, told us that the Anasazi lived there from 300 B.C. until about eight hundred years ago. They hunted with bows and arrows, she said, and they grew corn, beans, and squash, mined salt and turquoise, made pottery, jewelry, and baskets, and built pit-houses and pueblos. No one knows why they disappeared. All that remains of them are some knives, arrowheads, baskets, and shards of pottery. And hanging on one wall, a cradleboard woven of basket fibers, the cloth straps that held the baby in place dangling, untied.

The tour guide came up to us as we looked at it and raised her camera. "Smile, you two," she said, and I did.

THE NURSERY

During our three-day tour, we visited dozens of places in and around Las Vegas—several casinos, the Liberace and Bellagio museums, The World of Coca-Cola, The Little White Wedding Chapel, the Mormon Fort, the Ethel M Chocolate Factory, Glen Campbell's Area 51 Research Center. You name it, we saw it. Maybe because we'd visited so many different places, when we got home our house felt unfamiliar, almost like a museum, everything in it artifacts from a now-vanished civilization. We walked through the house, looking at everything like tourists. When we got to the nursery, we stopped. The Nursery. That's what we called the spare bedroom that we'd painted baby blue. We'd stenciled our son's name—*Joey*—in dark blue chevron letters over the crib and the changing table beside it. Amy's eyes teared up when she looked at the crib. She reached out and switched on the Winnie the Pooh mobile we'd attached to the crib, and Pooh and Tigger and Piglet and Eeyore came to life, rotating to the tune of Brahms's Lullaby. I can't explain why but hearing that music pissed me off. I left the room before the music stopped, but Amy stayed for a long time, playing that song over and over again.

We didn't say a word to each other until that night, at dinner, when she cleared her throat and said she thought we should turn the room back into a guest room. We could donate the baby furniture to Goodwill, she said, then repaint the room a pale green and buy a bookcase, a floor lamp, and an armchair to put where the crib and changing table were. "It'd be a nice place to sit and read," she said. I was so angry I wanted to scream, but I controlled myself and said, "Are you sure you don't want to try again?" She knew very well what I meant, but she pretended she didn't. "Try what?" she said, and I pushed away from the table and stormed out of the room.

ALL THE GOOD MEN

We continued to see the grief counselor once a week. She kept telling me to be patient with Amy but I was running out of patience. And I was lonely. So I started to see Ken on the sly again. And not just Ken, I admit: a woman, too. Her name is Edie, and she's a bookkeeper for Big South. She's very different from Amy. Amy's short and blond, a little heavy around the hips, but she moves with the grace of the gymnast she was back in high school. Edie's tall and lanky, even a bit gangly, and her hair is long and black and she always wears bright red lipstick, something Amy would never do. She got pregnant right after high school and was barely married long enough to divorce her husband. After her divorce, she lived with a series of guys but they all left her and her daughter Ashley high and dry. Then she moved back home with her parents and went to school at Pulaski Tech, where she earned an Associate degree in Accounting. She's been our bookkeeper for four years now. I've always liked her, and she's always liked me. A few times over the years she's smiled at me and said, "Why are all the good men taken?" She always said it like she was joking but I knew she wasn't. So one day, when I couldn't bear the thought of going home to another long night of silence, I asked Edie if she wanted to get a drink after work. She blinked hard, like she wasn't sure she'd heard me right. But then she said yes. And she said yes to everything else I asked her after that.

MEXICO

Our grief counselor was right: people do heal at different paces. About three months after our trip to Las Vegas, Amy started talking more and smiling from time to time, even laughing at something funny on TV. And one night, during dinner, out of nowhere she said, "I feel just awful about how I've treated Ken and Cynthia. We should have them over sometime soon." I told her I'd like that and she smiled. And a week later, we did have them over, and although everyone was awkward at first, by the time we all said goodnight, it was almost as if nothing had ever come between us. That night, Amy and I made love for the first time since we lost Joey. And after that, the list of foods to avoid was back on our refrigerator door and there was no more talk about turning the nursery into a guest room.

So I finally got what I wished for. I got my wife back, and my best friend. Ken and I go golfing every Saturday, if the weather's decent, and when our softball team plays, Amy and Cynthia sit in the stands and cheer us on. And Amy's pregnant again. She's well into her second trimester, and her gynecologist says the odds of losing another child are virtually nil. So everything's back the way it was. But at the same time, everything's different.

I know I should break up with Edie, and I've been planning to do it for a while, but I haven't been able to do it just yet. We still get together at least once or twice a week, usually at her apartment but sometimes, when she has a babysitter lined up for Ashley, at a motel outside the city. I've taken her with me on a couple of business trips, too, but she complains that there's not much to do while I'm working and that places like Shreveport and Waco aren't exactly tourist meccas. Lately she's been talking a lot about the two of us going to Puerto Vallarta. She has a friend who went there and loved it, and she says her mom would be happy to watch Ashley for a few days, just as she did when we went on my business trips. She's shown me photos of the place on the Internet, and it looks great. She gets all excited just talking about going there. And I get excited too, I confess. I imagine the two of us lying on the beach, snorkeling, going whale-watching, strolling along the El Malecón boardwalk, and drinking margaritas on our hotel balcony while the sun sets over the impossibly blue Bahía de Banderas. It all sounds so relaxing, so carefree and peaceful, that more and more I think I should take her there. I think I owe her that much at least. I could tell Amy I'm going on another business trip, and Edie and I could spend three or four days there, just the two of us, far away from everything that makes us unhappy. We could have a great time together, and then, a day or two after we got back, I could sit her down and tell her it's over. Yes, the more I think about it, the more I think a trip to Mexico would be the perfect way to end things, to make everything right again.

BLIZZARDS

It's been thirty-two years since my fiancée died in a car accident, and although I've thought about her less and less as the years have passed, she's been in my thoughts almost constantly the past few weeks, ever since my wife suggested that we drive through Sheffield on our way to visit her parents in Sioux Falls. Sheffield is the small Minnesota town where my fiancée and I grew up, and until today, I hadn't been back there since 1998, when my parents died, my mother in the spring and my father in the fall. For years now, Rachel has been encouraging me to go back home, to say goodbye to all my ghosts, including my own. I wasn't sure I was ready to do that, but I promised her and our daughters we'd stop there this morning on our way to South Dakota and put some flowers on my parents' graves, and I kept that promise. The sun has just set, and I can hear the girls downstairs in my in-laws' kitchen, laughing and talking with their mother and grandparents as they prepare dinner. I will join them as soon as I can calm down enough to stop trembling.

It's strange, but I miss the girls, even though we've been together all day and they're only one floor of a small house away from me. Lisa and Laura are twenty-one, twins, and they'll be graduating from college this time next year. This is probably the last trip we'll ever take as a family, a thought that saddens me, though it'd probably be a relief to them since they're anxious to be out in the world and on their own. For them, the present is already a part of the past they want lost to memory. The future is where they live.

When she died, my fiancée was only slightly older than my daughters are now. She had turned twenty-two earlier that spring, and we were planning to get married in June, after we graduated from the U of M. A light rain had been falling for much of that April day, but no one blamed the accident on the weather. Most likely Abby was simply preoccupied when she turned onto the highway and into the path of another car. I imagine her turning her head at the last instant and seeing its headlights and grille suddenly appear at her window. But that's where my imagination stops. Even now, all these years later, I cannot bear to imagine anything beyond that moment.

After Abby's funeral, I never wanted to go back home again. I stayed away all summer and fall. My parents begged me to come home for Thanksgiving, but the last thing I wanted to think about was giving thanks, so I stayed in Minneapolis, in the apartment Abby and I had lived in while we went to school. But I felt so guilty about disappointing my parents that I agreed to come home for Christmas. As it turned out, the worst blizzard I've ever experienced hit my hometown that Christmas Eve. I'll never forget that night; it's a night I've relived in memory hundreds of times, a night I think of whenever I think of Abby. I almost never think about the day of her death; it's that night, eight months later, that haunts me most.

When I drove down from Minneapolis Christmas Eve morning, a soft gauze-like snow was sifting down, dusting everything with a fine veneer of white. But as the day went on, it began to snow harder and harder, and by that night the wind was gusting up to fifty miles per hour. I remember standing at my bedroom window for a long time, watching the wind-blasted snowflakes detonate against the glass, then pressing my cheek against the windowpane and feeling the cold glass shudder in the wind. Somehow I found the violence of the storm more comforting than the consoling words I'd been hearing for months from my parents, friends, and relatives.

As I pressed my cheek against the pane, I remembered the first time I saw Abby naked, her dark hair just grazing her bare shoulders, her arms crossed over the breasts she thought were too small for me to love. And I remembered the trace of a Southern accent in her soft voice, inherited from her mother, who liked to say she'd married a Yankee to get revenge for Sherman's march through Georgia. The tiny mole in the hollow behind her earlobe. The way she chewed her lower lip when she was reading one of those historical romances she loved—"bodice-rippers," she called them, mocking her own taste. How the tips of her nostrils would turn white when she was angry. I remembered, too, our long talks about the future, about the kids we would have, the kind of house we wanted, and where we would live, and it seemed immensely foolish to have ever believed that such a life were possible.

I pressed my cheekbone against the window harder and watched the pane frost up from my breath. I thought about saying Abby's name, so I could watch its syllables cloud the glass. But I didn't say it, for fear I would start crying and never be able to stop.

A short while later, my mother tapped on the door. "Matt?" she said. "Can we come in?" Earlier that night, I'd left her and my father downstairs in the den, no longer able to endure their attempts at holiday cheer.

I didn't answer. I wanted them to think I was sleeping, so I wouldn't have to talk anymore. My mother knocked again, a little louder this time. "Matt?" she said. Still I said nothing. After a long moment, I heard my father clear his throat and say, "Come on, dear. Let's go to bed. He's not going to answer." He sounded so sad that I wanted to call out to them, open the door and hug them and cry with them. But I didn't. I just stood there, staring at the snow. It seemed odd that something so white could make the world seem darker. The snow obliterated everything. I couldn't even see the moon. I remembered, then, how my father told me when I was little that the moon was a hole in the sky and if I had a ladder tall enough I could climb up and crawl through it to heaven. When I asked him why we put dead people in the ground if heaven was the other way, he laughed and tousled my hair. "Silly boy," he said. But he never answered my question.

I decided to go out into the storm. I didn't know why, nor did I know where I would go; all I knew was that I needed to be outside, in the cold and snow, for as long as I could bear it. But I didn't want my parents to worry, so I made myself wait until they fell asleep. I listened to the distant murmur of their voices down the hall, their words dismantled now, sounds only, until finally the sounds, too, were dismantled, broken down into their essential silence. Then I crept down the stairs in the dark to the hall. The hallway smelled like blue spruce. In the darkened living room, I knew, the Christmas tree stood, ringed by presents, none of them bearing Abby's name. In the morning, we'd open them and pretend to be happy.

I walked past the living room to the entryway closet, put on the old khaki parka, felt-lined boots, and chamois mittens that my father always wore when he shoveled snow. Then I wrapped a woolen scarf around my neck and stepped out onto the porch, closing the door behind me gently, the way my parents always had after they tucked me into bed when I was a child.

As soon as I closed the door, the cold clamped down on me like a vise. I pulled up the parka's hood and wrapped the scarf more tightly around my neck, then went down the porch steps and out into the storm. The wind was so cold my eyes instantly watered, and the flecks of wind-flung snow stung my cheeks like slivers of glass.

I trudged through the knee-high drifts down the sidewalk and when I reached the street, I turned and looked back at the house through the scrim of snow. The drifts rose against it like frozen waves, covering all but the tips of the evergreen shrubs that lined the front of the house. The tips looked like miniature flocked

Christmas trees against the picture window, which was etched with frost. A row of icicles hung from the eaves. Somehow, the house didn't look real; it looked like something you'd see in a snow globe or on a Currier and Ives calendar, the kind of house in which everyone was happy and safe. I turned and headed into the wind, following my clouds of breath toward the streetlight on the corner, which seemed to be breathing its own bright cloud.

The snow was so thick that I couldn't see much farther than our next-door neighbor's house, which was lit by a string of red and blue and green Christmas lights framing the picture window and porch, lights the falling snow smeared together, like the colors in a child's finger painting. The Cooks had moved to our neighborhood from the other side of town several years before, when Abby and I were still in high school, and I'd heard my mother tell one of her friends that they'd moved because they couldn't bear to stay in their old house anymore: their two-year-old daughter had died there, after drinking some turpentine Mr. Cook had poured into a Mason jar to clean a paint brush. The girl's name was Kimberly, and although I'd never seen a picture of her, I'd always thought of her as a chubby little cherub with curly blond hair. Mr. Cook was a round-shouldered man who always walked slowly, with his head down, as if he were walking on ice. We rarely saw either him or his wife, except on Sundays, when he helped her down the front steps to the car, one hand on her back, the other holding hers, as if she were so old and frail that she might fall. But they were a young couple, in their early forties at most. Why, I wondered then, did they act so old? But now that I'm older than they were, I know that age has less to do with time than it does with grief.

As I walked past the Cooks' house, whorls of snow rose from drifts all around me and I thought of Sister Carmella telling us in religion class that if our souls were as white as snow when we died, they would rise to rejoin God because they were part of God. *The soul is the part of us that was made in His image,* she said, *so when we sin, it's just like throwing dirt on God's face. But if we keep our souls pure we'll be with God when we die and then we will understand all the mysteries of life and death because we will be one with God and know everything that He knows.* If the dead did know everything, I thought, what did they feel when they looked down on those they'd left behind? Did Kimberly ache when she saw her father help her mother down the steps? Or was her understanding so Godlike that she was beyond sadness now? And what did Abby think, watching me trudge through this storm? I tried to imagine the look she'd have on her face, but all I could see was the blue silk dress she was buried in, the same dress she wore the month before when we celebrated her birthday, the dress I lifted up over her head and raised arms that night and dropped on our apartment floor as if it were nothing but a dress.

Tears rose thick in my throat. The thought of her lying in the frozen earth, wearing only that thin blue dress, made the world seem colder. I felt the cold go through me like a spike, and I shivered, just as I'd shivered at the cemetery in the spring when the funeral procession passed the sexton's shed and I saw the backhoe parked behind it. Someone had tried to cover it with an olive-drab tarp, but its steel jaw was sticking out, its teeth still clotted with black dirt.

I hunched my shoulders to keep the cold from seeping down the back of my neck and continued walking through the onslaught of snow, my breath already turning to ice in my scarf. I wasn't going anywhere, I was just walking. I could have gone to a friend's house, or Abby's parents' house, but I didn't want to see anybody. I didn't want to be consoled: I wanted to give myself over to this sorrow, let it make me into someone else, someone who would one day look back on this night and not recognize the young man trudging through the deep snow, trying to discover if he could survive the blizzard of his grief.

Everywhere I looked, the landscape was alien, everything that made it familiar hidden beneath the pall of snow. There were no cars on the road, and no one else was out walking. I felt as if I were the only person in the entire world, the last person alive. And then I thought: no, maybe this is what it feels like to be dead.

By now each breath seared my nostrils and lungs, so I pulled my scarf up, covering my nose and mouth the way outlaws in westerns hide their faces with bandannas. But I was no outlaw, I'd done nothing wrong, I was not to blame for Abby's death. I wished I still believed in God, so I could blame Him, but I had lost my faith years before, something I didn't dare confess to my devoutly Catholic parents until many years later.

As I walked, breathing in my scarf's thick smell of wool, I felt the heat leaching out of my body, and my neck and back prickled. The drifts were so deep in places that I had to wade through them, and the snow worked its way down inside my boots. Before long, I knew, my socks would be crusted with ice. My hands, even inside the fur-lined mittens, were getting numb, so I pounded them together to warm them. The sound was like muffled applause, and it seemed to be coming from a long way away. The only other noise was the wind, a sound so continuous that after a while it became another kind of silence, more the shadow of a sound than a sound itself.

I was crying now, but my cheeks had been scoured numb by the wind and snow and I could barely feel the tears. I wiped them away with my mittens and for a moment thought about turning around and going back home. Then I realized I didn't know where I was, or how to get home. Although I had tried to stay in the middle of the street, I was now surrounded by trees. Their limbs creaked in the wind, and for a moment I was certain I had strayed into some woods I hadn't even known existed. But after a few panicked steps I knew where I was: I was on the playground of the elementary school I would have gone to with Abby if I hadn't been born Catholic. The school was dark, but the outside spotlights were on, and through the haze of their yellow glow I could see the dark outlines of the basketball court, tetherball poles, and monkey bars, and the steep mound of plowed snow that rose at the edge of the parking lot. When I was a boy, my friends and I would spend all day digging a tunnel into the middle of that mound, where we carved out a cave that somehow seemed as warm and cozy as a snowbound cabin with a blazing hearth. I remembered how it felt to be inside, burrowed beneath all that snow, a strange dove-gray light filtering through the tunnel's opening, and I hoped that was what Abby felt like now. I struggled through the waves of drifts until I reached the snow mound, hoping the children of the neighborhood had dug their own tunnel there, made a cave I could crawl into and escape the cold. But there was no way in.

I stood there a moment, listening to the far-off ocean sound of the wind through the bare trees that ringed the playground and, whenever the wind paused, as if to take a breath, the hollow clink of the tetherball chains against the poles. Then I lay back against the mound and looked up at the snowflakes swarming the sky. The flakes seemed to be flying frantically in every direction at once and I thought of how my physics professor described the moment after the big bang, how all the particles that eventually became the universe and everyone in it suddenly flew apart, filling the nothing that was with everything that would ever be. And I remembered Father DeGrote standing in front of our confirmation class, holding the Bible in his liver-spotted hands, intoning *In the beginning was the Word*, and I imagined the frozen flecks of white above me were the syllables of that first word, and what they said was nothing. The world was born of nothing, everything was nothing. From nothing it had come and to nothing it would return.

I lay there shivering, as much from my strange thoughts as from the cold that now seemed more in me than outside me, and I thought about staying there all night and letting the snow gradually cover me until there was no sign of me anywhere. But even as I imagined this, I knew I had no intention of dying. I only wanted to lie there long enough to feel the peace I'd heard came to those who froze to death, the peace that preceded their slow drifting off to sleep. I lay there a long time, trying to reach at least the edge of that peace, until my body was so numb I almost felt I didn't have one, that I'd become whatever was left after someone died—whether that be a soul, a mind, or just a memory, like the phantom pain amputees feel in their lost limbs. And there was no peace in that feeling. I stood up then and stamped my feet and clapped my hands until I felt the burning sting of blood returning to them, then started walking back home as fast as I could through the deep snow, to bring the rest of my body back to life.

I was remembering that terrible Christmas Eve this morning when I saw the exit sign for the highway to Sheffield—the same highway Abby died on. I felt my hands tighten on the steering wheel. I wanted to tell Rachel and the girls I just couldn't do it, that we'd maybe stop there on our way back from Sioux Falls, but I'd promised them—and, I have to admit, I'd promised myself too—so I took the exit and turned onto the highway. I was still so caught up in memories of that horrible night that I don't even remember driving the last forty miles to Sheffield. The next thing I knew we had passed the city limits sign and turned onto Black Oak Avenue, the street both Abby and I used to live on. It was a warm, sunny June morning, yet as I drove our minivan down the street I walked that night so many years ago, I halfway expected to see my young self trudging through thigh-high drifts of snow. I looked over at Rachel, sure she knew what I was thinking about, and the smile she gave me told me she did, and that she understood. She doesn't resent my grief—she says it has deepened me, made me the man she loves—but I know she feels there's a part of me that remains buried in the past, and she wants a husband who's whole. She's never said that, but I can hear it in the way she teases me from time to time, calling me Gloomy Gus or Mister Sad Eyes. Yesterday, when she found me in the den reading the journal I kept the year Abby died, she laughed and said, "Hey, good idea—maybe it'll turn out different this time!" I tried to laugh back, but couldn't.

As we drove down the street, Rachel reached over and patted my hand. "Things have really changed, haven't they?" she said, and at first I thought she was talking about my feelings for Abby, but when she looked out the window, I realized it was the town she was talking about, all the new houses, a new church and a Montessori school. But my feelings for Abby *have* changed, of course. Because she's remained twenty-two in my mind, she now seems more like a daughter to me than a lover and fiancée.

As we passed the house I still think of as Abby's, the house her parents eventually abandoned just as the Cooks had abandoned theirs, I slowed and looked up at the window of the room that was her bedroom, its shades drawn against the afternoon sun, and wondered who lives there now. For a moment I thought of pointing out the house and telling Rachel and the girls that that's where Abby used to live, but I didn't say anything. I've told Rachel about Abby, of course, even let her read my journal, but I've never mentioned her to Lisa and Laura, and although this morning would have been a good time to do it, I didn't. I did point out the elementary school when we passed it, though, and I told the girls about the huge mound of snow the plow would leave at the end of the parking lot and how my friends and I would dig a tunnel into its heart and make a cave there—a memory that of course meant nothing to them, or to Rachel. And why, I found myself wondering, does it mean so much to me? Why is it that some things from our childhood, even small, inconsequential things like the smell of burning leaves or the clacking of baseball cards clipped with clothespins to the spokes of a bike, not only remain in our memories but resonate there with the inexplicable power of a dream?

We drove slowly up the street, passing the Cooks' house, which I still cannot see or think of without recalling the smell of turpentine, and then stopped in front of my old house. I don't know who lives there now, but they must have small children: there was a red tricycle lying on its side in the grass, a soccer ball and some dolls nearby, and a jump rope lay curled on the sidewalk like a snake bathing in the sun. The house was white when I lived in it, but now it's a bluish gray, and the siding is vinyl, not wood. Sitting there, the engine idling, I wished that Rachel and the girls could see not only the house before us but also the one I see in my head, the one that exists in time but not in space. I felt a sudden lurch of sadness, a sensation of falling, as in an elevator that's descending too quickly. Still, I armed myself with a grin and told the girls, "And here's where your old dad grew up."

Laura said, "Fascinating, Dad," and Lisa added, "Are you sure this is the right place? I don't see any plaque saying this is a national monument or anything."

"Very funny," I said.

Rachel smiled at me, reached over and patted my shoulder. "You asked for it," she said.

I shifted the minivan into drive and headed toward the cemetery that was once at the edge of town but is now surrounded by neighborhoods with pretentious names like Grande Vue and Fairhaven Estates. The cemetery still has the same wrought-iron gate, though the sexton's shed is new. It looks like a miniature barn, only it's white instead of red. The road that horseshoes around the perimeter of the cemetery is asphalt now, so I heard the crunch of gravel beneath the tires only in my mind. I parked next to the path that winds up the grassy slope to my parents' graves, then we all got out and walked up there, each of the girls carrying one of the pots of yellow chrysanthemums we bought before we left Rochester this morning. When we got there, they set one on each side of their tombstone, then bowed their heads and folded their hands in prayer, as their mother has taught them to do. Rachel was praying too. But I just stood there looking at the stone, feeling guilty. We were there to remember my parents, but I had thought little of them all day.

When Rachel and the girls lifted their heads, I leaned over and picked one of the chrysanthemums, then turned to Rachel. "Do you mind?" I said.

She looked at me, a momentary flicker of uncertainty in her eyes, but then she understood and smiled. "Of course not," she said. "You go on. We'll wait here."

As I walked off down the path that winds between the rows of evergreens, I heard the girls ask their mother where I was going and then Rachel's answer: "He's going to lay a flower on the grave of an old friend." And I realized that she was right, that that's what Abby has become after all these years—an old friend. And if she had lived, perhaps I wouldn't feel much different than I do now—perhaps our feelings for each other would have changed, as so often happens with those who marry young, and we would have divorced and found new loves, started new lives. And maybe one day we would have met at a class reunion and kissed each other on the cheek in front of our new spouses, not even embarrassed by the difference between what we had been to each other and what we were now.

Once I was past the rows of evergreens, I felt a breeze lift the hair from my forehead. I walked down the slope through the monuments until I reached Abby's stone. It was smaller than I remembered, though it's nearly as large as the matching stone beside it, on which her parents' names and dates are chiseled in black granite. I bent over and laid the flower on the grass in front of her stone, and when I stood up, I felt dizzy for a second. But I didn't feel the sickening sadness I'd been expecting, and I wondered, with both fear and joy, if my grief was finally ending, if it would eventually become nothing more than a memento, a souvenir, of that time, something I'll keep tucked away in my mind the same way I keep some of the prized possessions of my youth in a box in our attic.

I stood there awhile, looking down the long rows of gravestones decorated with wreaths and potted flowers, past the rusting wrought-iron fence that surrounds the cemetery, toward the horizon beyond and the cloudless sky above it. From somewhere I heard the song of an invisible bird and, a moment later, another's answer. It was a beautiful day, and I stood there in the warm sun a long time, smelling the fresh-mown grass and feeling the breeze tousle my hair the way my father did when I was a child.

I know I am a lucky man. I was raised by parents who were devoted to me and loved me even when I left the church they believed in with all their heart. I have a wife and children who love me as deeply as I love them. I have not suffered the loss of a child, as Abby's parents and the Cooks did. I have many friends and no enemies. I have a beautiful life, and I know it. But still, when I looked at the sky this morning, a sky as blue as a robin's egg, I couldn't help but shiver at the thought that beyond it, hidden by the bright light of the sun, was the universe's vast blizzard of stars, through which we are all hurtling, still driven by God's first and last breath. And I shiver now, still not ready to go downstairs, where those I most love in this world are waiting for me to talk and smile and laugh with them as if nothing is wrong, as if none of us will ever die.

THE BRIDGE

If I had it to do over again, I'd still go to the funeral, but this time I wouldn't wear a disguise. And if I heard anyone say, "What's *she* doing here?" I'd just give them my Mona Lisa smile, then take a seat in a pew up front, right beside the grieving widow. Everyone would be staring at me, but I'd just sit there, ignoring them and looking only at the casket, trying to imagine what he looked like in there after the accident. And I wouldn't cry, not even once.

As it was, of course, I made a world-class fool of myself. And I don't even have the excuse of being drunk, since I've been on the wagon for nearly three years now—pretty much ever since he said he'd had enough of me. I don't know what made me decide to put on that stupid wig and sunglasses, but it wasn't a pitcher of margaritas. And it wasn't love. Don't you make the mistake of thinking that.

I read about his death in the Sunday paper. I was just turning the pages, and there his photo was, on the first page of the Arkansas section, right next to a shot of what looked like the Leaning Tower of Pisa but was actually a concrete bridge support stuck in a riverbank. I knew it was him even before I saw his name because of the missing eyebrow. I was with him the night he lost it on I-40. We shouldn't have taken the motorcycle out in the rain, but this was right after we were married and we were immortal in those days. I remember how the bike just suddenly disappeared out from under us, like we'd only been dreaming we were riding it, and we went skidding face-first across the wet asphalt. No helmets, of course. He's lucky he didn't die then. Me, too. I got a road rash you wouldn't believe, but at least I didn't lose an eyebrow. As he liked to say, you never realize how important it is to have eyebrows until you lose one. I think he grew the mustache so people would look at it, not his missing eyebrow. But it didn't work.

I wonder now if the undertaker drew in an eyebrow for him. He probably didn't, since the casket was closed, but I like to think he did. If I'd still been his wife, I would have made sure he did.

It's funny he died helping to build a bridge. He loved bridges, especially rickety old ones. One year he bought us a calendar of covered wooden bridges in Vermont or New Hampshire or someplace like that. And he once said that if he knew how to take photographs, he'd take a whole book full of shots of old bridges and make a fortune selling it. He said there was a real market for bridge nostalgia. And a few times he drove me up to Heber Springs on his bike just so we could stand on this old wooden plank bridge they call the Swinging Bridge and feel it sway a little in the breeze over the river. He loved that feeling, he said. He said he felt almost like he was about to float up into the air and fly away. Other people went to the Swinging Bridge to fish, but he went there just to stand. Frankly, I never thought the bridge was that big a deal. But I didn't say that to him, of course. I think he knew, though, because once when we were standing there, swaying in the wind, he started to sing, real slow and somber, that old song "Like a Bridge Over Troubled Water," and stupid me, I thought he was joking and started to laugh. He stopped singing right away then, and when I looked at him, I could tell he was hurt. I told him I wasn't laughing at him, that I was just thinking of a joke I'd heard at work, but I don't think he believed me. He was very smart, even if he did do some dumb things. Anyway, I've always felt bad about laughing at him that day. I should have known better. I should have remembered he had a deep, serious side.

According to the paper, what happened was, a cable on a crane snapped and dropped the bridge support on him. He'd been guiding the base of it into the hole they'd dug for it in the riverbank. The coroner said he probably died instantly, but it took his coworkers and paramedics seven hours to dig him out from under the concrete column. They had to jackhammer their way through it. Sometimes when I close my eyes I can hear what it must have sounded like. Like a machine gun, only louder. And I wonder if he heard it, if only for a second, and tried to figure out what that sound was.

It shocked me to hear that he'd been killed, but what shocked me more was that the paper said he'd remarried just a few months before. Why none of my friends told me, I don't know. I wouldn't have minded. I'd have been happy for him, and I would have gone to his wedding just the same as I went to his funeral. Only I wouldn't have worn a disguise to the wedding. I would have gone as myself. I would have waited in the reception line like everyone else to shake her hand and kiss him on the cheek. I would have said, "I hope you'll be happy this time."

I don't want you to get the wrong impression. I stopped loving him long before he stopped loving me. When he told me he'd had it, we were already history as far as I was concerned. But not loving someone doesn't mean you *hate* them. And I didn't hate him.

I didn't hate her either. In fact, the reason I started crying at the funeral was that I felt *sorry* for her. Even from where I was sitting, a dozen or so rows behind her to the right, I could see her lips and chin were quivering, and once when she reached up to adjust her black veil, her hand just fluttered. She was trying so hard not to cry that I felt I had to do it for her. And did I ever do it. I've always been a loud crier, but now I was crying so hard that I was gulping air, which made my sobs sound kind of like

seal barks. I can't help it. It's the way I cry. And isn't crying
normal at a funeral? The way everyone turned and looked at me,
you would have thought I was singing "Happy Birthday" or doing
a striptease or something. Even the minister stopped telling lies
about him to stare at me.

It was the same minister who'd married us, but it wasn't him
who recognized me, it was the wife. How she knew it was me
despite the curly blond wig and sunglasses, I don't know,
especially since we'd never met. Most likely she'd seen one of
the photos he took of me, maybe even that one where I was all
laid out on a blanket in a bikini like the main course at a picnic.
Or maybe he'd told her about the way I laugh, which is a lot like
the way I cry. He couldn't have told her how I cried. He never
heard me cry. Not once. Not even the day he took off his ring,
dropped it in my glass of José Cuervo, and walked out the door
without so much as a fare-thee-well. I just sat there, looking at
that ring. It looked so much like a dead, curled-up worm I almost
had to laugh. But I didn't. And I didn't cry either. There's no one
alive who could tell you otherwise.

Anyway, she said my name. She didn't shout it or anything. She
just looked at me and said it. Then someone said, "What's *she* doing
here?" and someone else said, "No respect for the dead." I also
heard the word *bitch*, and more than once. And the word *drunk*, too.
But like I said, I wasn't drunk. That's the thing about a reputation:
once you've got one, it's got you. To his friends and relatives, I'll
always be the drunk who cheated on him. He got to start his life
over with a new wife, but me, I don't get a second chance.

I could be bitter, but I'm not. And I suppose I could move
away from Little Rock, go someplace where no one knows me.
But I like it here, and I've got a good-paying job—lab tech at
Baptist Medical Center. I deserve my second chance here, just
like he did.

It didn't take me long to stop crying. One minute I was wailing
and the next I was stone silent. It was not a dignified silence, though.
I was trembling all over, and I could feel my face flush red-hot.

That's when his asshole brother came up to the pew where I was sitting and said, like he was trying to be polite, "Would you please leave?" I looked up at him, my mouth hanging open. Of all the people to ask *me* to leave!

"You've got some nerve," I said.

His face was so red it looked sunburned.

"Now's not the time," he said back, his voice shaking a little.

He got a second chance, too. My ex-husband forgave his little brother but not me. When he found out, I told him it takes two to tangle, but he still blamed it on me and me alone.

"I'm not going," I told his brother now.

The minister cleared his throat then and asked if he could resume the eulogy. The last I'd heard, he'd been saying something about the corpse having been a loving and devoted husband.

I stood up. "Go right ahead," I said. "Lie your ass off. The bastard left me."

Well, you can guess how people reacted to that. No one likes the truth. For a few seconds, there was nothing but arms and elbows and legs and shouting, and then I found myself outside, laying face-down on the sidewalk, my wig ripped off, my dress torn, and my head throbbing. There was a small crowd standing on the top step looking down at me, mostly men but also a couple of stocky women. One of the women was his brother's wife. She shook my wig at me and said, "You didn't even have the guts to face us. You're pathetic." I rose onto my skinned knees then and reached up to touch my eyebrows. They were still there. Then I started to laugh.

"Get out of here," a man's voice said. "*Now.*"

But I couldn't stop laughing. I stood up then, and my head went woozy, and for a moment I felt like I was back on the Swinging Bridge, my husband by my side, both of us swaying there in the breeze, so light somehow that the slightest puff of wind could lift us up off that bridge and into the blue, blue sky. And then I felt like I really *was* floating up into the sky, just like a balloon or a saint, and he was floating there beside me, holding my hand. I knew that any second I'd drift back down to earth, to the cracked concrete sidewalk, the scowls and jeers, to the realization that I'd been an utter fool and always would be, but I didn't care, at least not then. I was with him, and they weren't. I was with him, and he was holding my hand, and it felt so real, so real and so right.

FIRELIGHT

Jimmy hadn't planned to break the windows; he hadn't thought about it at all. He'd just been walking around the neighborhood, as he always did on the Saturdays his mother's boyfriend came to town. He'd left the apartment so quickly that he'd forgotten his mittens, and he walked with his hands balled in his jacket pockets. He thought about going back to get his mittens, but once when he'd gone home before he was supposed to, his mother and her boyfriend were in her bedroom with the door closed, making noises. He knew what those noises meant because one day at recess a third-grader named Evan was talking about what grown-ups do in bedrooms. "It's the same as dogs," he'd said. Jimmy couldn't imagine his mother doing such a thing with anybody, especially that vacuum salesman from St. Paul with his thick glasses and hairy ears. And maybe she didn't do it after all. Maybe they were in her bedroom because she was too tired to sit up in the living room and talk. She was always tired, even though she didn't work at the café anymore, and she spent most days in bed anyway. But what were the noises then?

He tried to think of something else. He thought about the Teenage Mutant Ninja Turtles and the frog his friend Greg brought to school in a jar once and let loose in the lunchroom. Michael Jackson kept a brain in a jar in his bedroom, and Greg said that proved he was crazy. But Jimmy thought he probably just wished he could put that person's brain in his head, and that didn't seem crazy to him. But maybe that was because *he* was crazy, too. If he had Greg's brain, he'd know if he was or not. He imagined lying in bed, with Greg's brain in his head and his own brain in a jar on the dresser, and wondered what he'd think. But he couldn't guess. If his brain was normal, shouldn't he be able to guess what someone else would think?

His mother's brain definitely wasn't normal. Ever since his father left them, she'd had to take pills for her mind. Jimmy used to blame the way she was on his father, but maybe she wasn't much different before he left. His father used to call her a crazy bitch, so maybe that was why he left, because she was crazy even then. Jimmy didn't know. He couldn't remember much about that time because he was so little. He barely even remembered his father. He just remembered that he was tall and had a mustache and smoked brown cigarettes. And he remembered how his big hands would hurt him when he picked him up under his arms, and how he liked him to pick him up anyway. Jimmy wondered where his father was now and what he was doing. His mother said he lived in Nebraska with his new family, and Jimmy wondered if Nebraska was a town or a state and how far away it was. And did his father ever pick up his new son the way he used to pick him up?

He was tired of walking around, so he decided to go over to the school playground. Kids were always there on weekends, playing on the swings and monkey bars or tossing a football back and forth. But when he got to the playground, no one was there. Even the houses across the street seemed deserted. Everywhere he looked, there was nothing. Not even a stray dog. And suddenly he felt all alone. A long shiver snaked up his spine, and he wanted to go home and sit on the edge of his mother's bed and talk to her. But it wasn't six o'clock yet. Her boyfriend would still be there.

He started walking slowly toward home anyway, kicking rocks as he crossed the gravel playground. But when he'd rounded the south wing of the school, he stopped. The sun was setting in the long row of windows, making them glow with a beautiful, cold fire. He'd seen those windows many times before, but only today did he realize how easy it would be to break one. All you had to do was pick up a rock and throw it. Anybody could do it, but nobody ever did. Maybe you had to be crazy to do it. He picked up a rock, to see if he would throw it. What would Greg think if he saw him now? Would he try to talk him out of it? And what about his mother and his father? What would they say? Jimmy imagined his father walking down the sidewalk and seeing him with the rock in his hand. "Hey, Jimmy," he'd say. "Is that you?"

Then one of the windows exploded, and Jimmy jumped back, startled, and looked at his empty hand. He couldn't remember throwing the rock, but he had. And now that he'd done it, he felt so good, so suddenly *happy*, that he kept on picking up rocks and throwing them, breaking window after window, until he heard a car coming down the street and had to run away.

By Monday morning, when Jimmy went back to school, the janitors had swept up the glass and taped cardboard over the eighteen broken windows. After the bell rang, all the kids in his class were still standing by the windows, talking excitedly about who could have done it, and they didn't take their seats until Mrs. Anthony threatened to keep them inside during recess. And even before the class could recite the Pledge of Allegiance, the principal's voice came over the loudspeaker and said the guilty party would eventually be caught so he might as well turn himself in now. *The guilty party*—that was Jimmy. He tried not to look guilty, but the more he tried, the more he felt everyone knew he had done it. Ever since he'd broken the windows, he'd felt like a stranger in his own life, someone just pretending to be who he was, and he was sure everyone would see the change in his face if they looked. He stared at his desk intently, as if merely to look up would be a confession.

Later that morning, as the class was on its way out for recess, Mrs. Anthony stopped him at the door and asked if she could

talk to him for a minute. He was sure, then, that she had found
out, but when the others were gone, she only asked if he was
feeling all right. He nodded. Her forehead furrowed then, and he
looked away. "Jimmy," she said. "You can tell me. Have things
been bad at home again?" Her husky voice was soft, like his
mother's when she was trying to make up for something she'd
said. Somehow it made him angry. "Yes," he lied, and the word
seemed to take his breath away. "My mother was mean to me."
And then he ran outside and sat under a maple tree near the
swings, trying to get his breath back. Greg came over then and
challenged him to a game of tetherball, but Jimmy said he didn't
want to play. "Why not?" Greg said. "You chicken?" And even
though Greg started to flap his arms and cluck like a chicken,
Jimmy did not get up and chase him.

School ended that day without anyone accusing him of
breaking the windows, but he was still certain he'd be caught.
Maybe somebody already knew, but they hadn't said anything
because they were testing him, trying to see if he would confess
on his own. He didn't know what to think. It was like he had to
learn a whole new way of thinking now that he'd broken the
windows. As he walked home, he tried out different things to
say when he was accused. He could say it was all an accident—
he'd been trying to hit some blackbirds that were flying past or
something—or maybe there was a robber, somebody breaking
into the school, and he'd chased him away by throwing rocks at
him and some of them hit the windows. But nothing he thought
of sounded good enough, and after a while he gave up and tried
to think of something else.

Though the afternoon was bright and sunny, the temperature
had dropped below freezing. He hunched his shoulders against
the cold and started down the street to the rundown clapboard
house where he and his mother rented an apartment on the second
floor. He was hoping his mother wasn't too tired to make hot
chocolate for him. But then he saw the social worker's yellow
Subaru parked in front of the house again and knew he wouldn't

get any hot chocolate—or even any supper. After Mrs. McClure's visits, his mother was always so exhausted she'd have to go to bed for the rest of the day, and he'd have to make his own supper, and hers too. And that meant he'd have to eat hot dogs or toast again because they were the only things he could cook. And he'd have to watch TV by himself all night, too, and every now and then he'd probably hear her crying in her room. He knew better than to go in and try to comfort her, though; that only made her cry harder or, sometimes, yell at him.

He didn't want to go inside while Mrs. McClure was there, but it was so cold he went in the dark, musty entryway of the old house and climbed the steps up to the second-floor landing. Outside their apartment he hesitated a moment, then opened the door quietly. He hoped he could sneak through the kitchen and down the hall to his room without Mrs. McClure seeing him. Carefully he set his book bag on the rug and hung his jacket on the coat rack. Then he heard his mother's voice coming from the living room.

"So I had a glass with lunch. I don't know what's the big hairy deal. Who appointed you my savior anyway?"

"Now, Marjorie, I don't think of myself as—"

"Look, why don't you just get the hell out of here. I'm sick to death of your stupid face. Just get out and leave me alone."

During the silence that followed, Jimmy's jacket suddenly slipped off the coat rack and landed with a muffled thud on the floor. "Jimmy?" his mother said. "Is that you?"

Jimmy sighed. "Yes," he said, and stepped to the doorway of the living room.

Mrs. McClure turned in her chair. "Why, hello, Jimmy! Aren't you getting to be a big boy?" She said things like that every time she saw him, as if she hadn't seen him just the week before. He hated that, and hated even more the times she tried to act like she was his mother. Last month, when it was time for parent-teacher conferences, she'd gone to his school and talked to Mrs. Anthony about the Unsatisfactory he got in Conduct. She had no right to do that; that was his mother's job, not hers.

"Aren't you going to say hello, Jimmy?" Mrs. McClure said.

"Hi," Jimmy answered. But that didn't satisfy her; she kept looking at him, as if she were waiting for him to say something else, and he thought again how her long nose and chin made her look like a witch.

"Come on in and sit down," she said then, as if it were *her* apartment, but Jimmy stayed in the doorway. Finally, she turned back to his mother, who was lying on the couch in her flannel nightgown and blue terrycloth bathrobe, an arm crooked over her eyes to block out the light slanting through the tall windows. Mrs. McClure always opened the drapes when she came. "No wonder you're down in the dumps," she'd say. "You keep this place too dark." Now she said, "I suppose I should be going. But don't forget what I said about a new hairdo. I think you'd be surprised how much better you'd feel about yourself." She nodded her bangs at his mother's greasy brown hair to emphasize her point. "And the Rosary Society at St. Jacob's is sponsoring a clothing drive. Perhaps you'd like me to bring around a few things in your size?" Jimmy looked at Mrs. McClure and tried to imagine his mother wearing her pink dress and nylons, her hoop earrings and silver and turquoise bracelets. But he couldn't and he started to giggle. He didn't think it was funny, but he started to giggle anyway.

"Shush," his mother said, without removing her arm from her eyes. Some days, that was the only thing she said to him. She got headaches easily, so he had to be quiet around her. Sometimes he even watched TV with the sound off, guessing at what people were saying. It was kind of fun, watching the mouths move and no sounds come out, and sometimes in school he'd pretend he was deaf and dumb until Mrs. Anthony threatened to send him to the principal's office. Just thinking about how red Mrs. Anthony's face got when she was mad made him giggle more. He wished he could have seen her face when she first saw all the broken windows. He imagined it getting so red that steam blew out her ears, just like in the cartoons, and he started laughing. His mother gritted her teeth. "I said, *Stop it.*" But he couldn't stop.

Mrs. McClure turned to look at him, her head tilted a little, like a bird listening for worms underground, and he began laughing hard. But then—he didn't know how it happened—he was crying. His mother didn't get up, but she pointed at him. "Now look what you've done," she said to Mrs. McClure.

"Look what *I've* done?" Mrs. McClure said. "Can't you see why he's crying? He's just come home from school and you haven't even said hello to him. All you've done is snap at him."

"Why don't you just shut the fuck up."

"I have a job to do, Marjorie, and I intend to do it. But if you're not interested in helping yourself, how can I possibly help you?"

His mother sat up slowly and leaned toward Mrs. McClure. "You can help me by getting the hell out of my apartment."

"Marjorie, you know that—"

"I said, *Get out.*"

Mrs. McClure sighed and shook her head, then she turned to Jimmy. "Don't cry, honey," she said. "Everything's going to work out in the end." She held out her arms. "Come here, sweetie."

For a second, he saw himself sitting in her lap, her arms around him, and he almost started toward her. That fact surprised him so much he stopped crying.

Mrs. McClure dropped her arms and sat there a moment, looking at him, then she slowly stood up. "Maybe I've done all I can do here," she said to his mother. "Maybe it's time to take your case to another level."

His mother glared at her. "Just what is that supposed to mean?" she asked. But Mrs. McClure only shook her head, then gathered up her manila folder and purse and started toward the door.

"You and your damned threats," his mother said to her back. "You can just go to hell."

Mrs. McClure didn't answer. She merely stopped for a second to tousle Jimmy's curly black hair and say, "Don't worry, we'll take care of you." Then she went out the door and down the steps.

"'A new hairdo,'" his mother said then. "She can just go fuck herself." Jimmy looked at her. Normally her round face was pale and her eyes looked wet, as if she had just finished crying or was about to start, but now her skin was splotchy and her eyes looked fierce. "What are you staring at?" she said.

Jimmy wanted to ask what Mrs. McClure meant by "another level," but he didn't dare. "Do you want me to make you supper tonight?" Jimmy asked. "I can make hot dogs if we got some."

"Just shut the damned drapes," she said. "Shut all the goddamned drapes and leave me alone. I'm tired and I want to sleep." She lay back on the sagging couch and hugged herself. "And get me a blanket. It's cold in here."

"Okay," Jimmy said, and went around the room, closing the drapes. Then he got a spare blanket from the linen closet and started to cover his mother with it. Her eyes were closed and he thought she was already asleep, but she opened them and said, "You're a good boy, Jimmy. I'm not mad at *you*. You know that, don't you?" When he nodded, she gave him the smile he loved so, the one that made her eyes crinkle up. "It's you and me, kid," she said. "You and me against the world." And then she closed her eyes again and turned toward the back of the couch.

For the next two weeks, no one mentioned the windows, and Jimmy began to believe that he wouldn't be caught after all. Then one day he came home from school and heard his mother talking on the phone in the kitchen. "Think about Jimmy," she was saying, her voice wavering. "He doesn't deserve this." Then she was silent a long time before she said, "I'll be there. Just give me a chance to explain." When she hung up, he went into the kitchen. His legs felt funny, as if his knees had turned to water. He was sure she'd been talking to the principal, or maybe a policeman.

"Oh, you're home," she said, and wiped her nose with a Kleenex.

He was about to tell her it wasn't true, someone else broke the windows, when she suddenly said, "Look at this mess!"

She gestured at the dirty dishes piled on the table and counters. "We've got to clean up everything right away." Then she began to fill the sink with water, but before it was even half-full, she abruptly turned off the faucet. "We'd better do the bedrooms first," she said, and hurried to her room, where she started picking up clothes and newspapers and empty wine jugs from the floor. "Just look at all of this!" she said. She carried the load out into the living room and dumped it on the sofa. Then she straightened the sofa pillows and wiped dust off the coffee table with her palm. "Don't just stand there," she said then. "Help me clean up this mess!"

"What should I do?"

"You can do the dishes while I do the laundry." She led him back into the kitchen. "First," she said. But then she closed her eyes and shook her head slowly back and forth. "Oh, God, why did they have to come today? Just a half-gallon of milk and a jar of jelly in the fridge. And me still in bed . . ." Then she looked at Jimmy. Her eyes were red and swollen, and he could smell the wine on her breath. "Damn it," she said. "Who the hell do they think they are?"

Jimmy realized then that the principal and the policeman must have come to the apartment looking for him. That frightened him, but he was relieved his mother seemed madder at them than at him. She must not believe that he broke the windows. Maybe she thought he was too normal to do it, and maybe that meant he really was normal. She was his mother and she would know, wouldn't she? "What's wrong?" he finally dared to say.

"Nothing," she answered. "Nothing for you to worry about." Then she said, "To hell with the dishes. We'll do them tomorrow." And she went to bed and stayed there the rest of the night. Every now and then, Jimmy heard her crying, and then she'd begin cursing. Finally, she fell asleep, and Jimmy lay in his bed across the hall, listening to her peaceful breathing and wishing he could dream whatever she was dreaming, so he'd know what could make her happy.

The next morning, his mother surprised him by coming into the kitchen in a lacy lavender dress with puffy sleeves. Her hair was combed, and she had put on lipstick and rouge. She frowned and said, "Do I look all right?"

"You look pretty," Jimmy said, and took a bite of his toast.

"But do I look like a good mommy?" she asked. "Do I look like I clean my house and go to church and love you more than anything in the world?"

He started to smile, thinking she was teasing him, but the frightened look on her face made him stop. He looked down at his plate.

"I think so," he said.

All that week and most of the next, his mother dressed up each morning and left the apartment. She was looking for a new job, she told him, but every afternoon, when he came home from school and asked her if she'd found one, she said no. "But I'll keep trying," she said one day, then knelt down and hugged him tightly. "I won't give up. No matter how hard I have to fight, I won't give up."

But eventually she stopped dressing in the morning and started staying in bed all day, drinking wine, just as she had before. When Jimmy asked her why she wasn't looking for jobs anymore, she said, "What are you talking about?" Then she said, "Oh, that. Forget about that. There aren't any jobs for bad mommies, not a single one."

Then one morning Mrs. McClure came to the apartment for the first time in weeks. It took Jimmy a few minutes to realize she had come to take him away. "You're going to live somewhere else for just a little while," his mother said, her voice quivering. "It's all for your own good." Then she took his small face in her hands and kissed him goodbye. "Remember I love you," she said, and her mouth twisted as if the words made it hurt. "Now go." Then Mrs. McClure took his hand and led him outside to her car.

It was several months before Jimmy learned he had not been
taken away from his mother because of the windows. That
morning, though, he believed they had finally proved he'd done
it and, because he was too young to go to jail, they were
punishing him by sending him to some strangers' house, where
they would watch him to make sure he didn't break any more
windows. As he rode away from his home, he thought of telling
Mrs. McClure he was innocent, but he was sure a teacher or
janitor had seen him. And he knew that none of the excuses he
had made up would work. So he didn't say anything; he just sat
there, looking straight ahead while Mrs. McClure went on and
on about Mr. and Mrs. Kahlstrom and how they had fixed up
their spare room just for him. "They've painted the walls sea
blue and they've put a huge toy box at the foot of the bed and
filled it with Transformers and Lincoln Logs and everything else
you can think of," she said. "How does that sound?" When he
didn't answer, she said, "You don't have anything to worry about,
Jimmy. Everything's going to be just fine. You know that, don't
you?" Jimmy nodded, so she'd leave him alone. "That's good,"
she said then. "I'm glad you're being such a big brave boy."

But at the Kahlstroms' house, he wasn't brave for long. Standing
in the entryway, Mrs. McClure cheerfully introduced him to the
strangers who would be his temporary parents. Mrs. Kahlstrom
was a small, bird-boned woman, and even though the house was
warm and she was wearing a bulky turtleneck sweater, she kept
hugging herself as if she were cold. She said, "Hello, Jimmy," and
smiled so big he could see her gums. Mr. Kahlstrom shook his
hand when he said hello. He was tall and thin and had an Adam's
apple like Ichabod Crane in the story Mrs. Anthony had read to
Jimmy's class. Jimmy was so scared he wanted to turn and run out
the door, but his legs were trembling too much. He didn't know
what to do, and he surprised himself as much as the others when
he suddenly lay down on the rug and curled up like a dog going to
sleep. The three adults hovered over him, startled looks on their
faces. From the floor they looked so different it was almost as if

they weren't people at all but some strange creatures from another world. Mrs. McClure took his elbow and asked him to please stand up like a good boy, but he jerked his arm away. They all tried to talk him into getting up, but he stayed on the floor, even when Mr. and Mrs. Kahlstrom tried to tempt him into the house by showing him some of the toys they'd bought. Finally Mrs. McClure said it might be best just to let him lie there until he was ready to get up. "I don't know what to say," she told the Kahlstroms. "I've never seen a reaction like this." Mrs. Kahlstrom offered him a sofa pillow then, but he shook his head, so she just set it on the linoleum beside him. Then Mrs. McClure shook their hands and said goodbye, and Mr. and Mrs. Kahlstrom went into the living room to wait for Jimmy to get up and join them.

For a time after Mrs. McClure left, Jimmy could hear them whispering. Then he heard a sudden sharp sob, and Mr. Kahlstrom saying, "There, there, dear. Just give him time." Then they went into another room, farther away, and he couldn't hear them anymore. After a while, a phone rang somewhere, and Jimmy heard Mr. Kahlstrom answer it, then say, "No, not yet" and "We'll let you know as soon as anything happens" and "Thanks for calling." A long time later, Mr. Kahlstrom came, squatted down on his haunches, and set a plate beside the rug. "It's lunchtime, Jimmy," he said. "Mrs. McClure told us you liked Sloppy Joes and potato chips. I hope that's right." When Jimmy didn't say anything, he let out a long sigh, then stood up and went away. Jimmy was hungry, but he wasn't going to eat anything until they took him back home. He'd starve himself, and if that didn't work, he'd just break all the windows in the house. And if Mrs. McClure took him somewhere else, he'd break all the windows there, too; he'd break all the windows everywhere, until she'd finally have to take him back to his mother again.

A half-hour later, when Mr. Kahlstrom returned, Jimmy still hadn't eaten anything, but he was sitting up now and crying. "I'm sorry," he said. "I won't break any of your windows, I promise. Just let me go home, please. Please let me go home."

Mr. Kahlstrom knelt down beside Jimmy. "Sorry? You don't have anything to be sorry about. And you don't have to worry about breaking any of our windows, or anything else either. Just feel free to play and do everything you do in your own house. And if something does break, don't worry about it—we can get it fixed. All right?"

Jimmy looked at him. Maybe he didn't know about the windows, maybe Mrs. McClure didn't tell either of them. "All right," he said.

"Say," Mr. Kahlstrom said then, "I bet your Sloppy Joe is cold. What do you say we head into the kitchen and make you another one?"

For the next two months, whenever Mrs. McClure asked, Jimmy told her that he liked living with the Kahlstroms. And mostly, he did. Mr. Kahlstrom taught music at the high school, and he played songs for Jimmy on the big upright piano in the living room. Jimmy's favorite was one called "Down at Papa Joe's." Mr. Kahlstrom showed Jimmy how to play the melody—he took his small hand with his big one and helped him poke out the notes with one finger—and Jimmy liked that. But he didn't like it when Mrs. Kahlstrom sat down on the corner of the piano bench beside them. She had scared him his third night there, when she tucked him into bed, by telling him that she and Roger—that was what she called Mr. Kahlstrom—had once had a little boy very much like him but that he had caught some disease called leukemia and died. It had been eleven years since he died and they still missed him, and that was why they had decided to become foster parents. She reached out her bony hand when she said that and brushed the hair away from his forehead. "He had curly hair too," she said, "only his was blond."

The Kahlstroms were nice to him. Mr. Kahlstrom took him up to the high school on weekends and let him play with all the different drums in the band room, and he bought him a Nerf football so they could play Goal Line Stand in the living room.

Mrs. Kahlstrom worried about the furniture and lamps, but she let them play anyway, and when Jimmy tackled Mr. Kahlstrom she'd clap and say, "Way to go, Jimmy!" Mrs. Kahlstrom made him bacon and eggs for breakfast nearly every day and helped him with his homework and took him to the matinee on Saturdays, but she was so nervous all the time that she made him nervous too. And she was always talking about love. She had loved him even before she met him, she said. And at night, after she read him a story, she'd kiss him on his nose just like he was a little kid still and say she loved, loved, loved him so much she could eat him up. Then she'd sit there a moment, as if she were waiting for him to say "I love you" back, before she'd finally get up and turn out the lights. And the stories she read bothered him too. They were stupid stories, little kid stories. Once she read one about a dog that was on the ark with Noah. The dog seemed to think the flood came along just so he could have a good time, sailing around and playing games with the other animals. He never even thought about all the dogs that got drowned. His own parents had probably drowned in the flood, and his brothers and sisters too. But he didn't seem to care. And when the flood was over and Noah picked him for his pet, he jumped up and down like he was the luckiest dog in history.

Each Friday, Mrs. McClure came to visit for a few minutes. She never mentioned the windows, but Jimmy knew she hadn't forgotten about them, because she always told him he couldn't go home just yet. He wished she'd tell him how long he was going to be punished, but all she'd ever say was, "It won't be much longer now, sweetheart." At first he thought he'd have to stay at the Kahlstroms' for eighteen days—one for each window—but when the eighteenth day came and went without her coming to take him home, he began to worry it'd be eighteen weeks. But then, a few days before Christmas, she called and told him to pack his things because she was coming to take him home. At the door, Mr. Kahlstrom shook his hand and hugged him. "Be good, Jimmy," he said, patting his back. Mrs. Kahlstrom wasn't there; she was upstairs in her room, and although he couldn't hear her, Jimmy knew she was crying. "Tell Mrs. Kahlstrom . . ." he said, but he didn't know what he wanted him to tell her, so he stopped. Then Mrs. McClure took his hand and led him down the sidewalk to her car. He wanted to turn around and see if Mrs. Kahlstrom was watching from her window upstairs, but he didn't.

On the way home, Mrs. McClure mentioned that his mother had been at a hospital in St. Paul. "What was she doing there?" he asked.

"Getting better," Mrs. McClure answered. "Wait till you see her. She's a new person now."

And she was, too, at least for a while. His first day back, she told him he was the best Christmas present she had ever gotten, and she baked a turkey and made mashed potatoes and gravy. And afterward, she gave him a present—"Just one, for now," she said. "You'll have to wait till Christmas Eve for the rest." It was a Nerf football, just like the one Mr. Kahlstrom had bought for him. He looked at her. Her chin was trembling. "Mrs. McClure told me you liked playing football," she said. "I thought maybe we could play a little sometime."

They only played a couple of times, though, before she started getting tired again. The first Saturday after Christmas she went to bed right after breakfast. Jimmy watched cartoons in the living room all morning, then made himself a peanut butter and jelly sandwich for lunch. After he finished it, he went into her room to ask her if she wanted something to eat, too. She was standing in front of her bureau mirror. She was still in her nightgown, but she was wearing a strange white hat with a pink ribbon around its brim. Jimmy wasn't sure, but he thought he'd seen that hat before. Then he remembered: it was her Easter hat, and she'd worn it back when his father lived with them and they still went to church. "Are you going to church, Mom?" he asked. She turned around, and he saw that she'd been crying. For a moment, he

was worried that she was going to say something about the
windows. But then she said, "While I was in the hospital, I got a
letter from Mr. Gilchrist. You remember Mr. Gilchrist, don't you?"
Jimmy nodded. Mr. Gilchrist was the vacuum salesman who
made the noises with her in the bedroom. "Well, he said he
wouldn't be coming to town anymore. He said his company
changed his route." She laughed abruptly, then frowned. "Men,"
she said. She looked at him. "I wish you weren't a boy, Jimmy.
You'll grow up to be just like the rest of them, and you'll leave
me too."

"No I won't," Jimmy said.

"Yes you will."

"No I won't," he repeated, shaking his head.

"Goddamn it, you *will*," she said, and tore the hat off her
head and flung it against the wall. Jimmy flinched and took a
step backward. "I'm sorry," she said then. "I didn't mean it." She
reached out for him. "Come here, honey. I'm sorry."

But he didn't move.

"All right then," she said, and dropped her hands to her sides.
"Do whatever the hell you want. You will anyway." She got back
into bed and pulled the covers up to her chin. Jimmy stood there,
watching her. "What are you waiting for?" she said. "*Go.*" And
he left.

The next day she was better—she even helped him build a
snow fort in the yard until she got too tired—and Jimmy thought
everything was going to be all right again. But by mid-January,
she was so tired all the time that she had to go back to the hospital.
Mrs. McClure said she was a lot better than she had been, but
she still wasn't quite well. When Jimmy asked what was wrong
with her, she said, "It's nothing to worry about. She just needs a
rest." Jimmy tried to convince her that his mother could rest at
home—he could clean the house for her and do the laundry and
cook—but she only sighed. "It's not just for a rest, Jimmy. Your
mother's not very happy right now. At the hospital they'll help
her be happy again."

Jimmy didn't say anything then. He knew why she was unhappy; it was all his fault. Why had he thrown those rocks? If he had just put that first rock down and walked away, she wouldn't have to go back to the hospital and he wouldn't have to go back to the Kahlstroms'. He didn't want to live there anymore. It wasn't that he didn't like the Kahlstroms—he did—but he missed his mother when he was there. Most people didn't know how nice she was; they only saw her when she was too tired to be nice. But sometimes when he'd tell her something funny that happened at school she'd laugh so hard she'd have to hold her sides and she'd smile so big there'd be wrinkles around her eyes. He loved that smile, and in the weeks that followed, he often stood in front of the Kahlstroms' bathroom mirror and tried to imitate it. He'd stand there for a long time, smiling at himself with her smile, until Mrs. Kahlstrom would get worried and come looking for him.

This time, his mother got out of the hospital after only a month, but Mrs. McClure said he couldn't go home just yet. He cried so hard then that the Kahlstroms agreed to let his mother come once a week for a visit. That Sunday, Mrs. McClure dropped her off in her Subaru. Jimmy was upstairs in his room when the doorbell rang. "Your mother's here," Mr. Kahlstrom called, and Jimmy came running downstairs just as he opened the door for her. It was snowing lightly and her hair and the shoulders of her coat were dusted with snow. "Come on in, Mrs. Holloway," he said, and helped her out of her coat. "Welcome to our home."
   She didn't look at him. She just cleared her throat and said, "Thank you," then looked at Jimmy, who was standing beside the potted fern in the hall. "Jimmy," she said, and knelt on one knee for him to come to her. He had been looking forward to her coming, but now that she was here, he felt strangely shy, and he walked toward her slowly, with his eyes down. Then her arms were around him and she was kissing his cheek. She didn't smell like herself, though; she was wearing perfume that smelled like

the potpourri Mrs. Kahlstrom kept in an oriental dish in the bathroom. He stepped back and looked at her. Her eyebrows looked darker and there were red smudges on her cheekbones. As she stood up, her silver earrings swung back and forth. She was smiling, but it wasn't her real smile, the one she gave him when they were alone.

"If you'd like, you can sit in the living room," Mr. Kahlstrom said. "I've just built a fire in the fireplace." He led them to the living room. "I'll leave you two alone," he said then, and went upstairs to join Mrs. Kahlstrom, who had told Jimmy at breakfast that she hoped he'd understand but she just couldn't be there when his mother came.

Jimmy sat in the wingback chair beside the white brick fireplace and swung his legs back and forth. His mother stood in front of the fire a moment, warming herself and looking at Mrs. Kahlstrom's collection of Hummel figurines on the mantel, then sat down on the end of the sofa next to the chair. He knew he should go sit with her, but he didn't. Then she touched the cushion beside her and said, "Won't you come sit with me?" He nodded and slid out of the chair and climbed up next to her. It felt strange to be alone with his mother in someone else's house—it was like they were actors in a movie or something and not real people. He didn't know what to say to her. He wasn't at all tired, but he stretched and yawned. He didn't know why he'd done that, and he suddenly wanted to be upstairs in his room, playing with his toys, the visit over and his mother on her way back home.

"Mr. Kahlstrom made a fire," he finally said, though she already knew that. Then he added, "He showed me how to do it. First you crumple up newspaper, then you stack up little sticks like a teepee over it and—"

"Jimmy," his mother interrupted. "I wish I could bring you home with me right now. You know that, don't you?"

He nodded.

"It may be a little longer, but I'm going to bring you home with me soon. Okay?"

"Okay," he said.

"And things'll be a lot better than they were last time, I promise. I still had a lot of anger in me then, a lot of hurt. But I don't feel like that anymore. I've got a new outlook, and I'm going to make a better life for us. You'll see."

Jimmy looked at her. "You're not mad anymore?"

"No," she said, and Jimmy smiled. But then she added, "At least not like before. I'm learning to deal with it. It was hard at first, but it's getting easier."

Jimmy looked down then. She was still mad, she still had not forgiven him.

"At any rate," his mother continued, "Mrs. McClure says it won't be long before I can bring you back home."

Then she was silent. She was looking at the flames in the fireplace. One of the logs popped and some sparks struck the black mesh screen.

Jimmy knew he should say something, but he thought if he opened his mouth, he'd start to cry.

"The Kahlstroms have such a nice house," his mother said then. "I've always loved fireplaces. When I was a girl, I used to imagine the house I'd live in when I got married, and it always had a fireplace in it. And after dinner on cold winter nights my husband would build a big, roaring fire and we'd all sit around it and talk, the firelight flickering over our faces." She shook her head and laughed. It didn't sound like her laugh. And the things she was saying didn't sound like anything she'd ever said before. "I had it all figured out," she said. "I was going to have five children. I even had their names picked out—Joseph, Kevin, Abigail, Christine, and John, in that order. No James—that was your father's idea." She laughed again. "I had everything figured out. Every blessed thing." Then she turned her face toward him. There were tears in her eyes. "Don't you ever have everything figured out, you hear? Don't you—"

Then she couldn't talk anymore.

"What's wrong, Mom?" he managed to say.

"I'd better go," she said, and stood up. She took a crumpled Kleenex from her purse and wiped her eyes with it. "This was a mistake. I shouldn't be here." She looked around the room at the large-screen TV, the piano, the watercolor landscapes on the walls, the philodendron in the corner, and added, "I don't belong here."

"Don't go," he said, but it was too late: she was already on her way out.

"Tell Mr. and Mrs. Kahlstrom thank you for letting me come see you," she said as she put on her coat.

"Mom," he said. "Mom!"

She leaned over and took his face in her hands and kissed him. "My baby," she said.

And then she was out the door, and he was standing at the window, watching her walk carefully down the icy sidewalk through the falling snow, not even a scarf on her head, and Mr. and Mrs. Kahlstrom were coming down the stairs asking why she had left so soon. When he tried to answer, a sob rose into his throat and stuck. He shook his head, unable to speak.

Mrs. Kahlstrom put her hands on his shoulders. "Don't worry, honey. You'll see her again next week," she said, but he wrenched himself out of her hands and ran upstairs and locked himself in the bathroom. And although Mr. and Mrs. Kahlstrom stood outside the door and tried to comfort him, it was nearly an hour before he came out.

Mrs. Kahlstrom hugged him hard then and said they'd stay downstairs with him next time, if he wanted, so they could make sure his mother wouldn't upset him again. Jimmy didn't say anything for a long moment. Then he took a deep breath and said something he'd been wanting to say for the past four months. "If I get a job delivering papers, and save all my money, and pay for the windows, will Mrs. McClure let me go back home?"

"Windows?" Mrs. Kahlstrom said, then looked at her husband.

Mr. Kahlstrom wrinkled his forehead. "What windows, Jimmy? What are you talking about?"

And then he confessed it all.

Mr. Kahlstrom took Jimmy to see the high school counselor the next afternoon. His name was Mr. Sargent, but he told Jimmy to call him Dale. He was a skinny man with a ponytail, and he was wearing a corduroy sport coat but no tie. He leaned back in his chair and put his scuffed Hush Puppies up on the desk. Behind him, on the wall, was a poster of a strangely dressed black man kneeling in front of a burning guitar. "So, Jimbo," he said, "what's a nice guy like you doing in a place like this?"

Jimmy sat there, looking down at his lap. His hands were shaking and he couldn't make them stop. He watched them tremble. Somehow, it seemed like it was happening a long way away, to somebody else maybe.

"You don't have to be afraid," Mr. Sargent said. "You can say anything in here. This is one place where you can say whatever you want. 'Cause I won't tell anyone anything you say. Everything you tell me will be confidential. And *confidential* means you can be *confident* I won't tell anyone your secrets."

Jimmy sat on his hands to make them stop. Then he tried to look up, but he couldn't. Finally, he said, "Did Mr. Kahlstrom tell you?"

"Tell me what, Jimbo?" Mr. Sargent said.

Jimmy didn't want to say. He was hoping Mr. Sargent didn't know.

"Tell me what?" Mr. Sargent asked again, more softly this time. "You can tell me."

"The windows," Jimmy managed to whisper.

"Oh, the *windows*. Sure, he told me about the windows. But who cares about the lousy windows?"

Jimmy looked up, startled. Mr. Sargent smiled and went on. "It was wrong to break the windows, of course, but I don't have to tell you that—you already know it. But once they're broken, there's nothing you can do about it, except admit it like a man and say you're sorry and go on with your life. Everybody makes mistakes. That's how we learn to be better people. If we didn't make mistakes, we'd never learn anything. So think of it that way—as a mistake you made that you can learn from." Here he took his feet down from the desk and leaned forward in his chair. "What have you learned from all of this, Jimbo? Is there anything it's taught you that'll help you on down the road?"

Jimmy didn't think he'd learned anything, unless it was that he wasn't who he'd always thought he was. He didn't know who he was now, but he was someone else. Someone crazy, like his mother. And once Mr. Sargent found that out, he'd make him go to a hospital too.

"Let me guess, then," Mr. Sargent said. "You tell me if I'm getting warm, okay?" When Jimmy didn't respond, he repeated, "Okay?" Finally, Jimmy nodded. "All right, then. Did you learn that—hmm, let's see—that it's best to talk about your anger instead of breaking things?"

Jimmy hadn't been angry when he broke the windows, but he nodded yes anyway.

"Good. That's a good thing to learn. And did you also learn that secrets make you unhappy? That the longer you keep something inside, the more it hurts?"

Again Jimmy nodded, though he thought he hurt more now that people knew what he had done. And even though Mr. and Mrs. Kahlstrom told him he wasn't taken away from his mother because he broke the windows, he didn't know if he could believe them. They wanted him to like them, so maybe they would lie. And they wanted to adopt him, so maybe they would tell Mrs. McClure about the windows and Mrs. McClure would tell his mother, and then she'd say she couldn't take him back because she couldn't afford to pay for the windows like Mr. and Mrs. Kahlstrom could.

"That's good. That's very good. And did you maybe also learn how much people care about you? Because if they didn't, I wouldn't be here talking to you. I'm talking to you because *I* care, and because Mr. and Mrs. K care, and because everybody who knows you cares about you and wants you to be happy. Is that maybe something you learned from all of this, too?"

Jimmy looked at him, then at the floor. He didn't see the floor, though; he was seeing his father, the morning of the day he left for work and never came back, trimming his mustache in front of the bathroom mirror.

It took him longer this time, but once again he nodded.

The following Sunday, Mrs. McClure's Subaru pulled up in front of the Kahlstroms' house, but Jimmy's mother was not in it. "What a terrible day," Mrs. McClure said to the Kahlstroms, as she flicked the snow from her boots with her gloves. "We must have a foot of snow already." Then she cocked her head toward Jimmy. "I'm sorry, sweetie, but your mother isn't feeling well today. She said she'd try to come again next week. I hope you aren't too disappointed."

Jimmy said, "You told her, didn't you."

"Told her what?"

"You know."

"Oh, that. No, I didn't say anything. I told you I wouldn't tell, and I won't." Then she frowned. "Is that why you think she didn't come?"

"You can tell her if you want," he said, sticking his chin out. "She won't come anyway."

"Of course she will. She'll come tomorrow or the day after," Mrs. McClure said. "It's just that today—" But before she could finish, Jimmy turned and started to run up the stairs. "Jimmy!" she called after him. "Let me explain."

At the top of the stairs, he stopped and shouted down, "Tell her I don't care if she ever comes—not *ever*!" And then he ran into his room and slammed the door.

A few minutes later, he heard Mrs. McClure's car drive away, and then Mr. and Mrs. Kahlstrom came up and tried to talk to him. "We know you were looking forward to seeing her, honey," Mrs. Kahlstrom said, but he just dumped his entire canister of Legos onto the carpet and started putting them together.

"What're you building?" Mr. Kahlstrom asked.

"Nothing," he answered.

"Well," he said, "that shouldn't take much time." But Jimmy didn't laugh. Mr. Kahlstrom cleared his throat and looked at his wife. "Maybe we ought to let Jimmy be alone for a while," he said. Mrs. Kahlstrom nodded and said, "We'll be right downstairs if you need us. Okay, Jimmy?"

Jimmy didn't say anything. And when they left, he got up and closed the door again.

He tried to play with his Legos, but after a few minutes, he gave up and sat on the edge of his bed, looking out the window. It had been snowing all day, and now the snow was so thick he could barely see the houses across the street. He watched the evergreens sway in the yard and listened to the wind whistle in the eaves, then pressed his warm cheek against the windowpane. The window was cold and it vibrated a little with every gust of wind. It felt as if the glass were shivering, and for a second he thought it might even break. But he didn't move his face away; he pressed his cheek against it harder, until he could feel the cold right through to his cheekbone. He wished he were outside, walking through the waist-high drifts, the wind making his cheeks burn and his eyes tear; he wanted to be so cold that nothing could ever warm him up. That didn't make sense, but Jimmy didn't care if it did or not. He had a lot of thoughts he didn't understand, but he didn't worry about them anymore. You couldn't do anything about the brain that was in your head. Even if you were as rich as Michael Jackson, you still couldn't buy a new brain. You could get a new mother, but you couldn't get a new brain.

Later that night, Mr. Kahlstrom built a fire, and the three of them sat on the sofa eating popcorn and watching *E.T.* on videotape. The movie was sad, but Mr. and Mrs. Kahlstrom were smiling. It was so easy to make them happy, he thought; all he had to do was sit on the sofa with them. And that thought made him feel bad, because he had stayed in his room almost all day, making them worry.

Outside, the snow was still falling, a thick curtain of it, and every now and then the wind would rattle the windowpanes. "My, what a storm," Mrs. Kahlstrom said when the picture on the television flickered and went dark for a second. "We'd better get the candles out."

"It looks like we'll be snowed in tomorrow," Mr. Kahlstrom said. Then he tousled Jimmy's hair. "No school for us, eh, buckaroo?"

Jimmy smiled and Mrs. Kahlstrom grinned. "I'd like that," she said. "We could sit around the fire and tell stories and play games, the way people did in the olden days. It'd be just like that poem 'Snow-Bound.' I memorized part of it when I was in high school, for a talent show." She lowered her head, as if it were immodest of her to say the word *talent*. But then she began to half-speak, half-sing the poem:

> What matter how the night behaved?
> What matter how . . . the north-wind raved?
> Blow high, blow low, not all its snow
> Could quench our hearth-fire's ruddy glow.
> O Time and Change!—with hair as gray
> As was my father's—no, my *sire's*—that winter day,
> How strange it seems to still . . .

"No, that's not right," she broke off. "I think I missed a line in there somewhere."

"It sounded great to me," Mr. Kahlstrom said. "Go on. Recite some more for us." And he pressed the pause button on the remote control, freezing E.T. as he raised his glowing fingertip.

"All right," she said, "I'll see what else I can remember." Then she looked toward the ceiling as if the words were above her, floating through the air, like snowflakes.

> Ah, brother! only I and thou
> Are left of all that circle now—

The dear . . . home faces whereupon
That fitful firelight paled and shone.
Henceforward, listen as we will,
The voices of that hearth are still;
Look where we may, the wide earth o'er,
Those lighted faces smile no more . . .

She stopped abruptly and looked down at her lap. Mr. Kahlstrom reached across Jimmy and patted her hand. "It's all right, dear," he said. "Don't cry."

"I'm sorry," she said. "Sometimes I just remember and . . ."

"I know, dear. I do, too."

Jimmy looked at their faces. He wasn't sure what they were talking about. He hadn't understood the poem either, but he'd liked the way it made him feel warm and cold all at once, as if he had just come out of a blizzard to stand by a fire. He liked the way she'd said it, too, pronouncing each word as if it were almost too beautiful to say. And she'd had such a strange look on her face while she said it, kind of sad but in a way happy, too. He didn't know how you could be happy and sad at the same time. But now she only looked sad.

Just then the wind rose sharply and the television went black. The only light left was the firelight. It cast long shadows up the walls around them, making Jimmy feel as if they were in a cave.

"I knew I should have gotten the candles out," Mrs. Kahlstrom said, and wiped her eyes.

"Don't worry, dear. I'm sure the electricity will be back on in no time. Let's just sit here and enjoy the fire."

He got up and threw two more logs on, adjusted them with the poker until the flames caught, then sat back on the sofa. "There," he said. "Isn't this cozy?"

They sat together a long time, watching the fire and talking. At first, Jimmy talked too, but after a while he started to grow tired and only listened to their quiet voices and the crackling fire and the wind. The way the wind battered the windows made the fire seem even warmer, and before long, Jimmy felt so drowsy and peaceful that he couldn't help but lean his head against Mrs. Kahlstrom's shoulder. She brushed his hair from his forehead while he listened to them talk and watched the fire through half-open eyes. Finally he couldn't keep his eyes open anymore, and he laid his head down in her lap and fell asleep.

When Jimmy woke the next morning, he was confused. It seemed as if only a moment before he'd been lying in front of the fire, and now he was upstairs in his room. How had it happened? Mr. Kahlstrom must have carried him up the steps and put him in his bed, but Jimmy didn't remember it. He felt as if a magician had made him disappear from one place, then reappear somewhere else. For a moment, he wasn't even sure he was the same person. He wondered if his mother had ever felt like that, waking up in the hospital, or if his father had the same thoughts when he sat down for breakfast with his new family. He didn't know, but he lay there awhile, thinking about it, before he got up and parted the curtains to look out the window. As far as he could see, everything was white—rooftops, the evergreens and yards, the street. The snow had drifted halfway up frosted picture windows and buried bushes and hedges and even the car parked in the neighbor's driveway. Here and there thin swirls of snow blew into the air like risen ghosts, and sunlight sparked on the drifts, the snow glinting like splintered glass. He'd never seen so much snow, not ever, and he wanted to run to Mr. and Mrs. Kahlstrom's room and tell them they were all snowbound, just like in the poem. But he stood there awhile longer, and imagined the huge fire they'd build, the yellow and orange flames rising up the chimney, and the three of them sitting beside it, unsure of what to say or even when to speak, but somehow strangely happy, their faces lit by a beautiful light.

DAVID JAUSS is the author of three previous collections of short stories (*Glossolalia: New & Selected Stories; Black Maps;* and *Crimes of Passion*), two collections of poems (*You Are Not Here* and *Improvising Rivers*), and a collection of essays (*On Writing Fiction*). He has also edited or coedited three anthologies (*Strong Measures: Contemporary American Poetry in Traditional Forms*; *The Best of* Crazyhorse*: Thirty Years of Poetry and Prose;* and *Words Overflown by Stars: Creative Writing Instruction and Insight from the Vermont College of Fine Arts MFA Program*). His short stories have been published in numerous magazines and reprinted in *Best American Short Stories, The O. Henry Awards: Prize Stories,* and, twice, *The Pushcart Prize: Best of the Small Presses,* as well as in *The Pushcart Book of Short Stories: The Best Stories from the Pushcart Prize.* He is the recipient of a National Endowment for the Arts Fellowship, a James A. Michener/Copernicus Society of America Fellowship, and three fellowships from the Arkansas Arts Council and one from the Minnesota State Arts Board. His collection *Black Maps* received the Associated Writers and Writing Programs Award for Short Fiction. A professor emeritus at the University of Arkansas at Little Rock, he teaches in the low-residency MFA in Writing Program at Vermont College of Fine Arts.

For 31 years, cover artist JACK L. GEISER worked as a professional photographer. His work covered industrial, legal, advertising and commercial fields. His assignments included working with many politicians, sports figures, dignitaries, celebrities and famous people as diverse as Mother Teresa and Bob Hope.

The last five years Jack has been artistically exploring the realms of digital photography on his own through Photoshop and the Internet. His work now covers texture, surrealism, abstraction, and realism. His day-to-day rambling artistry can be seen at www.flickr.com/photos/jg_photo_art/

Jack lives in Omaha, Nebraska, with his wife Shelly, who is a published poet and is currently working on her first novel. They run a small business together and try to spend time, when possible, with their four children and six grandchildren.